THE HOMEMAKER

MIRANDA RIJKS

INKUBATOR
BOOKS

Published by Inkubator Books

www.inkubatorbooks.com

ISBN (eBook): 978-1-83756-268-8

ISBN (Paperback): 978-1-83756-269-5

ISBN (Hardback): 978-1-83756-270-1

PROLOGUE

We all have to take impossible decisions at some point in our lives. Do we give more attention to one child over the other? Should we end a relationship even though we know it's going to break our partner's heart? Should we expose the office thief in the knowledge he'll lose his job?

Or should we kill someone because with *their* life extinguished, our life – or the lives of those we love – will be so much better?

Believe me, it's not an easy decision. We're taught that we should never take another person's life and under normal circumstances, I would concur. But I'm not facing normal circumstances. I need to act out of love and compassion. And I have no choice. It's a sacrifice. Human sacrifice has been part of cultures since the Bronze Age and probably before. It's just we don't talk about it today. We've become soft. And I'm as soft as the next person, a weak product of my twenty-first century upbringing. The strange thing is, I never thought I would be capable of something like this, but when it comes to family, most of us will do whatever it takes. Me included.

It's dark when I plan to do the deed. A damp, bitter autumnal evening, a time when most people are in the bosom of their family, eating supper, discussing the mundanities of their day. But my victim is alone with just the television for company.

I'm inside quickly, in a house that is warm and characterful and nothing like its owner. They say that he who hesitates is lost, so I move fast. I stab again and again, harnessing all the anger and conviction, which gives me almost supernatural strength. As the blood bubbles up and the air expels from the body, I watch life ebb away. It's almost as if I can see the soul wafting upwards, relieved to be free from its human form. I snap back to the present moment. I have a job to do; a mess to make; implements to clean. And finally, when I'm done, I pause for a moment and wonder about my impossible decision.

I've made the right one.

1

IMOGEN

I'm awake before the alarm goes off. The sunlight is pouring through the gaps in our curtains and I'm cold because Josh has sequestered most of the duvet. My eyes feel gritty and my limbs so heavy, I'm not convinced I'll be able to physically get out of bed. How many nights now has sleep been elusive? Eighty-seven. It's been eighty-seven long nights since Mum died and eighty-nine nights since she shattered my world.

Our bedroom door opens with a slight squeak. Ava pokes her head around the side and I grin at her, putting my finger over my mouth. She runs across the soft, worn pale grey carpet, her little feet making the old floorboards creak, but then she jumps on the bed and Josh wakes up with a groan.

'Sorry, Daddy,' she says in her high-pitched voice, with no conviction in her apology. She knows that neither of us are ever truly annoyed to be woken by her. Josh comes to quickly and grabs her, tickling her in the ribs. Ava squeals and thrashes out, wriggling like crazy. I edge away from our soon-to-be five-year-old and swing my legs around the side of the bed. My head is throbbing and exhaustion sits on my shoulders like a pile of bricks. It's just before 6 a.m. and I need to get a move on. I force myself to stand up and as I'm dragging myself to the bathroom a wave of nausea catches me unawares. I race to the toilet and only just make it in time, running the taps to block the sound. My first thought is, do I have a bug? I could have caught something from one of Ava's little friends at school. My second and more reluctant thought is, am I pregnant?

I drink water from the tap, brush my teeth and take a quick shower. I feel better afterwards. Perhaps not a sickness bug then. But no. Please, can I not be pregnant.

By the time I emerge from the bathroom, Josh has taken Ava to her room, so I dress hurriedly and dash downstairs. It's all quiet on the other side of the house so my guests aren't up yet.

We live in a beautiful old Georgian rectory. It was built around 1750 and was artfully extended by the previous owners. It's much too big for the three of us – four if you count Kyle, Josh's fifteen-year-old son from his first marriage, who visits every other weekend and occasionally in-between. But we both fell in love with it; Josh especially. It's a three-storey house, fine brickwork on the exterior with beautifully proportioned rooms and tall ceilings. It was beyond my wildest dreams to live in such a grand, expansive house, but my husband has his own dental practice and a lot of money in the bank. Not that we needed seven bedrooms. It just seemed greedy to me, so I suggested I turn the two bedrooms, both with en-suites, on the opposite side of the house with its own staircase into an upmarket bed and breakfast. Josh was reluctant at first, but it was my dream. And with my background, I should know what I'm doing. I went to hotel management college and spent eight years working in hotels in Singapore, Boston and Geneva. Tired of eking out a living abroad, far from my adored parents, I got a job working for a hotel consultancy and then four years ago, I branched out on my own. These days I only have a couple of clients and I don't do any marketing. Hotels tend to come to me and I choose the ones located near us in Sussex, passing other leads to colleagues. I don't have the time or inclination to travel.

Today just one of our bed and breakfast rooms is rented. An older couple are visiting cousins nearby and when I met them yesterday, they seemed quite charming. I've been lucky and so far haven't had any horrendous guests. I price the rooms quite high and I list them with an upmarket website that vets its properties. We had to buy new mattresses and extra-large fluffy towels, and our bathrooms were checked with a fine-tooth comb to make sure the water pressure was adequate and the taps were sparkling. The downside to running a B&B is I have to provide a cooked breakfast every morning. The upside is we get to meet interesting people. Today's couple asked for a full English to be served for 7.30 a.m. And that's a juggle.

My first task is giving Ava breakfast. Once she is digging into her bowl of cereal I get a few minutes' grace to prepare food for my guests. The small dining room, used solely by our guests, is tidy with tables already laid. I do that last thing at night so I have a little less to worry about in the mornings. I'm halfway through the fry-up with the bacon sizzling and the eggs (sunny side up today) cooking slowly in the pan. I yawn.

'You look exhausted.' Josh has padded silently up behind

me and he makes me jump. A smidgeon of oil leaps out of the pan and burns the back of my hand.

'Ouch,' I mutter, running it under the tap.

'Are you alright?' he asks.

'Honestly, I am exhausted. I wonder if I'm going down with something.' I assume he didn't hear me throwing up, otherwise he would have commented.

Josh tilts his head at me. 'You've been like this for a few weeks, love. Perhaps you should go to the doctor. He might be able to give you a short course of antidepressants.' I clench my jaw and tighten my shoulders. Grief is normal. Why do people think it's necessary to medicate it? And why doesn't Josh understand?

'Anyway,' he continues. 'What's happening about getting some help? Has the advert in the local shop yielded anyone?'

'Actually, yes,' I say. 'I forgot to tell you. I'm interviewing today.'

'Fingers crossed then.' He places a cursory kiss on my cheek and then heads for the fridge where he takes out the bottle of freshly squeezed orange juice and pours himself a large glass. My husband is a creature of habit and drinks his juice first thing every morning.

I welcome 10 a.m. By then, I've served breakfast to my guests and bid them goodbye, taken Ava to school and nipped into town to buy a pregnancy test from the chemist. Back at home, I'm cleaning the kitchen but the pregnancy test box keeps grabbing my attention. Eventually I throw down the tea towel, grab the box and go to the toilet. The irony doesn't escape me. For the past three and a half years I've been desperate to get pregnant. Both Josh and I wanted a sibling for Ava, close enough in age so they can play together. Yet month after month it didn't happen. Shortly before Mum died I even mooted a visit to the gynaecologist to find out why I wasn't becoming pregnant as easily as I did the first time. But then the bombshell hit me.

And now the very last thing I want is another child. It would be a curse, a ticking time bomb, an abhorrence. I place the stick next to the sink and follow the second hand as it creeps around the face of my watch. It doesn't take long.

I'm pregnant.

I burst into tears.

And then I feel terrible. How awful for this foetus to be unwanted. Will he or she know how I'm feeling? I pace up and down our large bedroom, tugging at my hair, angrily swiping the tears from my cheeks. I should be happy yet I'm not. I'm devastated, terrified and confused in equal measures. I walk over to Mum's urn on the dresser. It's not really an urn but rather a wooden box holding her ashes. I've propped up her photograph next to it but every so often I turn it face down. It hurts too much to see her face, to know that we'll never talk again, that she'll never put her arms around me or meet her second grandchild.

'Mum. What the hell am I going to do?' I murmur, my voice catching.

The doorbell rings, startling me.

I glance at my watch and actually read the time now, realising long minutes have passed and it's already 11 a.m. I'm not ready. I quickly splash some water on my face, pat it dry with a towel and run downstairs. I must look a fright. I swing the front door open.

'Sorry to keep you waiting,' I say breathlessly.

She's young, much younger than she sounded on the phone, and I make an instant and quite possibly unfair judgment. Do I want a young woman wearing ripped leggings and a stain down the front of her white T-shirt cleaning my house and making up my beautiful guest rooms? And then I catch myself. I never used to be like this, judgmental. It's a trait I abhor in others yet I'm just as bad. Worse sometimes.

'Please, come in,' I say. 'It's good to meet you, Kerry.'

She doesn't say anything but she follows me into the kitchen. Most people make some comment about our beautiful, fully-fitted kitchen with its bespoke carpentry and cupboards painted in a dark marine blue contrasted with pale grey. But Kerry is young and she's probably not the slightest bit interested in interior decor. She sits down at the kitchen table and starts biting her nails.

'Would you like a drink?' I ask.

'Nah.' She doesn't look at me when she speaks and the lack of a thank you grates. There I go again, being judgmental.

'Thanks for replying to my advert in the village shop,' I say, as I sit down next to her. 'Can you talk me through any cleaning experience you've had?'

'I've only cleaned for Mum. She says I need to get off my arse and earn some money but it's not like I want to do this. I'm gonna be an influencer. But yeah, how many hours do you want me to work, because I can't do too much?'

Clearly no one has taught this young woman how to conduct herself in an interview. I almost feel sorry for her. 'At least five hours a day,' I say. 'More when I'm very busy.'

She chews her thumbnail and looks pensively at the ceiling. 'Yeah, well, I'm not sure about that.'

It's obvious that Kerry doesn't want this job, and I don't want to employ her. I make small talk for five minutes or so just to be polite and then show her to the door. What a waste of time. If my next interviewee is no good, then I'll have to use an agency.

I make myself a cup of coffee and then tip it down the sink. I'm pregnant now, whether I like it or not. Instead I boil the kettle, find a peppermint tea bag at the back of the pantry and pour hot water into the mug. It's my favourite mug, painted in a delicate green and blue floral design, brought back from South Africa when my parents visited the country on holiday just before Dad died. I leave the mug on the countertop whilst I nip back upstairs and put a little makeup on my face. At least I don't look like I've been crying now.

On the dot of noon, the doorbell rings again.

This time I'm prepared and open the front door quickly.

'Hello. I'm Maria Hinks. Thank you for agreeing to interview me.' She must be mid to late fifties and she's wearing a pair of black trousers, a cream blouse with a pussy bow neck and a black tweed-like jacket. Her short hair is curly and largely grey. With a weathered, make-up-free face, she looks efficient and business-like, not as if she's here to interview for what is essentially a cleaning position.

We shake hands, but her handshake is limp and the palm of her hand damp. She's clearly not as confident as her initial words suggest.

'Please, come in,' I say, standing to one side of the door to let her pass. Her black trainers make a squelching sound on the tiled floor.

'You have a beautiful home,' she says, glancing around the hallway. The staircase sweeps upwards on our right with a curve, the wooden handrail a smooth mid-brown colour. There's an antique console table made from satinwood, inherited from Josh's grandmother, standing against the opposite wall, on which I've placed a lamp and a pale grey pot filled with lavender. It's fake, but the lavender is so realistic no one has ever noticed.

'Thank you. Yes, it is a gorgeous house, and rather big. We're very lucky to live here. Please come through to the kitchen.'

We walk along the downstairs hallway and into the large, square kitchen. I gesticulate for her to sit down at the table, the seat which young Kerry vacated. 'Would you like a cup of tea or coffee?' I ask.

'Wow! What a fabulous kitchen!' Her eyes are wide as she glances around. 'If I get the job I'd love to clean in here, although it looks like it's already sparkling.'

The interview goes well. Maria explains she used to be a live-in housekeeper for a wealthy family in Oxshott and has recently moved to West Sussex to be nearer friends and family. Her previous employers have relocated to Dubai and although she was asked to join them there, she declined.

'I'm happy to do a bit of everything,' she explains. 'Cleaning, cooking, shopping, school runs, general errands. I like to call myself a homemaker.'

'That sounds perfect,' I say, wondering for a moment if this woman is too good to be true. No doubt the sticking point will be pay, as I'm sure she must have been on a good salary before. But when I broach how much I'm offering per hour and the fact that the job might not be full-time, she doesn't seem fazed. I show Maria around the house and explain what needs doing in the two guest rooms and en-suites, and then we return to the kitchen.

'How soon could you start?' I ask.

'Tomorrow! My diary is empty as I've only just moved.'

'That's marvellous,' I exclaim. 'And references?'

She delves in her worn black leather handbag and removes a creased piece of paper with two names and phone numbers on it. Her writing is jagged and all in capitals. 'These are the people I've worked for most recently.'

'Great, thank you. Assuming all is okay with your references, I'd love to offer you the job,' I say. 'Shall we provisionally agree for you to start on Monday?'

'Perfect.' Maria grins broadly and thanks me effusively.

Surprisingly and fortuitously, the first name on the list of Maria's references answers immediately. She's gushing about Maria's cleaning skills and her positive attitude, saying they couldn't have done without her and they were gutted when they had to let her go due to their move. I put the phone down with a smile. Josh will be pleased; I'm going to have help.

The rest of the day is spent with Ava and she keeps me so busy, I have little time to think about the pregnancy. It isn't until I'm preparing supper that I realise I'm going to have to tell Josh. He'll be delighted, of course. We've always said we'd like two children of our own, three in total for Josh. We have the space and the money to provide our family with everything they need. All perfect, except it's no longer what I want.

I hear his car pull up into the driveway. The car door slams shut and his feet crunch on the gravel as he strides up to the back door. He walks into the kitchen and dumps his briefcase on the ground.

'How are my girls?' he asks, stepping towards me and reaching down for a kiss.

'Good,' I say. 'And how was your day?'

'Two root canals, dental bonding, a full set of veneers,

along with the normal day-to-day stuff. Ordinary. How about you? Have you employed someone?'

'Actually yes, I have. She's called Maria and she's in her fifties. She seems efficient, willing to do anything, and comes with great references.'

Josh throws his arms around me and hugs me tightly. 'That's great news.'

Josh runs his own thriving dental practice. When we first met, he ran a practice with his old friend Arun Devi. I remember how Arun and his wife Louise welcomed me into their friendship group. But then things got awkward and Arun left to set up his own practice. We don't see them anymore.

'Daddy!' Ava shouts, careering into the kitchen and throwing her arms around his legs.

'How is my munchkin?' he asks, lifting her up into the air. She giggles raucously.

The evening goes as most of our evenings do. Giving Ava a bath and putting her to bed, something Josh and I like to do together whenever he's home from work in good time. Finishing off the cooking for supper, followed by eating it at the kitchen table. Clearing up together. One or both of us finishing off our work and if we have time and there's something worth watching, we'll sit together in the capacious living room and watch television. It isn't until we're in bed with the lights off, Josh's arms wrapped around me, that I realise I haven't told him. Josh has no idea that I'm pregnant. I could tell him now but instead I think about Mum, and the tears slip silently down my cheeks.

'Are you alright?' Josh murmurs sleepily.

'Yes, fine,' I say and shift away from him. I remind myself how lucky I am living in this big house, wanting for nothing.

Married to a loving and generous man, working because I choose to, surrounded by caring friends. Except everything is different now and despite all the love and comforts around me, my past is tainted and my future uncertain. Eighty-nine days ago I was gripped with sorrow at Mum's impending death, stroking her hand as she gasped for breath, her voice cracking as she told me how much she loved me. Tears coursed down my cheeks. But then she broke my world and now there's a darkness that enshrouds my thoughts, a fear that makes me question everything. And no, despite what I tell Josh, I'm not fine. Not at all.

2

MARIA

For the first time in years, I got lucky. I haven't had a lot of luck so maybe it's my time now. Just a shame I've had to wait so many decades for it to happen. The one saying I loathe above all is that you make your own luck. Sure, if you're born into a family with money and status you might be able to change the trajectory of your life, but if you're like me, with a string of soured relationships and all alone, you can't make your own luck. Instead you're buoyed along at the mercy of others like a plastic duck on the high seas. But today Lady Luck helped me get a job with the delightful and rather beautiful Imogen Letwin.

I tried not to show how impressed I was with her fancy house, but heavens above, it's like a mini palace. I've seen places like the Letwins' Fairview House in magazines but I've never been inside such a grand property. I might have disliked Imogen if she'd been a lady of leisure but she explained how she rents out two of the bedrooms and she has some sort of a hotel consultancy job. And then there's her little one, so this is a woman juggling a lot of plates.

Perfect for me to swoop in and help. I mustn't get too carried away because it's only a cleaning job, but I fully intend to make the most of it. Perhaps it'll even be a way for me to get out of this dump.

I glance around my bedsit. It's the sort of place you might expect to find tucked behind the station in a large city, managed by an unscrupulous landlord, with drug addicts hanging around the doorway. But look hard enough and you'll find grotty places just like this one in every town in the country. The trouble is, when you've got no money, there's zero choice. And I've got no money. I suppose I should be grateful that I have a bed and a roof over my head, but it's hard to be appreciative living in a single room with damp crawling up the walls, paint peeling from the ceilings and a bathroom that stinks of raw sewage. I could try and make it my own, give the place a lick of paint and hang up some pretty curtains, but hopefully I won't be here too long. For now, I'm living out of the two suitcases that hold the sum of my worldly possessions. I don't have much to show for my fifty-five years on earth.

I'm up at the crack of dawn, pacing the tiny space, a flicker of excitement in my chest. I've got such a good feeling about this job and Imogen in particular. I put on a pair of grey slacks with an elastic waist and a long sleeved T-shirt. At 7.30 a.m. I walk out into the hallway, unlock my rusty bicycle and wheel it outside. I wish I had another mode of transport but there aren't any buses that stop near Fairview House, and it makes no financial sense to get a taxi. I wanted to look unflustered and confident for my interview, so I got a taxi to drop me at the bottom of Imogen's drive and then I walked home. It took ages and cost me a small fortune, so I won't be doing that again.

I hum away to myself as I cycle out of town and along the narrow country roads. I find it quite amusing how cars back up behind me, and I'm certainly not going to be intimidated by the chap in the white van who drives so close to my rear wheel he might knock me off. No, it's the car owners' problems if they don't know how to share the road with a cyclist. It's a sunny morning and the birds are singing. Some of the trees are just beginning to turn yellow and orange. I love the autumn, with the hint of decay in the air.

Fairview House has a wrought iron sign at the bottom of the driveway and the gravel crunches as I push hard on the pedals of my bike. It's truly a breathtaking house with its symmetry and sweeping driveway. I lean the bike against the wall near the back door and press the bell. My heart is thumping excitedly.

The door swings open and standing there is a very handsome man. His dark hair is slightly greying at the temples and his amber-flecked brown eyes crease as he smiles at me. I'd say he's quite a lot older than Imogen and he has one of those classically handsome faces that, like vintage wine, gets better with age. Then again, I can't see the beautiful Imogen marrying anyone who didn't match her in the looks stakes.

He extends his hand. 'You must be Maria. I'm Josh, Imogen's husband. Welcome!'

His grip is firm and he squeezes my fingers together. I wish I'd had the chance to wipe down my hands after gripping my handlebars for the last thirty minutes.

'Please, come in. Imogen is in the kitchen with our daughter Ava.'

I follow Josh through the utility room and into their fabulous kitchen. Imogen is at the sink but she immediately puts down a dish cloth and smiles at me. 'Hello, Maria. Welcome to our family.'

My heart melts, quite literally, and it renders me speechless. There's something about Imogen that is strangely familiar. Her colouring is the obvious – the honey blonde hair and pale blue eyes – but it's more than that. I can't work out if it's her smile that is ever so slightly lopsided or the way she moves so fluidly, almost like a dancer. It takes a beat for me to realise that all three of the Letwins are staring at me.

'Sorry. Thank you so much. I can't wait to get stuck in.' I walk towards Ava, who is a mini-Imogen with her mother's colouring and the cutest curly blond hair. 'You must be Miss Ava, the grownup of this family.' To my surprise, she holds out her hand so I shake it.

'I'm still a child,' she says with great sincerity. The three of us adults laugh and Ava looks affronted.

'Maria is going to be working with me in the house,' Imogen explains.

'And I can't wait.' I smile broadly and I don't even have to fake it.

'Would you like to see my room?' Ava asks. Once again, my heart swells.

'Maria will see it later,' Imogen explains. 'Because you, little monster, need to get ready for school. Daddy is taking you this morning.'

'I'm not a monster,' she says, pushing back her chair and skipping out of the kitchen.

'You have the most adorable daughter,' I say. This family is utterly perfect. Beautiful, polite, well-educated. I couldn't have landed anywhere more perfect. If only this position could be a live-in so I could get out of my rented dump. I can just imagine getting little Ava up in the mornings, preparing breakfast for all the family, perhaps taking Imogen a mug of tea in bed.

'Would you like to follow me,' Imogen says, breaking into my thoughts. 'It would be great if you could start by cleaning the guest rooms.'

Imogen leads me back to the utility room and shows me where she keeps all of her cleaning materials. There are myriad shelves and cupboards painted in a tasteful pale blue and I realise that this space alone is larger than my bedsit. I carry a bag full of cloths and spray bottles in one hand and the hoover in the other and follow her back into a hallway and up a staircase at the back of the house.

'My guests use the side door and this staircase,' Imogen explains. 'It's perfect, as it means our family living spaces and the guest spaces are totally separate.' She opens the door to one of the bedrooms. 'The guests left yesterday but I haven't gotten around to cleaning the room. My other guests are downstairs eating their breakfast. They'll be leaving within the hour. Can I leave you to it? Just strip the beds and put the linen in the washing machine downstairs. Clean the bathroom and bedroom, please.'

'Of course,' I say. Now isn't the time to tell the lovely Imogen that my cleaning experience is zero. But how hard can it be? I've always cleaned my own home and I'm a neat and tidy person.

Imogen leans against the doorframe and her face has turned very pale.

'Are you alright?' I ask.

'Yes, yes. Thank you. I'll be downstairs in the study so just shout if you need anything.'

And then she's gone. But that was weird. It was as if

Imogen had had a funny turn. Goodness, I hope she's not sick.

I look around the room. It has rose-pink curtains and bedspreads and is more old-fashioned than the rest of the house. I suppose her guests like the chintzy, olde English country-house style. It's not to my taste. I work the hardest I've worked in years, scrubbing the bathroom, hoovering throughout, dusting up high and stripping the sheets off the bed. I carry the dirty sheets and towels back downstairs and put them in the washing machine, but it's nothing like the one that I use at the launderette and as I stare at the machine, I realise I don't know how it works. I hurry along the corridor, past the kitchen and the fancy living room to a smaller study at the far end of the corridor. The door is slightly ajar and as I poke my head around I realise that my soft shoes haven't alerted Imogen that I'm here. My beautiful boss has her head in her hands and her back is shuddering. Why is she crying?

I take a step backwards and knock on the door. Imogen jumps, hurriedly wiping her eyes with the backs of her hands and swivelling around.

'I'm sorry to disturb you,' I say. She looks terrible, her eyes pink, her nose dripping. 'You're not alright, are you?'

She goes very still and I realise that I might be in danger of overstepping some invisible boundary. But surely it's okay to ask a distressed person if they need help?

'Can I do anything?' I ask, after a long and awkward pause.

'I'm just having a moment,' she says and gets up from her chair. 'My mother died three months ago and the grief suddenly hits me for no obvious reason. I'm told it gets better with time.'

'Oh, you poor love,' I say and immediately regret my words. 'It's the hardest thing in the world losing your parents.' People say that's the case but frankly when my parents died, it was a relief, so it's not like I have first-hand experience. 'I was just wondering if you could show me how the washing machine works. I'm not familiar with that brand.'

There's a flicker of a frown but then she leads me back to the utility room, turns the dial and presses the start button.

'Sorry if I seem a bit thick, because it is obvious now you're showing me. I just didn't want to wreck your lovely linen.'

'It's absolutely fine,' Imogen says with a weak smile. 'The other guests have left now so please can you clean their room next.'

'Where do I find the clean linen?' I ask.

'Oh, sorry, I didn't show you.'

'Sounds like you have too much on your plate,' I suggest. Once again she side-steps my comment.

'It's on the upstairs landing, the second door on your left. It's a large linen cupboard. Please take the linen from the left-hand side marked for guests.'

I hurry back upstairs and gaze at the stacks of linen and towels neatly piled up on slated shelves that stretch both sides of the long, narrow walk-in cupboard. I run my hands over the smooth Egyptian cotton sheets on the Letwin family stack. Similar to the rest of the house, it's of the finest quality, cool and almost silk-like to the touch. No cheap polycotton here. For a moment I wonder if Imogen would miss a bottom sheet if I took one for myself, but then immediately chastise myself. I'm no thief. I turn to the other side, which is marked B&B Linen, and select two bottoms sheets, two white duvet covers with matching pillow cases and a pile of fluffy white towels.

After making up the bed in the first guest room I then head for the second room. It's a tip. The duvet is crumpled up on the floor, the curtains half drawn. There are dirty tissues and mud on the carpet. Surely it isn't too much to expect the guests to put their rubbish in the bin? I glance in the en-suite and it's in an even worse state than the bedroom. I'm disgusted. Hair and scum in the bath; smeared toothpaste in the sink; makeup-stained towels dumped on the tiled floor. How can people treat a beautiful home like this? It's so disrespectful to Imogen and Josh and it makes my blood boil. I bet whoever these guests were don't treat their own home like this. I'm angry as I clean the place up, and the physical exercise of scrubbing and vacuuming does little to abate it. It really beggars belief that people care so little for beautiful things and the perfect family who facilitated their stay here.

Around midday I'm almost finished. I hear the slamming of a door and the high-pitched voice of a young child. Ava must be back from school. I wonder if she's only at school for half days. After vacuuming the corridor upstairs, I walk silently down the back staircase. I can hear Imogen and Ava chatting and it's the sweetest sound. That familiarity hits me again and chokes me up. I really have landed in the perfect family.

Ava and Imogen are both seated at the wooden kitchen table, their blonde heads close together.

'Excuse me,' I interrupt. 'Would you like me to make lunch for your little one?'

Ava looks up at me and grins. I want to squelch those little cheeks and scoop her up into a hug.

'That's kind of you, Maria, but we're sorted for lunch. Ava has the afternoon off school today. Have you finished the guest rooms?'

'Yes, I have. Would you like me to do the guest dining room?'

'Actually, I've already done that, but if you could clean our bathroom and Ava's, that would be great.'

'Of course, with pleasure,' I say. But I feel a little cheated somehow, as if she wants me upstairs and out of the way. I want to know what kind of food Imogen makes for Ava; whether the little girl is fussy or a good eater; what I can do to make myself indispensable to each member of this perfect family.

An hour or so later, Ava and Imogen have finished their lunch. I'm a bit disappointed that she didn't leave any food for me, but I suppose I'm expected to bring my own sandwich. I didn't bother so I'll just forego lunch. I've had to cut down on food a lot lately, now that prices are so ridiculously high. It's worked wonders for my figure, not that I'm bothered about that. Having a man in my life is the last thing on my mind. But hopefully once I get my salary, I'll be able to indulge a little more. I hear voices in the garden and see that Imogen and Ava are playing in a sandpit. There's a small slide and swing next to it. Now, that surprises me a bit – not that they have play equipment in the garden for their daughter, but surely Imogen must know that it's not healthy to do physical exercise straight after eating. What sort of mother did she have not to have taught her that?

I glance around the kitchen and see a recipe book lying on the countertop. It's called *Quick Meals for Your Tricky Toddler*. Hardly an inspiring title, but the pages don't lie flat and it's clearly well used. I flick through the book, noting the

Post-it notes sticking out on the pages that Imogen uses the most. I take my phone from my pocket and photograph the recipes. I'll have a go at making them and perfecting them at mine, so I'm ready to give little Ava delicious meals. There are a few pots and pans on the draining board so I wipe them dry and hunt through the cupboards to make sure I'm putting them away in the correct places. When I'm done, I stand back and smile. Lady Luck is smiling down on me today.

3

IMOGEN

It's Friday late afternoon and the front door opens. I wait for Josh to come into the kitchen where Ava is finishing her tea but the footsteps go upstairs, followed by the banging of a door.

'Finish your food, sweetheart,' I tell Ava. I run upstairs.

'Josh?' I shout. I hurry into our bedroom but he's not there. And then the loud music starts and I remember. It's Kyle's weekend to stay with us. I groan. How could I have forgotten?

Kyle is Josh's son from his first marriage to Guila. They married young and the relationship was, according to Josh at least, doomed from the start. Guila became pregnant to improve their marriage, but as is often the way, it only made matters worse. They remained married for the sake of their son for a further decade.

I try to get along with fifteen-year-old Kyle but he's decided that he loathes my guts and only stays with us on sufferance. What makes it worse is that he's polite to me in front of his dad. The barbed comments and obnoxious behaviour are strictly for when we're alone.

I knock on his door and push it open. He's lying on his bed with headphones clamped over his ears.

'What are you doing in here?' he asks, sitting up. 'You need to knock before you come in.'

'I did. How are you, Kyle?'

'What do you care?'

'Actually I do, which is why I asked.'

'When's Dad coming home?'

'Any time now. I'm making chicken for supper. Is that alright for you?'

'I'm vegan.'

'What? Since when?'

'Since I decided that it's inhumane to eat living creatures.'

I grit my teeth. He wasn't vegan a fortnight ago. I wonder whether he's really only eating vegan food or whether he's doing it to wind me up. 'How does your mum feel about that?'

'It's none of your business what my mum thinks, but as you're asking, she thinks that you're a money-grabbing social climber who's ruined our lives.'

I gawp at him. Kyle has said some vile things to me before, but this is the worst. I'm about to justify myself, to tell him that his parents' marriage was broken long before I came on the scene, but a wave of nausea takes me unawares and I have to sprint to the bathroom. I sit for a moment on the cool bathroom floor, leaning my head against the trunk of the sink. I'm glad I didn't say anything to Kyle because it would have been inflammatory talking about his parents' marriage, but how am I meant to handle him? I know he resents me and actually I can understand that. He sees how his father is with Ava and he must be consumed with jealousy, but he's fifteen now, attending an expensive private day school courtesy of his dad, and he needs to learn to be polite. I wonder whether I should secretly record him when he's firing off at me, but I think that would incense Josh even more. I drink some water from the tap and wait for my stomach to settle.

'Imogen, are you up there?' Josh shouts up the stairs.

I quickly get to my feet and hurry along the corridor. 'Sorry, just needed the bathroom.'

'I was worried. Ava was all alone and said you'd been gone for ages.'

'Five minutes, max,' I say, walking down the stairs, but in truth it could have been much longer than that. I feel a rush of guilt for leaving our little girl.

'Are you alright? You look pale.'

'Yup, fine. How was your day? Oh, and Kyle is here.'

'Great. I'll go and have a word with him.'

No doubt he'll be charming towards his dad, the parent who furnishes him with a much-too-generous allowance and bends over backwards to his whims, I suppose to ease his guilt for divorcing Guila.

The next morning I'm awake early but the second I sit up in bed, the nausea strikes again. I rush to the bathroom but with insufficient time to shut the door behind me or run the taps to conceal the noise. When I emerge back into the bedroom, Josh is sitting up in bed.

'Have you got something to tell me?' he asks.

'No,' I say without meeting his eyes.

'Imogen, you're pregnant, aren't you?'

I stop still, glancing down at my toenails that need a fresh coat of nail varnish. I'm not sure I can tell my husband a blatant lie; it really isn't fair.

'Yes,' I admit after too long a pause.

'But that's fantastic news! Why didn't you tell me?' His face lights up.

'I wasn't sure,' I lie. 'I'm sorry.'

'I can't believe you didn't tell me the moment you had an inkling. This is what we've been wanting for the past three years. What's come over you?'

'Pregnancy,' I say with a hint of sarcasm.

'How long have you known?'

'Only yesterday,' I tell another fib.

'Oh darling, come here.' He opens his arms to me and somewhat reluctantly I walk towards him. 'I know it's the grief,' he murmurs into my hair as I sink onto the bed next to him. 'I really think you're suffering from depression, sweetheart. It's nothing to be ashamed of and ever so easy to treat. If we had got pregnant before your mum passed, you'd have been ecstatic, but grief has clouded everything. I'll come with you if you don't want to go to the doctor by yourself.'

But I know I'm not depressed. I'm just terrified that the child I'm carrying might not be the sort of child that Josh wants. Of course, I'm missing Mum terribly, and yes, I'm sad but mostly I'm conflicted and terrified about being pregnant. It's just I can't tell Josh the truth.

We're all at the breakfast table, which is unusual because after his morning orange juice, Josh normally grabs a piece of toast and eats it standing up and Kyle, when he's staying with us, languishes in bed, unless it's a school day and then Josh chivvies him along. But this Saturday morning, Josh has promised Kyle a trip to Sports Direct so he can buy some new trainers. Bribery works wonders for rousing teenagers. Maria has arrived early and is cleaning up after the guests who have already had their breakfast and checked out.

'We've got some amazing news,' Josh says, his hands clasped around a steaming mug of coffee. He's unable to wipe the grin off his face.

It takes me a moment to realise what he's about to say. 'It's a bit soon–' But he cuts me off.

'We're pregnant!' he exclaims. 'You two are going to have a baby brother or sister!'

'Josh! I'm nowhere near twelve weeks!'

He reaches across the table and squeezes my hand. 'Let's think positively. We've been wanting this for ages.'

'Am I getting a sister?' Ava asks excitedly, as she jumps down from her chair and does a little jig around the kitchen.

'Or a brother,' Josh says. 'It's great news, isn't it, Kyle?'

Kyle grunts without looking up and carries on shovelling cereal into his mouth.

'Will she share my room?' Ava asks. 'And can we go to the climbing frame together and play with my dolls?'

'Not for a couple of years,' Josh says with a grin. 'You'll have to wait until he or she has grown up a bit.' Josh puts the emphasis on he. He hasn't articulated it but it's clear he'd prefer a boy. I might have preferred a boy as well a few months ago. Now I'd rather have another girl. Or not have another child at all. But no. I mustn't think like that. Whatever happens, I'm going to have to keep this baby.

Ava sticks her lower lip out and returns to her place at the table. I wonder if our second child will be as much of a tomboy as Ava is. She's permanently covered in bruises from when she takes tumbles, and as she likes to climb pretty much anything and everything, her knees are always scraped.

'Maria says she'll take me to the big climbing frames.'

'Maria?' I ask with a frown. Ava is referring to a playground on the edge of town that is frequented by much older children, predominantly because it has a skate park. I think she's too young to go there. 'When did Maria offer that?' I ask. Why would our cleaner offer to take Ava out somewhere? It's strange.

'Don't know,' Ava says, unhelpfully.

'She's super creepy,' Kyle interjects.

Ava thumps her hand on the table. 'No, she's not. I like her.'

'She's like a witch with that frizzy grey hair and the way she just appears out of nowhere as if she's been tiptoeing around the house.'

'Let's not talk about people like that,' Josh says. 'She's helping Mum and that's what we want.'

'She's not my mum and Maria's a weirdo,' Kyle murmurs.

'I'm very grateful that she's here,' I say, needing to have the last word, especially as Josh has chosen not to reprimand Kyle.

Whenever Josh and I aren't doing anything on a Saturday night, we have an early supper with Ava and Kyle if he's staying with us. It's our little tradition and Ava loves it. It's 5 p.m. and I'm basting a roast chicken, while the lentil stew I've made especially for Kyle is bubbling nicely.

Kyle thumps down the stairs and then the front door slams closed. I hurry into the hallway and pull open the door.

'Kyle!' I shout. He turns around and frowns. 'We're having supper at 6 p.m. I've made you a vegan dish.'

'Not hungry. I'm going out with some friends.'

'We agreed that we'll all eat together this evening,' I say.

'You can't tell me what to do, Imogen.' He mutters, 'Just piss off,' under his breath and climbs onto his bicycle, tearing out of our drive onto the main road.

'You're not wearing your helmet!' I shout after him.

I stomp back into the house and call Josh. There's no answer. He's been playing a game of squash with a friend and is either still on the court or in the shower. I'm tempted to call Guila, but I'm aware I could look ridiculous. I let out a puff of air. Am I over-reacting? What do I know about teenage boys? Nothing. But it's so inconsiderate disappearing off when we had agreed to have family supper, and then to talk to me like that is downright rude. I place a hand over my flat stomach. Is my response to Kyle because I'm anti-boys at the moment? I desperately hope I'm not carrying a boy but then I'm riddled with guilt. Nothing is a given. I try to work out how many weeks pregnant I am. Six or seven, maximum, and the earliest we can find out the sex of our baby will be, I think, twenty weeks. But do I actually want to know? Will I worry more if I know I'm having a boy? I've heard stories about babies feeling their mother's emotions, knowing if they're not wanted. I can't have that for my child.

I do a quick check on the food and put my head around the door to Ava's playroom. It's a small room next to my study lined with shelves that are stacked with toys and games. She has so much stuff, I'm permanently worried that she's going to grow up spoiled, but now that Mum's dead, the crazy over-indulgence in present-giving will stop, so perhaps I shouldn't worry so much. Ava is playing happily with her dolls, fully engrossed in some make-believe world. I go upstairs to our bedroom and sit for a moment on the end of the bed and stare at the urn on the dresser. Josh questioned me about having the urn in our bedroom. He's been nagging me to scatter the ashes but I can't do it while the weather is bad; or at least that's the excuse I give myself. The truth is, I'm not ready. I feel a morbid modicum of comfort knowing that Mum's still with me, albeit in a different form. Scattering the ashes will be like her funeral all over again and I'm just not strong enough to go through that, to completely let her go. Not when I still have so many unanswered questions and so many things to tell her, and not whilst I'm so angry.

'Anyone home?' Josh shouts.

I hurry back downstairs.

'Something smells good,' he says, kissing me briefly. Josh's hair is still damp from a recent shower. I marvel at how good looking my husband is. The only things that stops him from being a true Adonis is his slightly crooked smile and a scar cutting through an eyebrow, the result of an unfortunate fight when he was much younger. He's a true catch, and on more than one occasion I've seen my girlfriends eye him up with a lascivious expression. I frequently have to pinch myself that he's married me.

'Roast chicken for us and a lentil stew for Kyle.'

'It's kind of you to make him a special meal.' Josh sits at the kitchen table and pulls his phone from his pocket. He'll be checking the rugby scores.

'He's gone out and said he won't be back for supper. Kyle's so rude to me, Josh.'

'I'm sure he doesn't mean it. He's just a typical teenage boy trying to push back. I was just like him at that age.'

'The thing is,' I say, 'he's fine in front of you but the moment it's just the two of us, he's rude and hurtful.'

Josh frowns and looks up from his phone. 'That's quite a claim, Imogen.'

'I think he's resentful about our relationship,' I say.

'Come on, sweetheart. We've been together for six years. It's not like this is some new romance. I'll give him a call and see where he is.'

I grit my teeth. Why can't Josh accept that Kyle isn't all sweetness and light? I decide I will have to secretly record our conversations. Josh steps out of the kitchen and I can hear him laughing on the phone, then he reappears.

'Kyle will be home in twenty minutes, just in time for supper. He said he can't wait to try your lentil stew.'

Really? That doesn't ring true.

Sure enough, just as we're about to sit down to eat, Kyle returns home, the door slamming as normal, him scooting into the kitchen to take his place at our wooden table.

'Made it just in time.' Josh laughs.

'I wouldn't have gone out if I'd known about supper. Imogen said it was fine for me to be out.'

'Excuse me!' I exclaim. 'I said no such thing. In fact, I told you that we were having a family supper at 6 p.m.'

Kyle rolls his eyes while Ava shuffles uncomfortably. I hate having arguments in front of her. She's a sensitive child and the last time she overheard Josh and me having a tiff she asked if we were getting a divorce.

'She must have misheard me,' Kyle says. He looks at his dad with a poker face and I wonder how he got so good at lying.

'My name is Imogen, not she,' I snap.

'Come on, love. Let's not get into a fight,' Josh says. 'Who would like green beans?' He picks up a spoonful from the dish and puts some on Kyle's plate.

This is what it's always like. Josh seems to think that I take pleasure in starting fights with Kyle. Why can't he see that his son is needling me, playing a much cleverer game than I am? I try to quell the knot of fury in my sternum and dump a large dollop of lentil stew on Kyle's plate, right on top of the beans. He smirks at me, which makes me even more livid.

'Fancy a bike ride along the South Downs Way tomorrow?' Josh asks Kyle, totally ignoring the tension in the room.

'Sure. Can we stop off at the pub for a beer?'

'You're a bit young for that,' Josh says, but then he winks at Kyle. What the hell is Josh playing at? It's one thing letting him have a beer at home, but giving him one in a pub is breaking the law. It seems like I'm on a losing battle with those two.

'Can I come too?' Ava asks.

'To the pub?' Kyle laughs.

'No, darling,' I say. 'Kyle needs some one-on-one time with Daddy. You and I can do something together.'

'Can we go to the big climbing frame?'

'We'll see,' I say.

We're just finishing off our meal when the doorbell rings.

'It'll be my guests,' I say, jumping up from the table.

'It's late,' Josh murmurs. I know it annoys him that I put my bed and breakfast guests first and it's far from ideal that they're interrupting our supper.

'Sorry, but they asked for a late check-in.' I prefer my guests to arrive mid-afternoon, but I don't say no to a late check-in. Before having Maria's assistance, it helped me, giving me more time to prepare the room.

Mr and Mrs Cornish are a middle-aged couple. There's a sourness to the woman's face, her lips pinched together, greying blonde hair swept back off her forehead with a wide floral headband. She nods at me curtly but it's only her bald, flabby husband who extends his hand for shaking. In contrast to her silence, he doesn't stop talking, wittering on about their journey from Nottinghamshire and how they prefer to stay in a hotel but all the decent ones in the locality are booked up so staying at my place was very much a needs must choice. He's doing nothing to improve my already bad mood. They follow me up the back staircase and along the short corridor to the first of my two guest rooms. I step back to let them walk inside. Mrs Cornish heads straight for the en-suite bathroom.

'Where's the bath?' she asks.

'I'm sorry, but our guest rooms only have showers en-suite.'

'That's not good enough. I need a bath.' She crosses her arms over her chest.

'I'm sorry,' I repeat, 'but it clearly says on our website that we only have en-suite showers.'

'You have to be joking. All British people like a bath and I'm no exception.'

I have to bite my cheek to stop myself from laughing at her sweeping statement and remind myself that the guests are always right. She steps over to the bed.

'Oh my god!' she exclaims dramatically. 'There's a black hair on the pillow case!' She steps backwards onto her husband's foot.

I lean over to inspect the bed and unfortunately, she's

right. In addition, the linen looks creased, not up to my normal immaculate standard. I'm annoyed with myself for not checking on how Maria left the room.

'I'm terribly sorry,' I say. 'Perhaps I could offer you a drink in the lounge downstairs whilst I change the bedlinen.'

'A port for me and a large gin and tonic for the wife,' Mr Cornish says.

I've no idea if we have any port but hopefully Josh will have a bottle stashed away somewhere.

They follow me downstairs and I install them in the guest dining room. I hurry into the kitchen where I'm relieved to see that Josh, Kyle and Ava have finished their meal.

'Would you mind being bartender?' I ask Josh. 'I've got to change the linen.'

'I'll do it,' Kyle says. 'I'll give them drinks.'

Fortunately Josh agrees with me that that wouldn't be appropriate. 'He wants a port and she wants a gin and tonic,' I explain. 'Would you mind giving them those?'

Josh seems to find it quite amusing. Whilst my husband charms my guests (or at least I hope he does) I quickly change the linen and make sure there isn't a hair or a whisper of dust anywhere. I'm hot and bothered by the time I go back downstairs.

Josh steps into the hallway to meet me. 'I'm sorry, love, but they've left.'

'What? I thought all the decent hotels in the area were booked up.'

'They found a room somewhere else. They've demanded a full refund as well, otherwise they'll leave you a stinking review. I know this is the last thing you need right now.'

Josh is right. I'm livid. I'm angry with Mr and Mrs Cornish for being so unreasonable, with Maria for her lack of attention to detail, and most of all with myself for not double-checking everything. This is the first time I've lost guests, and it stings.

4

MARIA

I'm devastated. I let the delightful Imogen down by not paying enough attention to detail. I should have double-checked there were no hairs on the bedlinen, and I didn't. I winged it. She sent me a message last night saying that she's created a quality control list, whatever that means. So I rang her straight back and poor Imogen sounded close to tears. She lost some guests because the room wasn't up to scratch. Imogen explained that it wasn't all my fault but honestly, I felt like sobbing. I want to do my best for my new employer, to help her and make her life easier. It seems I've done the opposite. I offered for her to dock the money she lost off my wages but she refused. She said it was her fault for not explaining to me carefully enough. It just goes to show what a lovely person she is, shouldering the blame like that.

I slept badly last night and today I'm restless. She has given me Sundays and Mondays off and I really don't know what to do with myself. The truth is, I'm lonely. Desperately lonely. I don't have any friends around here and I miss being

in the bosom of a family. After a cup of milky tea, I walk out
of my miserable bedsit and glance at my old banger parked
up along the side of the building. She's silver, full of dents
and scratches, but she's mine and I love her. Unfortunately,
today my only mode of transport is my bicycle. I say mine,
but it's actually an old bike I found discarded at the end of
the street where I used to live. Okay, here's the truth. I lost
my driving licence. You could say I was a naughty girl and I
got caught. Extremely frustrating, especially when you live
in a small town as I do and it's vital to drive. Luckily, it's only
a twenty-minute cycle to Imogen's house and I'm sure if the
weather is truly vile, she'd be happy to collect me and take
me home. Although thinking about it, there's no way I would
want her to see the sordid place where I'm living. I can't
imagine what she'd think of it.

I don't plan to ride past Fairview House but I find myself
pedalling along the narrow lane, conkers on the side of the
road causing little hazards, colourful leaves making a carpet
of reds and yellows. The air is fresh and cold with a promise
of icy weather to come. Perhaps it won't be so pleasant this
year, because my bedsit only has a night storage heater
which I'm unlikely to be able to afford to run. My earnings
will firstly be spent paying off my debts, secondly my rent,
followed by food. Luxuries like heating and clothes will have
to wait. I shiver at the prospect of months of coldness. A car
overtakes me, driving a little too close, and I wobble
violently. I stick my finger up in the air but the car has long
gone. Inconsiderate bastard. I slow right down at the
entrance to Fairview House and glance up the driveway but I
can't see anything. Imogen and Josh park their cars in a
garage to the side of the house so I'm not sure whether
they're at home or not. I'm tempted to hop off my bike and

ring the doorbell, to see if there's anything I can do to help, but I know that will seem weird. Who in their right mind offers to work on their days off?

Reluctantly, I carry on cycling and soon reach the local pub, The Hanging Gate. It's a bit early at midday, but the car park is surprisingly full, packed with Range Rovers and fancy sports cars. There's an affluence in this area that I love. I lean my bicycle up against a dumpster bin at the side of the pub. No need to lock it around here. Then I stroll inside and make my way up to the bar. It's an olde worlde place with black beams, low ceilings and a warren of small rooms. There's a restaurant to the left of the bar and it's already filled up with families chattering away. I stare at a family with three generations: grandparents, parents and little children. I wonder if the older woman truly appreciates what she has.

'Excuse me?'

I turn to face the barman.

'What can I get you?' he asks. He looks down his nose at me, as if my scruffy clothes and shiny face courtesy of the long bike ride aren't good enough for this fancy establishment.

'A small white wine, please. The house wine.' Hopefully that will be the cheapest they have.

He pours me a glass and pushes it across the bar. 'That'll be £4.79, please.'

I hand over a five pounds note. I could have made myself a decent meal for that price, but then I remind myself I'm not here because of the wine; I'm here because I want to feel part of this community.

I sit on a bar stool at the end of the bar and slowly sip the tepid wine. After ten minutes or so an old bloke sits down next to me. He has a white mop of hair and a reddened nose, most likely from excessive drinking. He must be a regular because the barman says, 'How are you doing, Trevor?'

'Good, good,' he replies.

'The usual?'

'Yes and make it a double being a Sunday.'

'Coming right up.' He pours Trevor a large measure of whisky.

'Haven't seen you around here before,' Trevor says. 'You on holiday?'

'No, I've recently moved here. For a job.'

'Oh yes. Well, it's alright around here, if you like fresh air. People are friendly enough although me, I prefer the cattle.'

'Cattle?' I frown.

'My son runs the farm these days but I'm still up at dawn giving the cows a once-over.'

He takes a sip of his drink and swills it around his mouth before swallowing it with a gulp. 'That's better,' he murmurs to himself.

'Do you know the Letwins? Josh and Imogen?'

He scratches his chin. 'Oh, you mean the dentist and his young family in the old rectory?'

'They live at Fairview House.'

'Yes, that's them. Some silly bugger renamed the place. Why are you asking about the Letwins, then?'

'I've started working for Imogen, as her housekeeper but I prefer to call myself a homemaker.'

'Can't say I know them well. Joshua was married before; lived the other side of Horsham. I've got a few friends that go to him to get their teeth done but he's too pricey for me. I prefer his old business partner, Arun Devi. Get the fillings done on the NHS with him.'

'And Imogen? What's she like?'

'We keep ourselves to ourselves around here.' He clambers down from his bar stool. 'Enjoy your new job.' He nods at me, the former friendliness having dissipated, and then he hobbles across the room and out of my view. What was all that about? Why did he give me the cold shoulder when I asked about Imogen?

'Can I get you another?' the barman asks. I glance into my wallet and see I have the total of £2.40 in coins.

'No, thanks,' I say. 'I've got to get a move on.'

I cycle back home and this time it seems to take forever. My legs are sore by the time I get there, and feel like they're in danger of giving way. A wave of sadness envelops me as I push open the door to my bedsit. There's only one solution: the bottle of cheap wine I bought yesterday. I spend the afternoon finishing it off.

I wake up with a pounding headache. I used to be able to knock back a bottle or even two with no problem, but these days age has caught up with me and it's knocked me for six. I swallow down some own-brand paracetamol and despite wanting to curl up in bed, I force myself to go out. I'm a little wobblier on the bicycle today as I cycle towards Fairview House, but I need to do something and not wallow all alone. As I reach the drive, I dismount from my bike and wheel it onto the pavement on the other side of the road, where rather conveniently, there's a large tree. To my delight, I see Imogen and Ava holding hands sauntering out of their drive, turning right, towards the centre of the village. I can't hear what they're saying from here, but Ava is bouncing along clearly happy. That warms my heart. Keeping a good distance between us, I cross back over the road and wheel my bike, following them along the pavement. As I suspected,

they head for the children's playground. Despite being a
Monday morning, it's busy with kids on the swings and
mothers sitting on the benches, chatting away. It must be
half term if they're not at school. When Imogen approaches,
a couple of the women wave at her, smiling broadly. I'm glad
to see that she has friends. One woman gets up and hugs
Imogen, blowing a kiss to Ava, who is already at the top of
the climbing frame. I stand back, next to a hedge where the
blackberries have rotted on their stems. I've got a good view
of Imogen, and even when she's talking to the other women,
she never takes her eye off Ava. And when Ava seems to be
stuck on the highest rung of the climbing frame, she's there
in a nanosecond, ready to help her daughter. I'm so happy to
see how motherhood suits her; how Imogen and Ava clearly
adore each other. I hope that their special bond lasts a lifetime, but I fear it might be transient. Perhaps I should warn
Imogen that the mother-daughter relationship is precarious
and can snap catastrophically if it isn't carefully tended.

I wait and watch, and about half an hour later, Imogen
gestures to Ava that it's time to leave. The little girl pouts
with disappointment but she listens to her mother and soon
they're waving goodbye to their friends. As they walk back
the way they came, I wheel my bicycle towards them.
Imogen is deep in conversation with her little girl so it's up to
me to stop and talk to them.

'Imogen?' I say.

She glances up and looks at me with surprise. 'Hello,
Maria.'

'I was just on my way back from the village shop. How
are you both today?'

'We're good, thanks, heading home so I can do a bit of
work.'

'What does Ava do whilst you're working?' I hope she isn't plonked in front of the television.

'Colouring, playing with games and dolls. There's always something, isn't there, munchkin?'

Ava nods.

'What are you up to on your day off?'

'Nothing at all.'

There's an awkward moment where neither of us say anything. I'm holding my breath, hoping that she's going to ask me back to the house, perhaps ask if I could do a little overtime. But she doesn't. She just says, 'Have a lovely day and we look forward to seeing you tomorrow morning.'

I watch as they saunter away, my heart heavy. Should I have said something? Let Imogen know that I have so much more to offer her than just being a cleaner? No. I have to be patient and bide my time. I am confident that everything will go to plan, because destiny is impossible to fight.

As I'm cycling back home, I have a bright idea, a way that I can help Imogen from behind the scenes, without her knowing it was me. I lock the bicycle in the hallway and hurry up to my bedsit. I pull out the old laptop from under the mattress and fire it up. It's a cast-off and extremely slow but it should do the trick. I go onto one of those review websites and search for Fairview House Luxury Bed and Breakfast, and there it is, Imogen's pretty face beaming out at me, next to perfectly taken photographs of her home. She has thirteen five star reviews and two four stars. I'm surprised she doesn't have more reviews but perhaps I can find others on different websites. She definitely needs more. I take a long time refining my gushing review, extolling the beauty of the location and the superb facilities, writing under the pen name of Mary Smith. I'm really pleased with my five stars review, and warmth courses through my veins as I think how thrilled Imogen will be to receive so much praise. In a day or two, I'll write another review, this time using a male name. It takes very little effort on my part but will undoubtedly make a big difference to Imogen. Who knew it could feel so good to help someone else?

5

IMOGEN

It's still dark when Ava crashes into our bedroom and wakes me with a start. Everything aches and as much as I adore our daughter, I feel a desperation for sleep.

'Josh,' I murmur.

'I've got it,' he says, sitting up in bed, lit up by the hallway light that we leave on for Ava. 'Come on, munchkin. It's night time and you should be tucked up fast asleep in bed.'

'I'm sorry,' I whisper to Josh.

'Go back to sleep, love. It's fine.'

I feel like crying. I'm so grateful to my husband who has been on night duty ever since Mum died. I don't know why he isn't exhausted, working all day in his dental practice and then having to pick up the pieces from me when he gets home. I suppose he's able to operate on fewer hours' sleep than I can but it doesn't stop me from feeling guilty.

He tries to slip back into bed quietly, but I'm still awake.

'Thank you,' I murmur.

He holds me tightly and before long his breathing is slow and steady.

I have two best friends: Danielle, whom I've known since we were children, although we've become really close during the past six years, and Tom. Tom is a stay-at-home dad to Ava's best friend, Issy. He was, and I suppose still is, an architect, but his wife Julia has the higher paying job working for an investment bank in the city, and they decided that of the two of them, it would be easiest for Tom to pause his career, returning to it in due course. Tom and I have an easy friendship. He's bright and funny and frankly better with the kids than most of us mums, and because our girls are inseparable, we spend a lot of time together. This morning the kids are back at school and Tom is coming over to have a measure-up of our stone garages. I had the idea of turning them into a two-bedroom holiday let which will be much easier to manage than the bed and breakfast. Now that I'm pregnant again, it makes sense to reduce the commitment of making breakfast every morning for our guests. Not that I've shared my idea with Josh yet. I want to know the logistics and get an estimate of costs before discussing my proposition.

We're sitting in the kitchen drinking mint tea. 'How are you?' he asks, peering at me with narrowed eyes. 'You look tired.'

'I'm pregnant,' I blurt out. And there I was promising myself I wouldn't tell anyone yet.

'Congratulations, Imogen! That's amazing news. How are you feeling?'

'Um, yes, okay. Tired and nauseous but I guess that's normal.' I wish I could tell him what I'm really feeling but I suspect it would be the end of our friendship if I did. I wonder what Tom would think if he knew what a bad mother I can be, how if you peel back just a little of my façade, you might find evil.

He frowns at me so I change the conversation. 'I've opened up the garage. Shall we go and look?'

'Sure.' We walk side by side across the gravel drive to the stone buildings. 'How have Ava and Kyle taken your happy news?'

'Actually I hadn't wanted to tell anyone yet as I haven't reached twelve weeks, but Josh blurted it out to the children. Ava is ecstatic, Kyle his normal.'

'Uncommunicative or rude?' Tom asks.

'Both. I find him so difficult and really don't know what to do about it.' I probably shouldn't be sharing my thoughts of Kyle with Tom, but Josh doesn't listen and Tom is able to give me a much-needed male perspective.

'Teenage boys aren't interested in babies,' Tom says. 'Just give him time and I'm sure he'll be fine.'

I'm not so sure. I open the garage doors and Tom walks inside.

'I'm just going to measure up,' he says, pointing his digital laser measuring tool at the far wall.

My phone pings with an incoming email.

'I've got a new review,' I say. I glance at the name. Mary Smith. I don't recall having any guest called Mary Smith, but sometimes people use their maiden names or even pseudonyms when posting reviews. It's a five star review so I'm not complaining, but when I read it, it makes my skin prickle.

My stay at Fairview House was amazing. The rooms are beautiful and the breakfast delicious but it's the owners of Fairview House that make this place special. What a lovely family they are! Imogen is the hostess with the

mostest. Beautiful, smart, attentive and kind. Her hand-
some husband, Josh, is charming, and their gorgeous little
girl, Ava, is just the most adorable child you could ever
hope to meet. They welcomed me with a smile and made
me feel like a member of their family. They have such
good manners and really are the perfect family. I would
like to stay with them for ever but sadly I had to leave.
Ten stars from me and hugs to the Letwin family.

'I've just had the weirdest review,' I say to Tom, who is
scribbling something in a small notebook.

'In what way?' he asks, peering over the top of his wire-
rimmed glasses.

'It's got to be a fake, because my guests rarely come into
contact with Josh and Ava. It's more a review on our family
than the B&B.' I think of the couple who Josh gave drinks to,
and how they'd left. If they were going to leave a review, it
certainly wouldn't be effusive.

'Let's see,' he says, striding to my side and peering over
my shoulder at my phone.

He snorts with laughter. 'It's like a love letter to the
Letwin family.'

'It's creepy and I don't know who posted it. I had my first
lot of disgruntled guests at the weekend and assumed it
might be them, but this doesn't stack up. Also, I don't like
that they've listed all of our names.'

'Can you delete it?'

'No. I'd have to get in touch with the website and they'll
probably penalise me. I mean, people sometimes leave
anonymous or fake reviews if they're slating a place, but a
fake good review? It doesn't make sense.'

'It can't be a bad thing, can it? I think you should lap up

the fact that you're the perfect family!' He laughs. Tom works in silence for a while and then says, 'Right, I've got the measurements, but are you sure about pursuing this renovation, Imogen? You have enough on your plate with your consultancy work, the B&B and your family, and now you're pregnant again. If you want to maintain that perfect family image, perhaps now isn't the right time for doing building works?'

'We're hardly perfect,' I say. 'Oh, I don't know.' I rub my eyes.

'I'm just worried you're pushing yourself unnecessarily.'

This is what I love about Tom. We have such an easy relationship and he's blunt with me. I view him like the brother I never had.

'Fancy another cup of tea?' I ask.

'Sure.'

We wander back into the house and through the utility room to the kitchen. It's my favourite room in the house: square, with enormous flagstones on the floor, an Aga on one wall as well as a conventional oven. Josh insisted we install a new kitchen at vast cost when we moved into the house, and this is a dream come true for me. I still pinch myself several times a week that this is all mine. I switch the kettle on while Tom sits at the rectangular oak kitchen table.

'I can draw up some simple plans but give it serious thought, Imogen. You can do this renovation at any time in the future; it doesn't have to be now.'

I'm pouring the hot water from the kettle when Maria appears at my side like an apparition. Maria walks so silently that she startles me, and it isn't the first time. I spill some boiling water onto the countertop.

'Oh hello,' she says, stopping in her tracks with a mop in

one hand and a bucket in the other, standing a little too close to me. 'Sorry, didn't mean to disturb.'

'You're not,' I reassure her. 'Maria, this is my friend Tom. He's Issy's dad, Ava's best friend.'

'Hello, Maria!' Tom waves a hand at her. 'I've heard lots of good things about you.' He hasn't because we've barely discussed my new help, but that is typical Tom. Mister Nice Guy putting everyone at ease. Maria stares at Tom for a beat too long and for a moment I wonder if she knows Tom, but then she smiles warmly and says, 'I'll leave you to it. Just want to collect some bits from the utility room.'

But somewhat annoyingly, Maria doesn't really leave us to it. She's constantly popping in and out of the kitchen, fetching a broom or a bottle of window cleaner or some kitchen roll, so we move into the living room, but she appears in there too with a duster and then apologises profusely for interrupting us. I know she's only doing her job but it does seem a little intrusive. I tell myself that I'm not used to having someone clean my house and of course it's going to be awkward to begin with. Eventually Tom leaves and I spend a couple of hours working before collecting Ava from school.

As with every marriage, Josh and I play a game of checks and balances. I attend a weekly painting class on a Tuesday night and Josh goes to the pub with his friends on a Friday night. Tonight it's my watercolour class. I feel bad about going, leaving Josh to care for Ava yet again, but he doesn't seem to mind. And goodness, do I need this evening. When I'm mixing up colours and carefully placing them on the stretched paper, my head is empty of all the intrusive thoughts, and when I stop, Danielle is at my side, feeding me gossip and making me howl with laughter. Helping me forget.

The watercolour class is held in the village hall, a large room that doubles up as a music and theatre venue, a voting hall, a yoga space and a room to hire for parties. The walls could do with a sprucing up and the floor is squeaky vinyl, but this place is much cherished in our village. Alain Poitier is our teacher and as his name suggests, he's French. When he first started the classes, he was over-subscribed. Not because the local ladies particularly wanted to learn to paint but because Alain could have walked straight out of a film as the dashing, somewhat melancholic unshaven hero with hair that's a little too long, stubble and piercing blue eyes that don't only critique your work but see straight into your soul. Much to the ladies' chagrin, Alain is married to Yvonne, a solicitor. After a while, the class dwindled to eight of us. Although I'll never be a great artist, with Alain's tuition I have improved considerably.

There is one big fly in the ointment, and that is the fact that Danielle is having a passionate affair with Alain. She confided in me about a month ago. I was shocked – well, perhaps not shocked, because nothing Danielle does surprises me, but disappointed I suppose. She justifies herself by telling me that all French men have affairs, that Alain's marriage is on the rocks anyway. It's like I'm watching the slow motion car crash of the destruction of a marriage.

This evening I'm five minutes early and as I walk into the hall, Danielle and Alain pull apart. Her face is flushed and he runs his fingers through his unruly hair.

'Thank goodness it's only you,' Danielle says.

I clench my jaw and sit down at my usual table,

unpacking my paints and brushes. Danielle hurries over to sit next to me.

'When the door swung open, I thought we might have been caught,' she says breathlessly.

'So it doesn't matter that I see you snogging our teacher but if anyone else finds out, it's a problem?'

'Don't be like that, Imo. I'm in love. We both are. I want you to be happy for us.'

'I don't want you to get hurt. He's married and it doesn't look like he's going to be leaving Yvonne anytime soon, does it?'

'He said he is. We're going to be together.'

'Yeah, right.'

'You're such a cynic. If he doesn't leave her, then I'll get pregnant. He'll leave Yvonne then.'

'You what? For God's sake, Danielle, how can you even think like that? That's a terrible thing to do.' Anger bubbles up inside me at the thought of bringing a baby into this world as a fixing mechanism. And then I check myself. I'm in danger of being a hypocrite.

'Keep your hair on. I was only joking,' Danielle says. Alain is welcoming the other artists but he throws a concerned glance our way. 'We don't all have the perfect marriage and the model blended family that you have.' There's a hard edge to Danielle's voice. I had no idea she might be resentful of my life.

I lose myself in painting this evening's photo, the sun setting over an indigo sea, palm trees edging in from the sides. But Danielle's comment about my perfect marriage goes around and around in my head. Is that what people on the outside think? Her words remind me of that fake review. The perfect family. Is that how everyone views us? If so, it goes to show that no one knows what someone's marriage is really like, and that can also apply to the couple in it. Josh and I aren't perfect. In fact, sometimes I wonder how much we really know each other. He's forever wanting to fix things, but the feelings I have about Mum can't be sorted with some fast-acting dental cement or a visit to the GP for a dose of antidepressants. And just because he's permanently full of energy and upbeat doesn't mean I can follow suit. We don't talk like we used to, sharing our feelings and hopes for the future, and often, when I'm lying awake in bed while Josh is asleep next to me, I feel a deep sense of loneliness. And it's not the first time. My mind wanders back to the first year of Ava's life. Things were far from great then. Do I feel like something is missing from our marriage? At the moment I do, because I'm keeping so much from my husband, letting all my worries stew inside me.

'You're pissed off with me,' Danielle says after about fifteen minutes of silence.

'A bit,' I say. 'I just don't want you to be hurt.'

'I'm willing to take that risk for the passion I'm experiencing now. But let's not talk about me. How are you?'

This is my cue to tell Danielle that I'm pregnant, but for some reason I don't. I know Tom won't spill the beans because he only knows Danielle through me, and I'll tell her soon, just not today. 'I'm fine,' I say curtly.

'Have you heard that Caitlin, Phoebe's mum, reversed her car into Angie's brand new Audi and now Angie's threatening to sue Caitlin and saying it's because Caitlin's an alcoholic and was drink-driving?'

'No!' I exclaim. 'When did that happen?'

'Yesterday at pick-up. Angie is such a cow. Apparently it

only caused a small dent in her bumper. She wanted to call the police but Mrs Howard, the head, stopped her.'

'How's Caitlin?'

'She was in floods of tears. Angie has disinvited Phoebe from her son's birthday party at the weekend.'

'Who knew there could be so much gossip at a primary school.' I chuckle, the atmosphere between us easing. I enjoy getting the inside tittle-tattle from Danielle, who works at Ava's primary school as the Year Two teacher. Of course, she's totally out of line telling me what's going on, but she knows I won't divulge any secrets.

'And how's your work?' Danielle asks.

'I've been brought in to sort out a hotel in Brighton. They're haemorrhaging money and will have to declare themselves bankrupt if things don't improve in the next quarter.'

'What are you doing to help them?' Danielle asks.

'They're overstaffed and the general manager is totally useless. I'm going to have to sack him and make a few other people redundant.'

'You're going to have to do that?' There's surprise in her voice. She holds her paint brush above her painting and a drop of water falls into the middle of her work.

'That's awful,' she says. She dabs at the water mark but it's wrecked the painting. Danielle doesn't seem to mind; if it were me, I'd be livid.

'It's what I'm paid to do.'

'Yes, but you're still putting people out of work, ruining their lives.'

'It's better to lose a few people than for everyone who works there to lose their jobs. At the end of the day, we're trying to save a business.'

'You must have loads of enemies if that's what you do – go into businesses and cull them. I'm surprised you've never told me that before.'

'You make it sound like I'm a murderer,' I murmur.

'I don't suppose you're the most popular of people. Doesn't it bother you?'

I shrug. I've never really thought of it that way. I guess I might have a few professional enemies, but someone has to sack people and it's easier for me as a consultant to do it than the people who have been working together for years.

'I wouldn't be able to sleep knowing I've got to fire someone.' Danielle shivers dramatically. I think that's a bit ironic considering Danielle is likely to ruin Alain's wife's life.

I've viewed firing people as a skill, being able to be objective and to let people go in as gentle and professional manner as possible, but Danielle might be right. Is there something wrong with me, not feeling any real guilt? Is it a true reflection of who I really am? I had always considered myself to be a good person but now I'm wondering if I'm not. I can be bitchy and cruel. I lap up the gossip that Danielle feeds me and we're forever laughing at the mums at school, even saying mean things about the children. But now I wonder if there's badness inside me, whether it's been there all along but I've never realised it until now. Perhaps Mum saw that in me my whole life but somehow managed to suppress it, but now she's gone, now I know the truth, it's swirling out of me like a plume of dark smoke, weaving around me and contaminating everyone I come into contact with.

'Alain and I are going away for a dirty weekend,' Danielle murmurs.

I tut.

'When did you get so sanctimonious?' Danielle asks.

I glower at her.

'Joke, joke,' Danielle says. 'Alain knows he needs to tell Yvonne but he's too worried about hurting her.'

I'm not listening now. All I can think of is how Danielle is right. There must be a ruthless side to me because I never lie awake worrying about firing someone. It's just what I do, but is that normal? Is it normal that I hit a fox with my car a couple of weeks ago and I didn't stop to check if it was all right? Or perhaps it goes right back to my childhood when Mum saw the signs but I didn't have enough self-awareness to know that it was an act of violence cutting off all the hair of my dolls, and when I begged Mum for judo lessons she took me to ballet instead. I see it now. I possess a brutality and lack of empathy, yet for the whole of my life I thought I was a good person.

I was wrong.

6

MARIA

My favourite room in Fairview House is the master bedroom. In here, I feel the very essence of Imogen and Josh. It's where they spend most of their time, relaxed, in harmony with each other. I imagine it's where Ava was conceived, where they share their deepest secrets, where they feel safe in each other's arms. This morning, I'm all alone in the house, and I'm going to give the master bedroom a spring clean. Imogen hasn't asked me to do this, but I know she'll be happy with the results.

I stand in the doorway and look around the room. Opposite the door is a wide sash window with views onto the garden and the South Downs in the far distance. The window is framed with floral curtains in whites, beiges and greens. It surprises me as the fabric is quite fussy and really not to Imogen's normal taste. I wonder whether she inherited these curtains and she hasn't got around to changing them. The king sized bed sits on the left wall. It has a covered headboard in plain green, and cream-painted bedside tables, each with three small drawers, stand either side of the bed. There are metal lights sticking out of the wall above each bedside table, the sort you find in hotels. Opposite the bed is a wide and tall chest of drawers and on top of it numerous photos in frames, a couple of boxes and other trinkets. There's a door into the en-suite bathroom. On the wall opposite the window there's a large built-in wardrobe and today, I intend to have a little rummage. At some point I might ask Imogen if she'd like me to sort through her clothes, arrange them in colours perhaps, but right now, it might be a bit forward of me.

I start by making the bed. Josh and Imogen were probably in a hurry this morning because the duvet has been pulled up haphazardly. I tug it back, smooth down the bottom sheet and pick up the pillow on Imogen's side of the bed. Bringing it up to my face, I inhale deeply. There's the faint scent of her floral perfume and another smell, perhaps from her shampoo. I pick a couple of long hairs off her pillow. I then walk around the bed and breathe in Josh's pillow. There's a peppery scent combined with something exotic, like amber perhaps. It's cheap smelling, not like Imogen's perfume. When the bed is made to perfection, I lift off the detritus on top of Josh's bedside table. There's a small clock, a miniature torch and a pack of pills, the name of which means nothing to me. I pull open the little drawers and chuckle. There are a couple of sex toys and a tube of lubricant. Lucky them. Other than that, I find some cables, probably to charge his phone, a Kindle and a packet of tissues. There's nothing to suggest Josh has an interesting personality.

Imogen's bedside table yields a little more of interest. She has kept the wrist band tag from when she gave birth to Ava.

There's a little silver box holding some baby teeth. They must be hers because Ava still has her first teeth. There's a polaroid photograph of Imogen and Josh laughing, and in the bottom drawer, a stash of jewellery. I take out a string of pearls, squeezing them between my fingers, and wonder if they're real. I put everything back carefully, just the way I found them.

The chest of drawers is full of clothes. The top drawer holds Imogen's underwear; the second drawer Josh's underwear; and the third and fourth drawer are full of Imogen's sweaters. It's in the bottom drawer where I find a heavy leather-bound book. Carefully, I remove it and place it on the bed. I open the first page and gasp out loud. It's a photo album stuffed full with baby photos – not pictures of little Ava, but another baby from longer ago. A baby who looks so familiar it takes my breath away. As I flip through the pages, the baby morphs into a small girl with blonde fly-away hair and cupid lips. She's laughing in lots of the photos, holding the hands of an older couple who gaze at her with adoration. These are undoubtedly photos of Imogen as a baby and young child. My heart pounds as a rush of excitement buzzes through my veins, happy tears springing to my eyes. The familiarity is so overwhelming, I let out a little sob. With fumbling fingers, I undo the chain around my neck and open the tiny heart locket. It's hard to undo because I haven't opened it in a very long time and I squeal with frustration. But eventually I manage it and stare at the photo of the tiny baby girl. Her features are so similar to those of Imogen as a baby, I can't help myself from pumping the air and screeching *yes* out aloud. I take my old mobile phone out of the pocket of my trousers and photograph some of the photos in the album. Then I'll be able to enjoy them at my leisure.

Eventually, I put the album back where I found it and start dusting the items on the top of the chest of drawers. I lay the photo frames on the bed and I'm just picking up a large wooden box, but it's heavier than I expected and to my horror it slips through my hands, landing on the beige carpet, spilling out a mound of ash.

What the hell?

It takes me a few moments to realise what I've done. This is an urn, holding the ashes of someone who has passed, and now they're all over the floor. My heart is pounding in my eardrums as I bend down to the floor and carefully pick up the urn. Fortunately it's not broken but about half the ashes have fallen out. I scoop up as much as I can, pouring them back into the urn, but it's not easy because the ash slips through my fingers. I shiver as I realise I'm touching the remains of a human being. I stand up and stare at the mess. The ash is caught in the fibres of the carpet and I have no choice but to vacuum them up. When I'm done, the carpet is clean but the urn is definitely lighter and not quite as full as before. I feel terrible. Are these the remains of Imogen's mum? What if she notices?

I hurry downstairs into the living room. There's an open fireplace there and although it looks like it hasn't been used in a while, there is still some ash sitting in the hearth. I run into the kitchen and find a jug and a large spoon. Back in the living room, I scoop ash into the jug, trying to avoid the little segments of coal and unburned wood. I'm still not sure that there's enough ash, so I go outside and smoke several cigarettes, one after the other, collecting the ash in a little saucer. Yes, I'm a smoker, but I don't smoke before coming to work because I don't want Imogen to smell it on my breath. I glance at the time. I need to hurry because Imogen will be home soon with Ava. Back in the master bedroom I'm chewing mint-flavoured gum as I carefully tip the ash into the urn and leave it centred on the chest of drawers. I just hope Imogen doesn't notice and that if she ever finds out what I've done, that she'll forgive me. It isn't until much later that it crosses my mind the urn might belong to Josh rather than Imogen.

I reckon I have just enough time to make Ava's tea. No, Imogen didn't ask me to cook for her, but she's had such a busy morning, out at the crack of dawn, dressed up all smartly in a navy business suit, telling me she had a difficult meeting to attend at a client's in Brighton, and then she was whizzing back to collect Ava from school.

I've chosen one of the recipes I photographed from *Quick Meals for Your Tricky Toddler* and I've practiced the recipe twice at home because it needs to be perfect. It's spaghetti with roasted chicken and peppers and was a bit tricky for me to make because I don't have an oven in my bedsit, just a two-ring electric stove. I could follow the recipe and use Imogen's oven but I've never touched an Aga before and the electric oven looks complicated. Instead I fry up the chicken and peppers on the stove and when I hear a car pull up and Ava's excited chattering voice, her tea is ready to be served.

'Oh!' Imogen says as she steps into the kitchen. 'You're cooking?'

'I thought I'd whip up a little tea for you, knowing what a busy day you've had. I hope I've done the right thing. I just wanted to help.' I'm a little concerned by the expression on Imogen's face but then she breaks into a smile.

'That's so kind of you, Maria. Really thoughtful.' She

turns to Ava. 'Sweetheart, go and wash your hands and then you can eat.' She glances over at the table where I've laid out cutlery for two.

'Actually, I eat with Josh when he's home, so it'll just be Ava eating now.'

'Oh,' I say. 'I hope it tastes alright.'

'I'm sure it'll be delicious. Thank you so much.'

I leave Imogen to give the food to Ava, but I can't stop myself from lingering on the other side of the door.

'It's really dry, Mummy,' Ava moans. 'The chicken sticks to the roof of my mouth.'

My heart sinks. I wanted the meal to be perfect.

'Just eat as much as you can,' Imogen says. 'Maria has been so kind to make this for us.'

I remind myself that Ava is just an ignorant little girl, while her mother is a well-mannered, considerate woman. I hurry away to finish cleaning the guest rooms because I'm really behind on my schedule.

About thirty minutes later, I hear footsteps on the back stairs. Imogen pops her head around the door. 'You've done way more than your five hours today, Maria,' she says. 'You should go home.'

'Oh no,' I chime. 'I've been slower than normal and I made your tea so I'm at least two hours behind. I gave a couple of your bedrooms a good spring clean, so I want to finish up here.'

'That's really kind of you. I'll pay you the extra hours in cash.'

'Goodness, absolutely not,' I say, but Imogen produces a twenty pounds note and holds it towards me.

'I refuse to accept it,' I say, noting and rather relishing the surprise on Imogen's face. 'I'm only doing my job, and just because I'm a perfectionist, doesn't mean that you should have to pay for that.'

'Oh,' Imogen says. She seems a little confused by my reaction but she puts the note back in her wallet. 'I do want you to be fairly remunerated.'

'Please don't worry. I love working here and if we need to up my hours, then we can talk about it in due course.'

'Thank you,' she says, her eyes creasing in such a familiar manner. My heart soars. *Oh, Imogen, I've found you.*

7

IMOGEN

I'm exhausted. The morning sickness has taken hold and it feels like it's destroying my body, as if the life growing inside me is leaching my energy. I've just dropped Ava at school and had intended to do a shop, but the fatigue is overwhelming, so I've come straight home. Walking into the kitchen, my legs feel so heavy they can barely carry me.

'I've made you a cup of tea,' Maria says. She must have heard my car arrive. 'You look tired.'

'I am. Thank you. I think I'm going to have a quick nap.'

'You really are pale. Do you think perhaps you should see a doctor?'

I smile wanly, realising that as I'm going to be seeing her every day it would be easier to tell her the truth. 'Actually, I'm pregnant. Early stages so we're not telling anyone yet.'

'Oh, congratulations!' Maria claps her hands together with such exuberance it's as if she's just won the lottery. 'Well, that explains why you're so tired. You need to look after yourself and your wee one.'

Upstairs, I collapse on our bed and when I next wake up, my tea is stone cold and my clock tells me it's 1 p.m. I sit up in bed and sniff the scent of cooking. I haven't suggested that Maria cooks and it's certainly not in her job description, but she seems to enjoy it, and as I'm feeling nauseous and drained, I'm grateful.

I groan as I force myself out of bed. I'm behind on my work and I haven't kept a check on what guests we have arriving when. In the kitchen, Maria is bustling around.

'I've made a lasagne for you, which you can heat up for your supper. I used the conventional oven rather than the Aga, as I've never used one before. I hope it tastes okay.'

'I'm sure it'll be lovely. Thank you.' I notice the instruction manual for the oven lying on the countertop.

'I thought you could have a portion for lunch.' She stares at me expectantly.

'Yes, of course. Thank you.' I don't really feel like eating a heavy meal but perhaps it'll be good for me and settle my stomach. 'Just a small serving, please.'

Maria ladles up a square and places the plate on the table in front of me. She then hovers next to me.

'Would you like to join me?' I ask. I feel awkward, her cooking for me as if I'm a guest and she's behind-the-scenes staff.

'If you're sure?'

'Absolutely.'

Maria sits down in Josh's place. 'I'm so happy for you that you're expecting. Were you this exhausted when you were carrying Ava?'

'Actually, no.' I think back five years. During my first pregnancy, I was super-charged with energy and buzzing with excitement. This time it's the opposite.

'How's the lasagne? I realise it won't be up to your standard but I hope it's okay.'

In fact it's dried out, the pasta leaves brittle and lacking in seasoning.

'It's good. Thank you,' I lie. I'm making an effort to finish my portion but it's not easy. 'I'll show you how to use the Aga tomorrow if there's time.'

Maria's expression changes and I wonder if I've offended her, but then she's back to her smiley self. 'Have you got food cravings?' she asks.

'No. I didn't with Ava either.'

'Would you ever adopt?'

'What?' I exclaim. Why is she asking me that? I let my fork drop onto the plate with a clatter.

'If you couldn't have children, would you adopt?'

'But I can have children.'

'Well, hypothetically. Considering what you've been through.'

I stare at Maria, slack jawed. She looks bashful, as if she's realised she's put her foot in it.

'I'm sorry. I shouldn't have said anything. I shouldn't have seen it, but it was right there and I couldn't help it.' She's wittering like an idiot now and I realise with dismay what she's referring to.

'What have you seen?' I ask, my voice tight.

'Your adoption certificate. I'm sorry, I didn't mean to look. I was searching for the instruction manual for the flat iron. I've never used one of those before and I didn't want to ruin your beautiful sheets. And I wasn't quite sure of the settings on the oven.'

I stare at Maria. I hid my adoption certificate in the one place I knew Josh would never look: the drawer in the utility room where I keep all the instruction manuals for our household appliances. It was in a large white sealed envelope right at the back.

'I didn't want to bother you and when I saw the instruction manual for the floor polishing machine I assumed the flat iron instructions and the oven manual would be in there too, and I was right. I found them both.' Maria shuffles in her chair, looking increasingly uncomfortable.

'But you opened an envelope,' I say, feeling panic clench at my throat. Maria was snooping, although... was she really? It's not unreasonable for her to search for instruction manuals. It was my fault for hiding such an important document in a place where my cleaner could find it. Why on earth didn't I remember that?

'I'm so sorry. Please accept my apologies.' She looks distraught.

I can't eat any more. I place my cutlery on the plate and shove the remaining lasagne to one side. This is a nightmare. No one knows that I was adopted, not even Josh. 'You must be mistaken,' I say, but I find it hard to meet Maria's eyes. 'It wasn't what you thought it was.'

Maria tilts her head to one side and throws me a look of pity and disbelief.

'Okay, it was mine,' I admit eventually, my shoulders sinking downwards. 'But I'd be grateful if you didn't say a word to anyone about it.'

'Oh, Imogen.' She reaches her hand across the table to touch mine, but I pull away. I'm feeling increasingly uncomfortable.

'I know all about adoption,' she says, giving a little sniff. 'I had to give up my daughter and it was the most painful moment of my entire life. What do you know about your birth mother?'

'Nothing.' I'm not going to share anything more with this stranger in my house.

'If she knew the woman you'd become I'm sure she would be so proud of you, Imogen. No woman gives up her child willingly. There's always a heart-wrenching reason why she has to do it.' She sighs heavily. 'We always think of the adopted child, but the mothers suffer too. So much guilt and shame for giving up your child, a life-long pain and a feeling of loss that never goes away. I hardly ever talk about it, because people think less of me. They judge me for giving away my child.'

'I'm sorry,' I say. I'm sure Maria is right. Our natural inclination is to blame the birth mother for not being strong enough to fight for her child. But what do we know of the consequences and the mental turmoil that these women go through? Who are we to judge them?

'It was the worst thing I ever had to do,' Maria says in a whisper. 'Even if you think you're doing the right thing at the time, the loss never leaves you. You're forever looking for your child, wondering how they are, whether they miss you.'

'I suppose I only think about it from the adopted child perspective,' I admit. 'And I was lucky because I had wonderful adoptive parents. I miss them terribly.' My words catch in my throat as I think of Mum.

'You've lost both your parents?' Maria asks.

'Yes. Dad died two years ago of a heart attack and Mum passed away three months ago. It was devastating.'

'I'm very sorry to hear that,' Maria says. There's an awkward moment of silence. 'If you ever want to talk about your adoption, I know a lot about it.'

'Thanks,' I say, but it's the last thing I want to talk about. 'And please don't mention my adoption to anyone.'

'I wouldn't dream of it. My lips are sealed.' She does that crass movement of pretending to zip up her lips. 'Right, I must be getting a move on. You're not paying me to sit here and chat.'

I'm relieved when she puts our plates in the dishwasher and leaves the kitchen. That was a conversation I wish I hadn't had to have but it does serve to clarify one thing. Even if I'm unsure about wanting this child, in my heart of hearts, I know I couldn't go through with giving him or her away. Whatever type of human they grow into, I will learn to love them unconditionally.

When I was pregnant with Ava, Josh and I spent hours imagining what our child would look like – would he or she have Josh's eyebrows or my lips – and which of our characteristics they would inherit. It was then that Josh opened up about his best friend, Dominic. Dom's wife, Rhiannon, has schizophrenia in her family. Her father suffered from it, as did a couple of cousins. And then their daughter Carla developed distressing mental health problems. It started with anorexia when she was just twelve and developed into periods of mania and suicide attempts. She was, and still is, hospitalised frequently and the strain on their family is horrendous. Dom has broken down into tears on several occasions in front of Josh.

My husband is of the opinion they shouldn't have had children. That sounds harsh, and of course he's fond of Carla, has known her since she was a baby, but Josh is of the belief that nature is more important than nurture. If you have a potentially inherited disease in your family, you shouldn't risk passing it on to your children. I disagree and we've had heated arguments about it. Who are we to judge what another couple should or shouldn't do? The subject came up again when I wasn't falling pregnant. We both wanted another child, a sibling closer in age to Ava than her and Kyle. I asked Josh if he would consider adoption and he was vehemently against it. He said he understood how it was an option for couples who couldn't get pregnant but firstly we could get pregnant, and secondly we already had our own child. I was rather taken aback by his attitude, one which I didn't share. How very ironic it's all turned out to be.

As I'm tidying up it crosses my mind that although I've asked Maria not to mention my adoption to anyone, I haven't specifically told her that Josh doesn't know. What's she going to think about my marriage if I ask her not to tell Josh? I know it doesn't look good that I'm hiding such a massive secret but I have my reasons. I go upstairs and into the guest bedroom where she's dusting and ticking off every one of the tasks I've written down for her on a checklist.

'Um, Maria,' I say.

She turns and smiles at me.

'This is a bit awkward but when I said please don't tell anyone about my adoption, that means not mentioning it to Josh either. He's funny about that sort of thing so I need to pick my time. What I didn't tell you was that I've only just found out.'

She stares at me with a blank expression, which then morphs into one of pity. 'Please don't worry, Imogen. I would never share your secrets.'

I nod. 'I've got to make a couple of work phone calls. I'm expecting Tom to bring Ava back at 3.20 p.m. If I'm still on a call, would you mind letting them in, please?'

'Of course.'

The next couple of hours are swept up with work. I finish writing the staff manual for the hotel I'm working for in Brighton and then I have a lengthy Zoom call with the owner, discussing all the roles and job descriptions of his staff. I'm just finishing when I hear the excited chatter of Issy and Ava. I quickly save my documents and then hurry through to the kitchen.

'Imogen is too busy,' I hear Maria say. I pause in the hall.

'We normally stay for a cup of tea,' Tom replies, 'so the girls can play together.'

'Well, not today. It's not convenient.'

I stride into the room, concerned about Maria's words. 'What's not convenient?' I ask, trying to keep some lightness in my voice.

'I was just explaining that you're tired and overworked so probably aren't up to visitors.'

'It's only Tom and Issy,' I say smiling. 'They always stay for a quick drink.'

'Fair enough.' Maria nods but I think I see a quick scowl pass over her face. 'If it's alright with you, I'll be off for the day.'

'Absolutely,' I reply. Maria has already worked longer than her hours.

I put the kettle on and pour the girls a couple of glasses of juice. 'What was all that about?' I ask Tom as I watch Maria cycle away down our drive.

'Not sure,' he replies, 'but I don't think she likes me very much.'

8

MARIA

When Imogen opened up to me, I wanted to scoop her into my arms and tell her the truth. It's like fate has brought us together and I wish I could share my excitement with her. But I've learned over the years that we all come to deep realisations at different times. I'm instinctual, with quick reactions, but I see that Imogen is more measured, with a strong logical brain, and I can't risk scaring her off. I need her to trust me, to lean on me more, to allow me to become part of her family.

When I finish work, I don't go straight home. Instead I bike to the park where the young mums and nannies congregate, watching their little ones, chattering away to each other without a care in the world. When Imogen's baby arrives, she's going to need much more help, especially now I know that her parents are deceased. She may not realise it yet, but helping with the cleaning won't be sufficient; she's going to need childcare assistance too.

I lean my bike up against an oak tree and wander through long grass to the playground. There are two benches but they're occupied. The other mums are huddled in groups, standing on the shorter grass, chatting away. I want to pick their brains, find out more about being a nanny or an au pair. I choose a group of three young women and sidle up to them. They're young, late twenties, early thirties at a guess. When the woman wearing baggy jeans and an oversized pink sweatshirt rushes to the assistance of a little girl on the swings, I turn to the other two.

'Hi. I'm Maria. Which of the kids are yours?'

The woman standing nearest to me, her hair caught up in a messy bun, a muslin over her shoulder as she cradles a baby, frowns at me. 'Haven't seen you here before.'

'No. I've just got a job working as a nanny and house-keeper to a local family. I thought I'd come and check out the best places to bring their little ones.'

'Oh,' she says.

'Are you all mums or are there any nannies here?'

'Bianca's a nanny.'

'Which one is Bianca?'

'Long black hair playing with the kids in the sandpit.'

'Right, thanks,' I say. As I walk away, I glance back over my shoulder and the woman I've just been talking to is whispering something behind her hand and throwing furtive looks my way. I wonder what I did wrong.

At the sand pit, I crouch down and ask, 'Are you Bianca?'

'Yeah.'

'I gather from the mums over there that you're a nanny. I'm a nanny too.'

She sneers ever so slightly and turns back to the little boy in the sand pit. What the hell was that look for? I grit my teeth and continue.

'I was wondering if I could ask you a few things about your job?'

'Why?' She shuffles a bit further away from me.

'Because I'm new to the role and just wondered what other nannies do.'

She stands up, wiping sand down from her jeans, and turns her back to me. 'Okay, Archie. Time to go home.' I realise then that she has an accent – Italian perhaps?

'Are you full time?' I persist.

'I'm sorry but I don't know you and we need to go.' She picks up the little boy and ignoring his wails, hurries over to a pushchair. What a rude young woman. I stand watching her, my hands on my hips. If that's what the young generation are like, heavens help us. This bunch of stuck-up women clearly don't want to befriend me, so I stomp back to my bike and pedal hard all the way home. I'm just glad that Imogen is nothing like them. She has good manners and a kind heart.

Back at the bedsit I power up the old laptop and search for Imogen Letwin. She has a website for her hotel consultancy business, a website for the bed and breakfast, and she posts regular articles on LinkedIn abut hotels and hospitality. Unfortunately for me, her Facebook is set to private and her Instagram account is just for the bed and breakfast. I don't discover anything personal about her. Giving up, I start researching stories about adopted children and soon I find a forum where mothers share their experiences. Many of the stories are sad, where mothers fail to find their adopted children, but there are a few that are happy and uplifting. I focus on those. I find a video of a woman called Seema who was forced to give up her baby for adoption. She has one of those hyper-mobile faces that contorts whenever she's expressing an emotion. Seema is sitting on an armchair opposite the interviewer, and their knees are so close together they're almost touching. I suppose it's so the camera can see both women in the same shot.

'Seema, tell us about your situation when you became pregnant,' the interviewer says.

Seema winces, her lips tightening, and her cheeks move upwards. *'I was seventeen, much too young to look after a baby. Both my parents and the parents of my boyfriend decided adoption was the way forwards.'*

'Did you have any say in the matter?'

Seema shakes her head sadly. That's a good expression so I rewind by a couple of moments and try to mimic the way her eyes well up and how she tilts her head to one side as she shakes it. I restart the video.

'Did you consider terminating the pregnancy?'

'No. It was too late anyway, but I wouldn't have wanted to terminate.'

'Too bloody right!' I mutter under my breath. Imagine if I'd terminated? The Letwin family wouldn't exist.

'How did you find your adoption family?'

'Mum did it. We used an agency and they found a family that seemed a good match. We agreed to have contact via letters and they still send me photographs of Leo every six months.'

'How does that make you feel?'

'In some ways it's good because it feels like I'm still part of Leo's life but I also feel such sadness and guilt.' Seema's eyes well up and she brushes the tears away with the back of her hand. I try to do the same but am not successful at making my eyes well up. Perhaps I'll need to keep a bit of cut onion in my handkerchief and bring it out whenever tears are required.

'Guilt?'

Yes, terrible guilt. Perhaps I should have fought harder to keep Leo. It's not natural to give away your baby, is it? And is he growing up hating me, knowing he was abandoned?'

I pause the video again. Is that what Imogen feels? Hatred? And is that what I feel? Guilt? I'm not sure I know what guilt really feels like. I do a Google search on *What guilt feels like.* Well, that's interesting. It can show up in your body, making your muscles tense and your stomach feel wobbly. Yes, I get that occasionally. And you go over and over your actions, questioning them, feeling bad or sorry for someone else. I feel that for Imogen – sorrow that she's hurting. Sadness that I abandoned her. I return to the interview and press play again.

'Do you regret giving Leo up for adoption?'

Seema takes a long time to answer and her face contorts into multiple expressions. *'Yes and no. I think I did the right thing because Leo's adoptive parents are in a much better situation to give him security, a good education and love, but every day I wake up and remember him. I miss him. It's a bit like he died but he didn't.'*

'Haven't you made the ultimate sacrifice, giving your son away so he can have a better life?'

'Yes, maybe,' Seema says softly.

I jab the pause button and then click the interview away. Sacrifice! If anyone knows about sacrifice, it's me. I think of the years of pain and emptiness, the not knowing how her cries sounded, not holding her hand on the first day of school, never seeing a school report or meeting her best friend. Never explaining the facts of life or waiting up until the early hours to make sure she returned safely after a date. Not being at her wedding or by her bedside when she gave birth. That's sacrifice, and surprisingly tears do spring to my eyes. Whether they're tears of anger or self-pity, I'm not sure.

I look at the photograph of Imogen once again and those kind blue eyes stare back at me. I can banish all the negative feelings, because fate is finally smiling on me and we've been brought together once again. I stand up and walk the three paces to the bathroom, wiping the scratched mirror with my towel so I can see my face better. I think of Imogen and I think of Ava, then I stretch out the corners of my lips into a broad smile. Yes, life is looking so much better.

9

IMOGEN

It's one of those mornings where I wake up with an overwhelming sense of loss, loss tinged with anger. I miss Mum. I need her; her old-fashioned but nevertheless relevant advice on child rearing; her ability to stay calm in any situation; her food and the way she solved every problem with tea and cake.

Mum chose to be cremated. It's not what I wanted. I would have preferred for her to be buried in the graveyard of our local church, somewhere I could visit and leave flowers, making sure that she is remembered for generations to come. But she wanted to do the same as Dad, so I respected her wishes. The church is ancient – I think it goes back to Norman times – and the churchyard is on the top of a hill with views across fields and ancient woodland. What Mum didn't say was where she wanted her ashes to be scattered.

The sky is bright blue and the trees have turned to golds and oranges. Although I have a mountain of work, I decide to walk up to the churchyard and see if it's possible to get a plot. At least then she'll have a headstone and somewhere for me to go, rather than randomly scattering her ashes in the sea or the woods. I stuff a packet of tissues in my jacket pocket and walk briskly through the village and up to the church. It's the first time that I've been back here since we had Mum's funeral service, and my throat feels choked as I approach the graveyard.

The church was packed for Mum's funeral. She was popular in the village, even though my parents only moved here after we did. Mum threw herself into local activities – flower arranging for the church, fundraising coffee mornings and the like. Everyone was shocked how quickly she died. She'd been feeling tired for a while but put it down to her grief over losing Dad. Then one day she popped by to see me, announcing that she had lung cancer. How ironic for someone who never smoked and was vehemently anti-smoking. But it was more than lung cancer. That was just the secondary tumour. Her bones were riddled with it. The disease was brutal and so rapid. She died three months later.

The churchyard is tranquil but just being here drives a spear of grief through my chest and I have to lean against the old yew tree to stop myself from doubling over. I wipe away the tears, take a few deep breaths and walk up to the curved wooden door. The church is open but there is no one inside and the scent of furniture polish and old flowers just adds to my grief. I force myself to walk in and I sit on the end of one of the pews near the back of the small church.

'Oh Mum!' I murmur out loud.

Two days before Mum passed away, she ruined my life. Sometimes I'm so angry with her. Why did she need to unburden herself right before she died? Why didn't she tell me years ago, so we could have had time to discuss it? But mostly, why did she tell me at all? I could have happily lived my life without knowing the truth.

I was sitting next to her bed in the hospice. Her room was lovely and bright, with a view to a well-manicured garden and vases of flowers on the windowsill and dresser. I thought she was asleep as I held her hand, but no.

'Darling, there's something you need to know.' Her voice was faint and breathless. 'Dad and I adopted you when you were just a few weeks old. We've always loved you as if you were our child. Loved you so much.'

'What?' I said, recoiling from her. My initial reaction was this was a hallucination, a result of the morphine being pumped into her veins. Sure, I didn't look much like Mum and Dad, but there had never been any hint that I wasn't their birth child.

'I know this will be a blow to you, darling, but you need to know.'

A blow? It was deep and overwhelming shock. I couldn't speak for many long minutes.

'Who was my birth mother?' I asked eventually, anger in my voice. Why had Mum dropped this bombshell now?

'She was very young. From Guildford. The poor girl had been raped. They locked the man away but she couldn't cope with it. She took her own life.' Mum's breath shuddered and her eyes flickered closed.

'Mum!' I jumped up, putting my face near to hers, terror that I'd lost her squeezing my sternum. I called out for a nurse, who checked Mum over.

'She's still with us, Imogen, but she's very poorly.'

In fact Mum never spoke again. She passed away in her sleep two days later. The woman I'd spent a lifetime loving shattered my world with her dying words.

That is why the past three months have been so horrendous. Not only am I grieving my mother, I'm grieving a life of fakery and I'm trying to make sense of the horrific circumstances of my birth. I think that knowledge is in danger of ruining my life. I can't stop wondering whether the child I'm carrying might have the same genes as his rapist grandfather or the mental fragility of her grandmother. Are such genes always passed down or could I somehow break the cycle? It's not as if I have violent tendencies or suffer from mental health problems. But it could skip a generation or perhaps only show up in the male ancestors. I think about my Ava. She seems like a perfectly normal little girl with kindness in her heart but who knows what type of young woman she'll grow up to become. And what about me? I'm not a good person. I think of how Tom religiously recycles, how he shops at the local village shop to support the local community even though the selection is inferior to that at the farm shop which is part of a chain. I don't. I do whatever is expedient for me. And I'm easy to anger, shouting at Ava if she's dawdling. What if that is just the precursor of what is to come? What if I let the omnipresent anger bubble up until I become violent? All these thoughts are whirling around in my head day and night, thoughts that I know I should share with Josh but I can't. He's made it perfectly clear what he thinks about adoption, mental health and all of that. Perhaps I should find a psychologist, share my concerns with an objective professional. Maybe I could get Ava assessed too, just in case.

'Oh Mum, what should I do?' I whisper out loud.

I say a silent prayer and leave the church. It was stupid coming here today. I need to speak to the vicar, find out what the possibilities are.

I can't stop thinking about my birth parents, wondering whether my father is out of jail, whether my birth mother's parents are still alive. Do I have grandparents out there, grandparents who might be missing me? For the past three months I've been burying my head in the sand, scared to do any research in case the story of my parents is too horrific for words. But I do recognise that ignoring the issues isn't helping me and the speculating just adds to the pain. When Maria talked about giving up her child for adoption, it got me thinking. No big decisions like that are ever straightforward. My poor birth mother must have been so ashamed, so broken, and my birth father... Was he simply an evil man? Had he raped before, and how long was he in prison for? Is he still locked away?

Tears are pouring down my face as I leave the graveyard, loss combined with anger and futility. I take out a tissue and dab my eyes, trying to take some deep breaths to calm myself. As I walk out of the small carpark and along the footpath next to the road, I hear heavy footsteps behind me. They seem to be in sync with my own. I glance over my shoulder and there's a broad-shouldered man walking just a few feet behind me, a hood pulled low over his forehead. As I walk faster, he does the same. My heart is hammering in my chest. The road is quiet here and he could easily loop an arm around my neck, stuff my mouth with a handkerchief and pull me behind the hedge. I'm almost running now, my breath loud in my ears, masking the sound of footsteps. As I round the corner, I glance backwards again. The man has gone. I let out a pathetic little whimper. I'm seeing monsters everywhere and it's all because of what Mum told me.

'Imogen, are you alright?'

I jump.

'Hey! You look like you've seen a ghost.' Tom gets off his bike and leans it against a lamppost. 'Where have you been?'

'To the churchyard.'

'Oh Imogen!' He steps forwards and envelops me in a hug. He feels very different to Josh; tall and lanky, less solid somehow. 'You've been crying.' He says it as a statement rather than a question.

'Not looking my best,' I say, trying to bring levity to my voice.

'It's still early days. Of course you're going to miss your mum. It all happened so quickly. What can I do to help?'

'Nothing. You're kind. Maybe I need a bit of distraction.'

'In which case let me walk you home. What's the plan for Ava's birthday? Issy practically exploded with excitement when she received the invitation.'

'I've booked a magician. I remember having a magician to a party when I was a kid. He took a white rabbit out of a hat. But we weren't so sophisticated when I was young and now I'm worrying that a magician might not cut it with four- and five-year-olds.'

'I'm sure they'll love it. Is there anything I can do to help?'

'Just the normal – keeping an eye on the kids during the party. I've got to get around to baking a cake.'

'I can't help with that one, I'm afraid.' He laughs. Tom may be a brilliant dad but cooking isn't his forte.

'I thought I'd ask Maria to help put up the decorations. I've got pink everything.'

Tom doesn't comment so we carry on walking in a comfortable silence, Tom pushing his bike. Once again it strikes me that I find it easier talking to Tom than I do to Josh. Is it just because I see Tom a lot during the daytimes, or is there something wrong with my marriage? I'm so desperate to tell Josh my secret but every time I make the decision to bring up the subject, I bottle out. I'm perfectly aware that the longer I leave it, the harder the truth will be. Yet I love Josh. It's just I can't face the disappointment in his face, the disgust that I'm not the person he thinks I am, the worry that his children may somehow be tainted. Perhaps that's another reason why I should talk to a therapist. I need advice on how to save my marriage.

When Josh and I first met, my job took me all over the country. I was auditing a hotel in Manchester. It was a dive of a place and although I was booked in to stay the night there, I had no desire to wake up covered in bed bugs. Instead, I rang around to find a room for the night. There were two big conferences going on in town and rooms were sparse. I spent too much money on a room at the Hilton and then wandered down Deansgate in search of somewhere to eat. It didn't bother me, eating alone. I rather enjoyed listening in to conversations, trying to work out the dynamics of strangers' relationships. I stumbled across a little Italian restaurant down a side street with a menu that seemed authentic. Pushing open the door, I was met by wonderful aromas and a welcome warmth. Just as the door was closing behind me, a man walked in.

'Good evening. How can I help you?' the waiter asked in an obviously assumed Italian accent.

'I'm looking for a table for one,' I said.

The waiter frowned as he glanced from me to the man standing closely behind me.

'You're not together?'

'No.' I turned to look at the man. He was wearing a thick black coat, cashmere by the looks of it, and with his chiselled face and sparkling eyes, he could have walked straight out of a magazine shoot.

'And you, sir?'

'Also a table for one, please.'

'I'm sorry but we only have one table left. The lady was here first.' He let the words hang.

'Of course,' the good-looking stranger said.

And to this day, I don't know why I spoke up, but I suggested that if he didn't mind sharing my table, then we could both eat in the restaurant. Josh's smile made me weak at the knees and for the first half an hour or so, I was rendered mute. It turned out that Josh was in town for a dentistry conference but having been surrounded by dentists for the past three days, he needed to have some time out. After I pulled myself together and had drunk a couple of glasses of wine, conversation flowed easily between us. At the end of the meal we split the bill, only because I was insistent on paying my half. Outside the restaurant he told me what an enjoyable evening he'd had, how it had been a pleasure meeting me and then, much to my disappointment, he wished me goodnight. I thought I'd never see the handsome stranger again.

But just the next day, I was at Piccadilly Station, walking through the train carriages, searching for my reserved seat (in first class because I'd booked it far in advance) when to my delight, there was Josh, reading some papers.

'Hello,' I blurted out. 'We meet again.'

'Well, this certainly is a pleasure. Where is your seat?'

'I think in the next carriage.'

He glanced up at the seat reservations above his head. 'There's no one sitting here. Why don't you join me?'

Neither of us did any work during the two hours and

twenty minutes it took to get to London. And then when we discovered we were both taking the train from Victoria to Horsham, it seemed as if destiny had played a hand. In the early days of our relationship, we never stopped talking. We shared our innermost thoughts and our dreams for the future. And then there was that glitch in the months after Ava was born, a time I try not to think about. Then, for a long time, things were good between us, but during the past year, there's been a change. Perhaps it's just life getting in the way, the fact we have a young child, are both working so hard. But it's like we rarely have time for each other. I miss those easy years, the closeness that was so much more than just physical.

Tom and I arrive at the entrance to Fairview House.

'Thanks for coming to my rescue,' I say. 'Would you like a cup of tea?'

'I've got a lot on so I'll pass. But you know you can call me any time. I've got broad shoulders.'

'Thanks, Tom.' I stand on my tiptoes and plant a quick kiss on his cheek. As I'm stepping away from him, a curtain twitches upstairs.

'What is it?' Tom asks.

'I think someone is watching us from inside the house.'

'Guests?'

'No. There's no one staying at the moment. It must be Maria.'

'Mmm.' Tom crosses his arms over his chest.

'What is it?' I ask. Tom rarely holds back from expressing an opinion.

'She's a bit odd, don't you think? She was actually quite rude to me the other day.'

'I'm sure she didn't mean to be. I think she's just a little socially awkward but honestly, I don't know what I'd do without her help.' I think of the conversation I had with Maria about my adoption and it creates a clenching in my stomach. One moment I feel a bond with her, the next I'm worried that I over-shared with an almost-stranger. And she was a bit rude to Tom, true, but was that just because she was being protective over me? I'm not too worried because she's still in her probation period and I can always let her go if it doesn't work out.

10

MARIA

When I found Imogen's adoption certificate, I just knew. The dates fitted. The location fitted. After more than thirty years of hoping, my dreams have been answered. I've found my daughter. Of course, the certificate doesn't mention my name, just the names of her adoptive parents, but it does list Imogen's birth date of 10th June 1988, and Guildford, the district of her birth. But I don't need a piece of paper to confirm what I instinctively knew the very first time I laid eyes on my adult child. We share the same colouring, the wide-set eyes, the tenderness in our hearts. As much as it pains me to admit it, Imogen's adoptive parents did a fine job. My daughter is most definitely a more refined, better version of myself. She's had opportunities I never had. A good education, university, and a career where she uses her brains. And now she has the most beautiful family. A handsome debonair husband, a stepson who is a bit of a handful but no different to how my friends and I were at his age, and a gorgeous little girl. Ava, my perfect granddaughter. After searching for so long, it feels as if my life is complete.

The only problem I have now is telling Imogen. I could come straight out with it, reveal the truth to her when she returns from her morning meeting, but I feel it needs to be a momentous occasion, something with pomp and circumstance. Perhaps over a dinner at a fancy restaurant or watching the sun go down over the sea. I can't underestimate how much of a shock it will be for Imogen but I hope that having got to know me, she'll be thrilled. The timing couldn't be better; she's gaining a new real mother so soon after losing her adoptive mother. And however much Imogen loved her adoptive mother, nothing beats the bond between blood relatives. I'm going to be the perfect mother and grandmother. At long last, my time has come.

After finishing cleaning the guest bedrooms, I saunter downstairs and am surprised to hear clattering coming from the kitchen. I didn't realise Imogen was home already.

'Hello!' I say cheerily. 'Are you baking?'

Imogen has put two cake tins on the countertop and is folding egg whites into the batter.

'Yes. It's Ava's birthday tomorrow and I need to make a birthday cake before I collect her from school. I'm going to use the conventional oven because I struggle with baking in the Aga. I know some people swear by it, but I still haven't gotten the hang of it. Actually, I forgot to ask; I was wondering if you'd help me put up the decorations in the conservatory. I'll keep Ava out of there until the morning.'

'With pleasure!' I say. This is exactly what a granny should do. In fact I want Imogen to lean on me more and more. She shouldn't have to do everything all alone.

With a big grin on my face, I wander into the utility room

to put the cleaning materials away. I rinse the cloths in the sink and empty the vacuum cleaner. When I'm finished I go back into the kitchen. Imogen has put the cake tins in the oven and piled the dirty bowls in the sink. I'm washing them up when I have a bright idea. Drying my hands, I step over to the oven and check the temperature. She's set it to 160 degrees on the fan setting. I turn the oven up to 220 and return to the sink. By the time I've dried everything and put all the cooking utensils and pots away in the correct places, there's a smell of burning. I wait another couple of minutes and then go in search of Imogen.

I find her in her little study, a small room off the living room, where she has a desk and a wall full of filing cabinets. She's hunched over a laptop. I knock on the door.

'Sorry to disturb you, Imogen, but I think your cake is burning.'

She jumps up, glances at her watch and frowns. She hurries through the house to the kitchen with me just behind her.

'Oh no!' she wails, opening the oven door and removing the cake tins. 'I've burned them. I can't believe I did that.' She peers at the temperature dial. 'I could have sworn I put them on at 160 degrees but I must have set it to 220 instead by mistake. I'm such an idiot! I was thinking about some work and obviously wasn't concentrating.' She groans as she removes the burned cakes.

'It happens to the best of us,' I console her. 'It's probably baby brain. The joys of being pregnant.'

She sighs. 'I never believed in baby brain. I was fine when I was pregnant with Ava but then I didn't have morning sickness with her so perhaps things are different this time.'

'It's definitely a thing. I've worked with a few people who have had it, becoming forgetful and a bit fraught. It all goes back to normal after the baby is born.'

Imogen runs her hands through her hair and glances at her watch. 'I haven't got time to make another cake before Ava comes home. I'm going to have to do it later tonight and I'm so tired. It's the last thing I feel like doing.'

'How about I make it for you?' I suggest. 'I used to be a professional cake baker so it's right up my alley. I can bake something especially for Ava and bring it over later tonight so it's ready for when she wakes up in the morning.'

'I couldn't possibly ask you to do that.' Imogen looks really distressed, close to tears even. The poor girl is truly taking on too much and I can't have her breaking down.

'I insist,' I say. 'It would be a real pleasure and it's not like I've got anything else to do later this afternoon.'

'Thank you, Maria. That's so kind of you. You must let me know what I owe you for your time and all the ingredients.'

'We'll worry about that later,' I say.

As I climb on my bike to go home, that earlier glow of being able to help Imogen morphs into panic. I don't think I've baked a cake ever in my whole life. Maybe years ago, but I don't have much of a sweet tooth so I've never particularly wanted to learn. And of course in the bedsit, I don't even have an oven. I think I read somewhere that you can bake a cake in a microwave but my microwave is tiny, just big enough for one. And I'm sure you can't bake a cake on an electric ring. I realise if I'm not going to let Imogen down – which I absolutely can't do – I'm going to have to buy a cake. I cycle as quickly as I can to the only bus stop in the village and just pray a bus will be along soon. If not, I'll have to order a taxi, which will be an unnecessary expense I can't afford. I wait twenty-five minutes, during which time my patience is tested. I pace backwards and forwards, letting out little yells every time I hear the rumble of heavy tyres, just to be disappointed that it's a truck. When the bus eventually arrives, I'm on it in a second.

It's only fifteen minutes to the centre of Horsham, but I haven't got long until the shops shut. My first stop is Waitrose because I'm sure they sell quality birthday cakes. It's not a shop I normally visit because it's a bit posh for me, but as it turns out, there's only a choice of two cakes. I suppose stock is low at the end of the day. There's a chocolate caterpillar which seems too young for a five-year-old or a pink unicorn cake. The cake is only for eight people. Will that be enough? I send Imogen a text.

> Forgot to ask how many people I should bake the cake for?

Fortunately she answers me back immediately.

> Twenty-two, please. I hope that's ok!

Twenty-two! I'll need to buy three of these cakes for that many people, but there's only one unicorn cake left. I find another simple Victoria sponge, so I get two of those plus some ready-made icing. I'll have to improvise putting the three cakes together and hope it doesn't look like a dog's dinner. I am literally counting out my last pennies as I pay for it, wondering whether I'll have to ask Imogen for an advance on my monthly pay. But that would be so humiliating. I wonder what she'd think if she knew how tough things are for her mother; whether she might dole out a few grand to tide me over. They say that blood is thicker than water so perhaps she wouldn't mind. But I've got pride and I'm certainly not going to tell her that I'm her birth mother in one breath and that I need her financial help in the next. No. I'll just have to scrape by as I always do.

Back in my bedsit I take the three cakes out of their boxes and lay them side by side. The unicorn cake is wider in diameter than the two plain Victoria sponges. I delve into my fridge and find a jar of old jam. It's gone a bit manky with the sugar crystallising and a layer of mould on the top. I scrape off the gunge and put a thin layer of jam over the top of both the sponge cakes, placing them one on top of the other. Then I place the unicorn cake on the top. The sides hang down and it looks top-heavy, which of course it is. I decide to cut away around the circumference of the unicorn cake so it's vaguely level with the cakes underneath. Then I take the ready-made icing out of its pack. I don't have a rolling pin so I improvise with the bottle of jam. It's hard to roll it out evenly but I manage to attach it to the sides of the three-layered cake. It's white and bumpy whereas the top of the cake is just perfect and pink. If only I had some ribbon to tie around it, to hide the poorly applied icing. I stand staring at my creation for a while and then have the bright idea of using the fabric belt to an old summer dress. It's pink, yellow and white – the perfect colours. I tie it around the cake and immediately it looks better. Home-made, but that's exactly the look I want. I hope my girls will be as thrilled with it as I am.

11

IMOGEN

Maria sent me a message late last night to say that the cake wouldn't be ready until this morning, but she'd bring it over first thing. I can't believe how kind she's being about it. Unsurprisingly, Ava wakes us up at the crack of dawn, wired with excitement to be turning five. I tell Josh to go back to sleep and I'm downstairs with Ava at 6 a.m. when I hear the crunch of tyres on the driveway. By the time I get to the front door, the car has gone, but lying on the stone porchway is a cake in a brown cardboard box. I pick the cake up and carry it through to the utility room, wanting to inspect it before Ava sees it. I'm sure she'll love it. It's a strange mixture of professional looking and rather homemade. It looks like Maria might have run out of time, or possibly patience, when it came to the finishing touches. I hope she wasn't up most of the night baking and decorating. I stick five candles into the top and carry it into the conservatory.

'Do you want to come through?' I ask Ava, who leaps from her chair carrying a bunch of pink balloons with her.

She squeals with delight when she sees the birthday bunting, more balloons, a table piled high with wrapped presents and the birthday cake.

'Can I open the presents?' She claps her hands excitedly.

'No. We need to wait for Daddy to get up.'

'Can I wake him?'

'No, sweetie. Let's have some breakfast and I'm sure Daddy will be down soon.'

'Can I eat some cake?'

'Before breakfast? What do you think?'

She looks at me with an exaggerated expression of forlornness. 'Please!'

'Nope. The cake is to have with your friends at your party but as it's your birthday, you can have Coco Pops.'

'Yippee!'

Ava opened her gifts in record time, ripping off the paper and gasping with delight. Her favourite gift so far is a Disney nail studio followed by a rubber camera that produces instant small polaroid photos. Josh has already left for work, so I'm in the conservatory playing with Ava and her new toys. There's a gentle knock on the door. Maria is standing there looking a bit red in the face.

'Sorry to disturb but I've got a present for Ava.'

Ava races over to Maria and stands there expectantly. 'Do I get a kiss from the birthday girl first?' Maria asks.

Ava glances at me, her forehead knotted. It's obvious she doesn't want to give Maria a kiss but how can we say no when Maria has gone out of her way to help me.

'Go on,' I urge her. Maria bends down and Ava gives her the briefest kiss on the cheek. Maria hands over a small parcel.

'Thank you,' Ava says politely as she rips off the paper. 'Oh,' she says, disappointment in her voice.

'I thought it matched your cake rather well,' Maria says.

It's a small plush unicorn toy, more suitable for an infant than a five-year-old, but it's so kind of her regardless. I leave Ava to play and walk with Maria along the corridor to the kitchen.

'Thank you so much for making the cake and dropping it off so early this morning.'

'No problem. I asked a friend to bring it around as I couldn't carry it on my bike.'

'I could have come and picked it up from your house,' I say.

'Really, it was no bother.'

'How much do I owe you, for your time and ingredients?'

'Don't worry, Imogen. I haven't added it up yet, but I'll let you know. What would you like me to start on this morning?'

'I was wondering if you'd like to help me make the food for Ava's party? Sandwiches, jellies and the like.'

'Of course, but I warn you, I'm not a great cook. But you've probably already sussed that one out. The only thing I know how to do is bake.'

'Your cooking is great.' I laugh, thinking that at best it's mediocre. 'Besides, it's only for a bunch of five-year-olds.'

Aided at various points by Ava, we work alongside each other in companionable silence, and when Maria goes off to clean the bedrooms, I wrap a pass-the-parcel and prepare the going home bags, stuffing them with little gifts and lollipops. Ava is restless and impatient for her party so by the time 3 p.m. arrives, it's a relief to us all.

Before long, our big house feels like it's bursting at the seams with people. The children are in the conservatory being entertained by the magician, whilst parents mill around the kitchen and the hallway. The only person who is missing is Kyle. He promised to be here. I catch Josh as he's pouring himself a beer.

'Where's Kyle?' I ask my husband.

'He's probably got a weekend match or something.'

'But he promised Ava he'd be here. She'll be upset.'

'I'm sure she won't even notice.'

I'm annoyed that once again, Josh takes Kyle's side. Ava had been so eager to show off her big brother to her little friends, and he promised to do some magic tricks for her, tricks that he swore were better than the professional magician would do. I was doubtful, obviously. Nevertheless, I bought a present for him to give Ava as I was sure that Guila wouldn't think of it, and I'm frustrated that he's not here.

'I'll send Kyle a message,' Josh says in response to my stony face.

Maria is a godsend. She's filling up the glasses of the parents, accompanying children to the toilet, and generally helping without me having to say a word. Her cheeks are flushed and there's a broad smile on her face.

'That's the new housekeeper woman?' Danielle asks, her voice low.

'Yes. She's such a help. I burned the cake yesterday and she made the new one. She was a baker in a previous life, apparently.'

'Umm, I don't think so.' Danielle says, her voice laden with sarcasm.

'What do you mean?'

'That top layer, the unicorn cake, it's Waitrose own brand.'

'But she made it,' I say.

Danielle takes her phone out of her pocket and starts scrolling. 'Here. £8.99. All she's done is take that cake and plonk it on top of two plain cakes.'

'I'm sure you're–' But I'm interrupted because at that moment, Maria appears carrying a tray of miniature sausage rolls.

'Maria?' Danielle says. I put my hand on Danielle's arm in the hope of stopping her, but she shrugs me off. 'I'm Danielle, Imo's best friend. I was just admiring the cake. Did you make it all yourself?'

'Um, yes. Last night. I like baking.'

'Because it looks really familiar, like a design that Waitrose sells.'

Maria's neck flushes red and I wish I could push Danielle away, stop her from this car crash of a conversation. 'You're right.' Maria looks bashful. 'I copied the design from a bought cake. I'm not that imaginative, you see, so I looked up cake designs online.' Maria shifts her eyes from side to side and it's obvious she's uncomfortable.

'Well, I'm just grateful for whatever you've done,' I say. 'If it had been left to me, we wouldn't have had a cake at all.'

'I do think that's it's a bit off to pretend–'

I steer Danielle away.

'What are you doing?' I ask in a whisper. 'You're totally embarrassing her and the woman has done nothing but help me.'

'I can't believe she's got the gall to pretend she made that cake, because she sure as hell didn't.'

'Does it really matter? I don't know what's got into you, Danielle.' It's like she wants to catch Maria out and it's embarrassing for all of us. Danielle and I used to be of like minds in most things, yet since she's fallen for Alain, I barely recognise her.

'I'm only here to support you, Imo.' She strides away, her shoulders bunched up high.

'Great magician,' Tom says as the children start pouring out of the conservatory into the kitchen. It's a relief to see him. The noise of screaming children starts to overwhelm me and all of a sudden I feel so dizzy, it's as if I'm going to faint. I lean against the wall but my legs give way and I sink to the floor.

'Imogen! Are you alright?' Tom's voice sounds weirdly distant and then it disappears altogether.

I wake up on my bed, Josh pacing up and down the bedroom.

'Darling, are you alright?'

I blink a few times and try to sit up in bed but it makes me feel dizzy and nauseous. Josh rushes to the side of the bed and picks up a glass of water. 'Would you like some?'

'Yes, please.' He supports my head as I gulp it down.

'The baby?' I say.

'I've called out a doctor and he's on his way.'

'It's Ava's party. I can't disappear. We can't!' I try to swing my legs over the side of the bed but Josh puts a hand on my shoulder.

'You're not going anywhere until the doctor has checked you over.'

'We can't miss the party. You need to go back down.' I feel panic at letting Ava down.

'I'm staying with you. The party is fine. Maria is sorting all the food and drink and she'll give out the party bags as people leave. Your friend Tom says he'll keep an eye on Ava.'

'He's Issy's dad.' I realise that Josh barely knows any of the parents of Ava's friends.

'You mustn't worry. Everything is under control.' Josh holds my hand.

About five minutes later, I hear footsteps coming up the stairs and there's a knock on the bedroom door. Josh strides over to open it.

'The doctor is here,' Maria says. 'I really hope Imogen is okay. When everyone has gone, I'll clear up downstairs and keep an eye on Ava so you don't have to worry about anything except getting Imogen better.'

'Thank you, Maria. Much appreciated.'

The doctor is probably late thirties, dressed in jeans and a jumper. He introduces himself as Dr Thomas.

'My wife fainted,' Josh says. 'And she's pregnant. Early stages.'

Tears spring to my eyes because however much I don't want this baby, I do. It's totally conflicting.

'Let's check your blood pressure first.' Dr Thomas has a reassuring manner and kindly amber eyes. He puts the blood pressure sleeve around my upper arm and pumps it up.

'Your blood pressure is high. It's not dangerously high, but higher than it should be. How many weeks pregnant do you think you are?'

'About ten weeks probably.'

'And no bleeding or stomach pain?'

'No. All that happened was I felt dizzy and fainted.'

'I think we should get you booked in for an ultrasound but from what I can assess at the moment, you just need to take it easy. Have you been very busy or under pressure?'

'Yes, she has,' Josh answers for me. 'Her mother passed away three months ago, Imogen is working too hard and not sleeping well. I think she might be depressed.'

'Grief isn't linear and can take a long time. I'd prefer not to give you anti-depressants during this early stage of your pregnancy.'

'I'm not depressed,' I say. 'I just have a lot on my plate.'

Both the men look at me with expressions of pity and it chokes me. Perhaps I am depressed. I have been finding things difficult recently. It could be another gene that I've inherited because if my mother took her own life, she certainly struggled with her mental health. Is this the beginning of a downward spiral for me too?

'I suggest you rest as much as possible over the next few days and make an appointment for an ultrasound scan. Do you have a home blood pressure monitor?'

I shake my head. 'We'll get one,' Josh says.

'Take your blood pressure morning and night for the next few days and book in to see me at the end of the week. If you feel faint again, then get yourself to the hospital. We need to make sure you don't develop preeclampsia.'

'Thank you,' I say weakly, as Josh accompanies the doctor out of the room.

A couple of minutes later, Josh returns and sits on my side of the bed. 'You need to cut down on your work, darling. How about stopping the bed and breakfast until after the baby is born?'

'No, I don't want to do that. It's going really well.'

'It's not like we need the money.'

'I'm not doing it for the money. I'm doing it because I love it.' That's not strictly true. I do my consultancy work and run the bed and breakfast because I don't want to be dependent on Josh for everything; it makes me feel empowered earning my own money, buying things for us as a family, or clothes for myself, without having to ask Josh for permission. It's my independence and not something I'm prepared to give up.

'But it just gives you a headache. Having to get up early to make breakfast for strangers. Worrying about reviews. Keeping the house permanently spick and span. It's not necessary. Or maybe give up your consultancy work.'

'Please, Josh. Just leave me alone.'

He throws me a pained look and when he's in the doorway, he turns and says, 'I love you, Imogen, and I want to keep you and our baby safe.' Talk about piling on the guilt.

I lie on the bed for another five minutes but I can't stay here. I want to be with Ava on her birthday, see what presents she's been given. I get up slowly, and fortunately the dizziness and nausea have passed, so I make my way downstairs.

'Mummy!' Ava squeals, running towards me and grabbing my legs. 'I've had the best party ever and look how many presents I've got!'

'I see that you have been eating chocolate.' Her mouth is covered in it.

'Maria gave me an extra big bar for my birthday. And she's given me a bag of gob stoppers that are so big I'm not sure they'll fit in my mouth!'

I'm not so pleased about that. I do my best to make sure that Ava only eats sweets on special occasions and brushes her teeth after eating sugary things. I know it's her birthday today but I might have to talk to Maria about not giving Ava sweets. We saunter into the kitchen and to my relief I see that Maria has done a fantastic job clearing up. There are three rubbish bags tied at the top ready to be taken out to the bins and she's working her way through drying a pile of plates and dishes.

'How are you?' she asks, peering at me with concern.

'Feeling much better, thanks.'

'Josh mentioned the doctor says you need to slow down and rest more.'

'Fat chance of that,' I scoff.

'But it's important.' She knots her eyebrows together. 'Your health is everything. You know, I was thinking, perhaps you might like me to work more hours.'

'That's an excellent idea,' Josh says, striding into the kitchen. 'Maybe you could take over the breakfasts so Imogen gets a big longer in bed?'

'We can't ask Maria to get here for 6.30 a.m. in the morning!' I exclaim.

'I could live in,' she suggests, her voice faltering slightly as if she's embarrassed to make the suggestion.

'That's a marvellous idea.' Josh claps his hands together.

'But we've only got the box room and you'd have to share Ava's bathroom,' I explain.

'I don't need much space and I'm more than happy to share the bathroom,' Maria says, a broad smile on her face. 'I could take on some of the cooking and perhaps I could do the school run, taking Ava backwards and forwards from school. That would mean you could have a rest every afternoon.'

'We're happy to increase your wages, of course,' Josh says. 'Hopefully this arrangement can suit everyone, at least until the new baby is born.'

It isn't until a bit later that I remember how Maria knows

my secret, and now she's going to be in our house and around Josh much more than before. What if she says something about my adoption? I really hope that she keeps her promise and doesn't say a word. For a moment I'm uncomfortable but then I bat away my worries. Maria has done nothing but go out of her way for me. I got lucky employing her.

Ava is over-excited and hyperactive and it takes much longer than normal to get her settled in for the night. My exhaustion has crept up on me again so I'm relieved and grateful that Josh has scrambled together some of the leftovers from the party and is making an attempt at cooking an omelette. As I sit down at the kitchen table, the front door opens and Kyle strides in nonchalantly.

'You've missed Ava's party,' I say. 'She was disappointed.'

'I'll go and say goodnight to her.' He dumps his rucksack on the floor and takes the stairs two at a time.

'I've only just settled her!' I shout, but he ignores me.

A door slams and I hear laughter and footsteps from upstairs. I'm about to get up to tell Ava to go to sleep, but Josh stops me. 'Let him say goodnight to his little sister. Another ten minutes isn't going to make any difference.'

To give him his due, Kyle lopes into the kitchen exactly ten minutes later. 'She zonked out on me,' he says, yawning without putting his hand in front of his mouth. 'Can I have tea with you and stay over? Mum's gone out tonight.'

'Of course you can.' Josh beams.

We're midway through eating when we hear a key in the lock yet again.

'Who's that?' Kyle asks with his mouth full.

Josh jumps up and I hear him talking. 'Maria! Back already?'

'Thought I'd move in this evening.'

'So soon?' Josh exclaims.

'Your wife needs me. I'll lug these cases upstairs and make up the bed in the small box room. I don't want to disturb your evening.'

'I'll ask Kyle to give you a hand with your bags.'

Josh reappears and instructs Kyle to help Maria.

'Why's she staying here?' he asks.

'She's moving in to give more help to Imogen.'

'Moving in?' he exclaims. 'You mean you trust her to live here?'

'Keep your voice down,' Josh says.

'Why shouldn't we?' I ask. Kyle shrugs his shoulders and scrapes his chair back.

He reappears just a couple of minutes later. 'She told me she didn't need my help but have you seen how much stuff she's got? Two big suitcases. I asked her how long she's staying and she said forever. That creepy woman's going to be here forever?' he asks.

'You must have misunderstood,' Josh says. 'We've asked her to move in until the baby is born.'

'She told me she's got all her worldly goods here. Why would she bring everything she owns?'

'I'll check on her later,' I say. I'm sure Kyle is wrong, that Maria has just brought her clothes. A fifteen-year-old isn't going to know how much stuff a middle-aged woman has. 'Shall I ask Maria if she'd like some supper with us?'

'I'll be off home, then,' Kyle says, scraping his chair back.

'This is your home,' Josh says.

'Not so long as she's here.'

Josh no doubt sees the expression on my face and inter-jects. 'That's rude, Kyle.' I'm glad that for once Josh is reprimanding his son but it proves to me that Kyle is against me at every turn. No doubt if I said something negative about Maria, he'd declare his liking of her.

'I don't get it!' Kyle exclaims. 'Why do you want her here? Maria totally creeps me out.'

12

MARIA

This couldn't have worked out better if I'd planned it myself. I am living in my daughter's home with access to my granddaughter every day of the week. I am literally ecstatic. For the first time in years, I am in the bosom of a family. My family. It must be fate because how else could everything have fallen so neatly into place? I don't even care that I have the worst room in the house because it is so much nicer than my grotty bedsit.

The box room is a small space under the eaves with a single bed and a wardrobe painted with some kind of Scandinavian design. It is across the hallway from Ava's bedroom and bathroom and I'm delighted that I'll be sleeping so close to my granddaughter, checking on her at night, being able to rock her back to sleep if she awakes with a nightmare. I've packed in such a way that only one of my suitcases needs opening. The case that can stay closed holds my summer clothes (of which I don't have many), my bedding and towels, which I won't need because I'll be using Imogen's. I would have liked to bring my other bits and pieces such as a couple of saucepans, plates and the like, but Imogen might have thought that weird. I checked the terms and conditions of my lease and I need to give them a month's notice. Hopefully I'll never have to revisit that dive.

I overheard Josh ask Kyle to help me with the suitcases, but he hasn't appeared so I'm lugging them up myself. There's a hatch in the ceiling near my room that leads up to an attic space. Imogen told me she stores luggage up there, as well as some boxes left over from clearing out her parents' house. If her mother only died three months ago, she did that quickly. With some difficulty, I shove the full suitcase up into the loft. Then I unpack my clothes and hang them up in the wardrobe. I go to the linen cupboard and select a bottom sheet and duvet cover. I use an old set that has seen better days because I don't want Imogen to think that I'm using her best Egyptian linen. After half an hour or so, Imogen comes upstairs and, in a whisper, says, 'Knock, knock. Is everything alright?'

'It's perfect, thank you. Are you feeling better? You should probably have an early night. I'll get up to do breakfast for the guests and I can prepare breakfast for you too.'

'That's kind of you. I'll show you how I do it in the morning and then you can take over going forwards. Are you hungry? Please help yourself to anything in the fridge or larder.'

We say goodnight.

I wake up about 1 a.m. and look up at the Velux window above my bed. I can see the stars and the moon from here and it's beautiful. I tiptoe out of bed, open Ava's door and just stand there watching her sleep. She's like a little angel with her hair splayed out on the pillow, her arms flung out either side. My granddaughter.

The next morning, Imogen shows me how she makes the full English breakfast for her guests and then goes upstairs to get Ava ready for school. When she comes back, her face is pale and she has dark rings under her eyes.

Josh hurries into the kitchen. 'Imogen is exhausted today. Would you keep an eye on her? I've got to dash to work. I'm already late.'

'Of course,' I say. 'That's why I'm here.' It sends a warm feeling through my veins.

'Perhaps you could take Ava to school for her so she can go back to bed?' Josh suggests.

He doesn't wait for me to answer.

Ava looks so sweet in her school uniform, the grey skirt that's a little too long for her and the royal blue jumper with its sleeves rolled up. Imogen helps Ava put on her jacket.

'Josh suggested I take Ava to school,' I say. 'Is it alright to use your car?'

I can tell that Imogen is conflicted. She desperately needs to go back to bed but at the same time she feels she should take her daughter to school.

I crouch down in front of Ava. 'Would you mind me taking you to school?' She shakes her head.

'I'll ring the secretary and tell them to put you on the approved list,' Imogen says. She grabs the keys off the small rack where all the keys hang and hands them to me. 'It can be a bit tricky to park sometimes. Leave the car on the next street over and walk Ava to school if you can't park out front.' She throws her arms around the little girl and hugs her tightly. 'Have a lovely day, darling.'

I hold Ava's hand as we walk out of the house to the garage.

'You're squeezing me too tight,' Ava says.

I release my grip a little. 'I'm sorry, sweetie.' But I know why I did it. I'm conflicted about driving. Officially I'm not allowed to, but who is ever going to know? Besides, I'm a good driver, careful and considerate. Taking my licence away was a travesty.

Imogen has a navy-blue Volvo which looks brand new and sparkling. I'm not used to an automatic, so I reverse out ever so carefully. It's only a five minutes' drive, but I go ridiculously slowly because my cargo is so very precious. Imogen is right. There isn't anywhere to park and as I'm not confident in parking this car, I leave it quite far away.

'Do you like school?' I ask Ava as I clutch her hand with my left hand and carry her little rucksack over my shoulder.

'Yes.'

'I was thinking, sweetie. Do you like secrets?'

Ava nods.

'Because I'm now living with you, it's like I'm your secret granny. Why don't you call me Gangan rather than Maria? It can be our big secret so you only call me that when we're just the two of us. What do you think?'

'Gangan?' she asks.

'It'll be our special word. A secret between us. Do you like that?'

She nods again.

'You'll have to be very grownup and not mention this to anyone, even your mummy.'

We walk up the path to the school and that dreadful friend of Imogen's is there, Tom, looking ridiculous dressed in Lycra.

'Is everything alright with Imogen?' he asks.

'Hunky-dory, but I'm living with the family now and I'll be doing more of the school runs.'

'Oh,' he says with a frown. 'I'll give her a call shortly.'

'I wouldn't bother,' I say. 'Imogen is up to her eyes in work. She's on a deadline so I don't think she'd appreciate being interrupted. That's one of the reason's I'm here.'

I ignore Tom and bend down to be level with Ava. 'Have a wonderful day, sweetie, and see you later.' I give her an awkward little hug which she quickly wriggles out of, but that's fine. I can't expect her to love me on day one.

Back at Fairview House, I manage to park the car without any incident and go to the kitchen to clear up the breakfast things. I hear loud footstep coming down the stairs and turn around, wondering if it's one of the guests.

'Oh, hello,' I say, realising Kyle has stopped still in the doorway.

'What are you doing here?' he asks.

'I live here now. Didn't your mum and dad tell you that?'

'She's not my mum.'

He turns around.

'Hey, wait!' I say. 'Do you have a lighter? I've left mine at home and I can't find any matches.'

He turns around slowly and narrows his eyes at me. He's tall for a fifteen-year-old, clearly taking after his dad. I expect he'll be handsome too, although right now he's lanky, like a giraffe that hasn't grown into its legs.

'I'll give you a cigarette if you can find me a lighter or matches,' I say.

'You won't tell on me?'

'Of course I won't. I don't want to get into trouble either, especially as it's my first day living in.'

'Alright then,' he says, padding with bare feet to a drawer next to the Aga. 'They're here.' He removes a box of matches.

Of course, I was perfectly aware where they are kept, but

I need to engage with Kyle. He'll help me learn more about the family.

'Fancy a ciggie?' I ask quietly.

'Yeah.'

'Where's the safest place where we won't be spotted?'

'Behind the garages. I'll show you.'

I'm rather pleased with myself as I follow Kyle out of the back door to the rear of the garages. Teenagers think they know it all and are so cool, but they're the easiest of all to bribe and manipulate. I take a packet of Benson & Hedges out of my pocket and offer him a cigarette.

'You have done this before, right?' I ask.

'I'm not a kid, you know.' He sneers at me. I decide not to correct him.

I flick a match and hold it up to his cigarette. He takes a puff and tries to conceal his cough. I have to bite the side of my cheek to stop myself from laughing. So much for the tough boy image.

'How long have your parents been divorced?' I inhale deeply.

'Six years.'

'So they weren't divorced when your dad met Imogen?'

'Nope.' Now that surprises me. I can't imagine for one moment that Imogen would have been instrumental in a marriage breakup. It must have been Josh who was playing away.

'Do you blame Imogen for your parents' split?'

'What's it to you?'

'Honestly, I'm just being nosey.'

That elicits a chuckle.

'And your mum, has she got a new partner?'

'Yes. But he's a jerk.'

'It must be hard living between two homes.'

He shrugs his shoulders.

'At least you have a kind stepmum.'

'She's not my stepmum and she never will be. And kind? Really? All she does is nag, nag, nag. Everything's always about Imogen. I don't know what Dad sees in her. I thought he might leave her but now they've got another kid on the way, I don't suppose he will.' He grinds his cigarette butt with the heel of his trainers. 'Thanks for the cig,' he says.

'Aren't you meant to be at school?' It only crosses my mind now to ask the question.

'Inset morning. Got to go in this afternoon.'

'If you want another smoke anytime, just message me.'

'Alright.' We swap phone numbers and I watch him lope back towards the house. I can tell that Kyle is going to be an excellent ally and source of information. Poor boy.

When everyone is out of the house, I go into Josh and Imogen's bedroom and take her photo album out once again. I have a cunning little plan. I swap out some of the photos of Imogen as a baby with my photos. It's uncanny how similar they are; the cute, rounded faces with the sprinkling of blonde hair. It's just the backgrounds and clothes that are different. I wonder how often Imogen looks at this album, whether she'll notice the changes.

When Imogen returns from wherever she's been she's still looking peaky and I offer to collect Ava from school.

'It's kind of you,' she says, 'but I'll do it.'

I'm worried about her; I really am. Whilst she's out I decide to make supper – a meal for Ava and a decent meal for the three of us. I rifle through Imogen's fridge and find four chicken breasts, a medley of vegetables, and in the larder, a jar of rice. I find a recipe for chicken and vegetables on the *BBC Good Food* website and carefully follow every step of the instructions. When Imogen and Ava return home, the meal is bubbling along nicely.

'Something smells good,' Imogen says.

'Thought I'd whip us up a bit of supper to save you from cooking.'

'That's kind of you but it really isn't part of your job description.'

I wish I could run my fingers down her forehead to ease that frown. 'I think it should be. I should be taking over as much of running the household chores as possible. I'm happy to cook for you. Perhaps not every night but shall we say three or four times a week?'

She winces slightly and I'm not sure whether it's because she's not feeling well or the thought of me taking over her kitchen is something she's uncomfortable with. The last thing I want to do is overstep the mark. Nevertheless, Imogen's natural politeness shines through and she simply says, 'Thank you.'

As much as I would love to sit at the kitchen table with Imogen and Ava as the little girl plays and then eats her tea, I realise that might be awkward, at least until I tell Imogen the truth. I disappear to my room under the eaves and flip through all the photos I've taken. She was such a delightful baby and as I run my fingers over her face, it brings tears to my eyes.

Whilst Imogen is bathing Ava and putting her to bed, I nip back downstairs and finish off our supper. I lay the kitchen table with three places, putting out wine and water glasses. I find some cotton napkins in a drawer and attempt to do a little origami to fashion them into an attractive design like they do in restaurants. I can't get them quite right and by the time I've finished, the napkins are creased and I'm furious. Instead I roll them up and place a little sprig of rosemary from the bush by the backdoor on top of each. Finally, I light a couple of candles. The table looks lovely, romantic even.

'Something smells good,' Josh walks into the room and then stops suddenly.

'Oh, hello. I thought it was Imogen in here.'

'No, just me,' I say lightly. 'Imogen is putting Ava to bed.'

'Right,' he says and disappears upstairs.

Ten minutes later and Imogen appears. 'What can I do to help?' she asks.

'Absolutely nothing. Perhaps you could tell Josh supper is ready and then have a seat.'

I let Josh and Imogen take their places at the table as I don't want to unwittingly sit in one of their chairs, and then I sit down next to Imogen.

'A bit of everything?' I ask Josh, as I start ladling out the food. He throws Imogen a strange glance and then nods.

'Well, this is lovely, isn't it?' I say, as I settle into my meal. 'I'm sure the food isn't up to your standard, Imogen, but hopefully I can learn.'

She smiles but there's tension in her face. I try to make polite conversation during the meal but both Josh and Imogen are rather quiet. I wonder if there's an issue in their relationship or whether they're both worried about Imogen's health. When we've finished eating, I insist that they leave the clearing up to me.

'That's so kind,' Imogen says. She's thanking me so much it's as if she's forgotten they're paying me to do this work. I am thrilled. It's as if she already accepts me as an integral member of their family. 'We'll go and watch something on Netflix next door,' she says.'

After putting as many dirty dishes as possible into the dishwasher, I decide to ask Josh and Imogen if they'd like a tea or coffee, or something stronger perhaps. I'm just outside the living room door when I hear Josh speaking.

'Did she just invite herself to eat with us?'

'I can hardly send her up to her bedroom, can I?'

'Maybe she should eat with Ava. I'm not sitting with her every night, Imogen. It's our time, family time. You'll have to discuss it with her. She's our employee, not a member of our family.'

I can't hear Imogen's response but then Josh says, 'Well, I'll talk to her. I'm not prepared to feel awkward in my own home.'

The bastard. I'm not just some second-rate employee, I *am* a member of their family. But now I'm wondering whether I want to be related to Josh. He's a self-centred, arrogant man and Imogen deserves so much more.

'And the chicken was dried out and not a patch on yours.'

'She means well,' Imogen says. Her voice gets louder and I realise she's walking across the room. I race back to the kitchen and grab a tea towel, but I don't have to pretend. Imogen disappears upstairs.

As I finish the cleaning up, that familiar anger bubbles inside my veins. Josh's attitude towards me and his insensitivity to what Imogen needs is making me furious. He's going to have to pay. I wonder how resilient he is to pain. No doubt his designer clothes and fancy car and 'look-at-me, I'm a super successful dentist' is all a façade. I bet he's a wimp at heart. I grin to myself. I look forward to finding out.

Upstairs in my room, I'm getting ready for bed when my

mobile phone beeps. I pick it up and drop it back down on the bed. It's Clare, yet again. She's sent me three text messages and left a voicemail. I'm tempted not to listen to it, but curiosity gets the better of me.

'I'm worried about you, Maria,' she says. To hell with that. I press delete before she finishes talking. I do the same to the text messages and mutter under my breath. 'Just leave me alone. Leave me the hell alone.'

13

IMOGEN

My phone rings. 'Good morning. This is Deirdre Staplehurst. We're staying with you tonight for three nights. I was just wondering if we could arrive in the next hour rather than after 3 p.m. as you normally request?'

'Mrs Staplehurst?' I ask. My stomach lurches. 'Could you just hold on for a moment, please?'

Hurriedly I rush to the study and open my online diary with details of my guests. She only booked last week and it's as I thought. The Staplehursts are booked in for next Wednesday, not today.

'I'm sorry, Mrs Staplehurst, but you're booked in next week. I'm fully booked tonight and tomorrow.'

There's a heavy silence before she speaks again. 'I have an email from you confirming our booking for today. Do you want me to send it to you?'

'Um, no. Just let me have a look.' I go through my sent emails and sure enough, there it is. I've got it wrong. For the first time, I have double-booked.

'Goodness, I'm so sorry, Mrs Staplehurst. I have made a terrible mistake.'

'Well, what are you going to do about it?'

'I can ring around other properties in the area and see if I can get you a room somewhere else, at my expense, obviously.'

'We're attending my best friend's funeral. I hope you understand what a difficult time this is for us and how desperately we need a room.'

'I'm so sorry. Leave it with me and I'll get straight back to you.'

'You have an hour to sort this,' she says. I hear a threat in her voice.

'Shit!' I let out a scream as I put the phone down. I have a list of other bed and breakfasts and hotels in the area, which I pass on to guests if we're fully booked. I start ringing around. Every single place is booked. Other than a very down-market hotel, there are no free places within twenty minutes of here. I don't know what to do. I let out a groan and bury my face in my hands.

'Is everything alright?'

I jump at Maria's voice. How come the woman walks around so silently?

'No. I've just double-booked one of the guest rooms and I can't find anywhere else for them to stay.'

'What about your spare room in the house?'

'It hasn't got an en-suite. As you know, the bathroom is down the other end of the corridor, which is why whenever we have friends to stay I put them in our B&B rooms.'

'You could just say you can't help?'

'But then they'll slate me on the review websites and I'll lose my gold standard status.'

'Hmm,' she says, scratching her chin. 'Your bedroom then?'

I hadn't thought of that, but Maria is right. We could give up our bedroom for three nights; clear away anything personal and Josh and I can decamp to the spare room.

'It's a good idea,' I say, thanking Maria.

'Do you want me to get started on emptying your wardrobe and drawers?'

'Yes, please. I'll be up to join you in a moment. I'll just call the guests back.'

It takes us the best part of two hours to depersonalise our bedroom and bathroom, but at least when the guests arrive, they have the best bedroom in the house. Mr Staplehurst is effusively grateful; Mrs Staplehurst doesn't say a word.

The problem comes when Josh gets home. When I tell him what I've done, he literally hits the roof.

'You've turfed us out of our bedroom to make way for some strangers! What the hell were you thinking, Imogen? I've already told you we don't need the money!'

'Please keep your voice down,' I say, but that seems to anger Josh even more.

'Didn't you think to call me and ask how I might feel about this?'

'I'm sorry but –'

'You're not thinking straight.'

'Please stop shouting,' I say. I haven't seen Josh this enraged for ages and it's scaring me.

Josh strides to the back door, slams it behind himself and disappears. It's not the first time he has stormed out but it is for the longest time. He only returns at 10.30 p.m. by which time I'm in bed.

'I'm sorry,' I say again.

'And I'm sorry for shouting at you.' But when he gets into bed, he doesn't touch me. Instead, he turns over, his back to me, and falls asleep almost instantly.

The next morning, I decline Maria's offer to take Ava to school and drive her there myself. As we're walking up the path, swept up amongst the other parents and children, with a sinking feeling I realise that they're all dressed up in costumes. Ava is the only child in school uniform.

'Mummy, it's fancy-dress day.' She squeezes my hand and I see tears welling up and her bottom lip shuddering. 'I was meant to come to school in costume.'

'But why didn't you–?' I stop myself. It's not Ava's fault – she's only five. It's my fault for not reading the school letters that appear in her rucksack. I pull her off the path to one side and bend down. 'I'm sorry, darling. I forgot it was today.' I'm forgetting too much. 'Let's have a word with Miss Wilson.'

'I'm not going into school dressed like this,' Ava cries.

I'm relieved to see the mother of one of Ava's friends walking back down the path. 'Leila, could you keep an eye on Ava whilst I go to talk to Miss Wilson? I forgot it was fancy-dress day.'

'Sure.'

I hurry inside and to my relief, Miss Wilson says she has some spare fancy-dress clothes and Ava can spend the day as Pippi Longstocking. It seems to appease Ava and when I leave her, she's grinning. I walk slowly back to my car but once I'm inside, I can't stop the tears from coming.

I'm letting everything slip at the moment. It's as if ball after ball is coming crashing down and despite having Maria's help, I'm still not coping. How I wish Mum was still here. She'd have made Ava a wonderful costume. I remember how I used to win every fancy-dress competition because she was so adept at creating magical creatures out of fabrics and boxes and cartons. Mum was so creative. I pull the visor down and look at myself in the mirror. My eyes are raw and red. As I'm staring at myself, it hits me how I look nothing like Mum. Why didn't I realise that before? Why did kindly people say I had Mum's eyes and Dad's lips? Because I don't. I wasn't even their child. I have the genes of strangers, and terrible strangers at that. Have my bad genes turned me into a bad person? Or was I intrinsically bad anyway, and it's just my parents' strict upbringing that kept me on the straight and narrow. Now that they're both gone, perhaps my true self is beginning to emerge. Josh was so angry with me last night, and that was over something relatively mild. Surely he'll divorce me when my big secret comes out. Will he reject his own children too, the grandchildren of a rapist?

I remember when we talked about his first marriage to Guila. How he said the relationship broke down because she wasn't honest about who she was; how dismayed he was that Guila went on to have a relationship with a woman, although for the past eighteen months she's been with a man. Josh wasn't angry that Guila came out as bisexual, it was the fact that she had hidden that side of herself from Josh for so many years. Honesty is everything to Josh. He's told me that repeatedly. Then I wonder if I'm self-sabotaging my marriage, but what else can I do? I can't tell Josh the truth; I should have done that the day that Mum told me. Now it's too late; I've been keeping this horrible secret for over three months.

There's a knock on my window and I jump. Hurriedly I wipe my eyes with the back of my hand. It's Tom.

'Hey, you,' he says, as I wind down the window. 'What's with the tears?'

'I'm just being stupid. It's nothing.'

'Doesn't look like nothing.'

'It's just I'm screwing up everything at the moment,' I say.

'Want to go for a coffee? We could grab a drink at the farm shop and I'll ride the bike home if you don't mind me putting it in the back of your car.'

'Of course,' I say. Tom opens the passenger door behind me and pulls the seat down and then wedges his bike inside the car. He then hops into the front passenger seat. As I'm starting the car, he places his hand over mine and squeezes it.

'I'm sorry you're having such a tough time at the moment.'

I throw him a wry smile. I wish I could tell him the truth about my adoption, and I know of anyone that Tom won't judge me, but if I share my secret with him, it will make the betrayal of Josh even greater. I can't risk it.

We are lucky to have a fabulous farm shop just two miles down the road. It has expanded in size year on year and now there's a butchery counter, fresh fruit and veg, as well as locally produced food, far nicer than anything found in the supermarkets. Last year's addition was a coffee shop, and it's permanently full. Tom insists on buying me a coffee so I sit at a small table for two, throwing a smile to a bunch of mums from Ava's school who are seated at an adjacent table. I pick up a leaflet that has been left on our table. It's promoting a fun fair. I'll take Ava – a treat for my letting her down today.

Tom hands me a mug of coffee and places his freshly squeezed orange juice on the table in front of him.

'A problem shared is a problem – I've forgotten the ending, but you know what I mean. Has the grief hit you again?'

'Yes. And I double-booked one of our rooms so I put them in our bedroom. Josh was livid.'

'Sorry, Imogen, but I'm with Josh on that one. If Julia chucked me out of our bedroom to install some strangers, I'd hit the roof.'

'Mum has thrown my life into chaos.'

'What do you mean by that?'

I bite the side of my mouth. I've already said too much, but I look at Tom's kind face and I realise that our friendship is probably the only one where there is no judgement. We just get on. There's no romantic spark; it's a pure and easy friendship. And then the words just slide from my mouth.

'The day before she died, Mum told me I was adopted.'

Tom's eyes widen and his mouth falls open. 'You didn't know?'

I shake my head.

'No wonder you've been out of sorts. Everything you thought you knew about yourself has been a lie. Did she give you any detail? Do you know who your birth parents are?'

'No.' But of course, that's not true. I may not know their names but I know what happened to them; what he did.

'The thing is, I haven't told anyone what Mum said.'

'That's understandable. Why would you want to tell your friends?'

'But I haven't even told Josh.'

'Oh,' Tom says, tilting his head to one side. 'Any particular reason?'

'He's more of a nature-over-nurture sort of person and the longer I don't tell him, the harder it gets.'

'I see that.'

I glance to the right and see one of the school mums staring at us. I realise that Tom and I have been speaking quietly, our heads close together. I sit back in my chair.

'You must tell him, Imogen. He's your husband.'

I look away. I don't need Tom to tell me that.

'Do you know anything about your birth parents?' he asks.

I shake my head.

'Are you going to try to find out about them?'

'I don't know.'

But it crosses my mind that I've been avoiding investigating my birth parents, burying my head in the sand rather than risking finding out more horrors about them. Perhaps that isn't the correct course of action. Perhaps it would be better to know the true story, and armed with that, then maybe I can pluck up the courage to tell Josh. If I'm lucky, Mum might have got her facts wrong. As soon as I've finished my coffee, I tell Tom that I need to get home to do some work, and we part ways.

In the study, I close the door, although Maria is upstairs and she has no reason to come into my work space. I fire up the laptop. All I know is that my birth mother lived in Guildford, that she was raped, and that her rapist was prosecuted and sent to jail. I don't know either of their names. I dig out the adoption certificate and it has my year of birth, 1988, and my place of birth, Guildford. With trembling fingers I type *rape, Guildford, 1988* into the search engine. But there's nothing that really tallies. I realise the internet didn't even exist back then, so any public information would have been disseminated by local newspapers. I take out a subscription for the British Newspaper Archive website and try again.

The local Surrey newspaper comes up with multiple hits. I click on the first article, dated December 1988, a month after I was born.

Surrey man convicted of rape of under-age girl.

A man who raped a teenage girl has been jailed for eight years. Guildford-born Anthony Stanbridge, 18, was yesterday convicted of the rape of a 15-year-old girl. No further details have been made public.

Could Anthony Stanbridge be my father, and my mother the unnamed girl? If my mother reported the rape at the time of my conception, then it's quite reasonable to think that it would take ten months for the case to go to trial. These days it's likely to be nearer eighteen months. I carry on looking through the search results, but it's only this brief article that seems to fit.

So where is Anthony Stanbridge now? It's a reasonably common name but for all I know he might have changed his name upon his release from prison. If he was 18 when he was sentenced in 1988, that makes him 53 years old now. It hits me then that Stanbridge should have been my family name. What sort of person would Imogen Stanbridge be? Evil, like her father? I wish I knew what my mother was called, but unsurprisingly, there are no articles mentioning her by name. Yet without her name, I can't search the births, deaths and marriages register. I simply have no way of finding out more.

That sensation that I had earlier, of heaviness, as if I'm in total overwhelm, makes me sink into my chair. My heart is thumping too loudly, yet I don't know why. It's as if there's a sense of impending doom. I pick up the telephone and call the doctor's surgery, because I need to know what's wrong with me. Am I feeling like this because I'm pregnant, because I'm hiding a secret, or because there really is some unknown threat and my world is about to come tumbling down?

I'm number seven in the queue. It takes fifteen minutes for the phone to be answered. After telling the receptionist that I'm pregnant, that we had to call out the doctor and that I think I need to see him again, she's magically found me an appointment in an hour's time. I place my hands over my stomach and murmur a quiet apology to the life that's growing inside of me.

14

MARIA

Imogen looks deathly pale and I'm worried about her.

'I'm going out for an hour or so,' she says, as she emerges from her study.

'Are you sure you're well enough?' I ask.

She gives me a strange look and I realise I've probably overstepped the mark, again.

'Actually, I've got a doctor's appointment.'

'That's good. Hopefully the doctor can put your mind at rest.'

She frowns slightly and I wonder what I've said wrong this time. 'Is there anything I can do for you whilst you're out?' I ask.

'We're a bit short on food. Would you mind going to the farm shop and buying some food for supper?' She slaps the side of her leg. 'Oh sorry, I forgot you've only got your bike. Don't worry, I'll do it later.'

'I can go to the village shop instead,' I say. 'That's nearer.' Cycling to the farm shop would take me about half an hour each way; the village shop is just ten minutes away, if that.

'Good idea,' Imogen says. 'Are you sure it's okay to go on your bike?'

'It's absolutely no problem. I've got a rucksack and it'll take half an hour, max. You get yourself to the doctor and I'll sort out here.'

'Thanks, Maria. I don't know what I'd do without you. I have an account there, so just put everything under my name.'

As Imogen hurries away, I relish the feeling of warmth, of being needed. I glance into the study and I see that her laptop is still lit up. Yes, I'm nosey, but this is my daughter and I want to find out more about her. I sneak into the study and sit down at the chair Imogen has just vacated. It's warm. The page she was looking at is about a rapist who was convicted in 1988. I let out a little whimper. That was the year of Imogen's birth. What a blow. What a terrible blow. Oh poor, poor Imogen, to have found out like this. No wonder my girl is struggling. It's up to me to help her out, to do whatever I can, whatever a good mother would do. As I'm walking through the utility room to the back door, I notice that the washing machine is on. I stop it mid cycle and remove a little cardigan that Ava was wearing during her party from the drum. It has chocolate stains down the front. I pop it back in the machine and turn the temperature up to high. It'll probably shrink on the high temperature, but then again, Imogen is really losing it, and let's face it, it's easy enough to press the wrong buttons when you've got other, bigger things on your mind. I tug on my coat, grab my rucksack and head out to do the shopping.

I've got to know the lady who runs the village shop. When you don't have any friends in a new area, I've found that there are certain people you should hone in on. The owners of the local pub or the regular assistants in the village shop or post office. These days many of the pubs are too fancy. The gastropubs are staffed with posh young people on their gap years and run by snooty management. But I struck lucky with the village shop owner. Hazel and her husband have run it for the past twenty years. She's forever complaining about the farm shop that has stripped them of business, but I couldn't care less about that. I just like to listen to the local gossip.

'Good morning!' I say cheerily as I enter the shop. 'How are you today?'

'Same old,' Hazel moans. 'The arthritis gets to me in this weather, but I shouldn't complain.'

I fill up my basket with a few bits and pieces: some salmon fillets that look a little past their best, various vegetables and a loaf of bread. I choose a small chocolate bar for Ava and another pack of Benson & Hedges for me, which I'll share with Kyle should he want to join me for another smoke.

'Have you made up with your estranged daughter yet?' Hazel asks.

'Actually, yes, I have.' I smile broadly.

'That's wonderful news. Family needs to stick together come hell or high water. That's what I tell my boys.'

'I'm staying with her now.'

'So you're out of the bedsit?'

'Yes. She took one look at it and said she couldn't have her mother staying in such a dump.'

'There you go. Family to the rescue. I'm really pleased for you.'

She rings up all the items. 'I'm buying these on behalf of

Imogen Letwin. Would you mind putting them on her account?'

'Such a lovely family, aren't they? And that little Ava, she's a doll,' Hazel says.

There's a woman behind me holding a basket with a pint of milk and a bottle of white wine. She snorts straight after Hazel has spoken and then covers it up with a cough. I glance at her, frowning. *What was that about?*

I grab the items I've bought and shove them haphazardly into my rucksack.

'How are you, Hazel?' The woman asks, ignoring me. I step towards the door but not before I get a good look at her. She has smooth, coffee-coloured skin and black hair that tumbles in big curls over her shoulders. Early forties, at a guess, she has an air of high-maintenance. I take a while to repack the shopping into my rucksack and wait until the woman emerges from the shop. She ignores me as she strides to her black Porsche Cayenne, parked on the side of the road. Within a few seconds, she's started the engine and driven away. I take note of her personalised number plate:

T33TH LD

I'm tempted to nip back into the shop to ask who the woman was, but by now a few other people have wandered inside. Instead, I commit that numberplate to memory and cycle home. Yes, Fairview House is my home now and I'm loving it.

I'm unpacking the groceries when Imogen comes home.

'How are you?' I ask.

'My blood pressure is a little high but otherwise I'm okay.'

I've got an ultrasound scan at the end of the week.' She walks back into the utility room and I hear her swear.

'Everything alright?' I ask, as I walk into the room. She's holding up Ava's little cardigan and it's shrunk to the size of a doll's outfit, the red embroidery on the front running to create pink patches on the white.

'I've ruined it! I've totally ruined it.' Tears are welling in Imogen's eyes. 'This was the last present my mum gave Ava and I've destroyed it.'

'Let's try and stretch it.' I take the cardigan from Imogen and try to tug at it, but it's well and truly boiled into a felted mess.

'It's as if I'm doing everything wrong at the moment. I double-booked, I forgot about dressing Ava up in fancy dress, and now I've shrunk her cardigan. I'm permanently on edge and feel like my life is disintegrating.'

'Why don't we go next door and I'll make you a nice cup of tea and you can tell me all about it.'

I boil the kettle and even though Imogen doesn't take sugar with her tea, I pop a couple of cubes into the mug.

'Here you go,' I say as I hand her the mug. 'Are you still worrying about your birth parents?'

She shivers slightly.

'Don't worry, your secret is safe with me. Just because you might have inherited some of the bad genes from your parents doesn't mean you're a bad mother. I've met a fair few people in my life and you are without doubt one of the best mothers I've ever met. Look how upset you are over shrinking Ava's cardigan. Most people would be a bit annoyed but they wouldn't care like you do. Ava is so lucky to have you as her mum.'

'Thank you, Maria,' Imogen says. She takes a sip of her

tea and winces, but she's too polite to comment on the sweetness. It'll do her good to get a bit of sugar in her system.

'How did Ava cope with not being in fancy dress at school?'

Imogen narrows her eyes. It's just the tiniest little movement and for a horrible moment I wonder if I've screwed up.

'You told me that you forgot it was a dressing-up day.' In fact she hadn't. I found the notice in Ava's school bag and shoved it in the bin. I felt a little sad for my granddaughter that she would be the only child in school uniform, but needs must. It's not like the experience will scar her for life. A little adversity makes us stronger.

'I felt really bad for letting Ava down. I thought I'd collect her from school and take her to the fun fair in Billingshurst.'

'That's a marvellous idea. I was planning on going myself after work. I love a fun fair.'

There's a beat of silence before my lovely Imogen says, 'Why don't you come with us?'

'Are you sure?' I ask, trying to appear bashful.

'Of course. Ava would love to have you there.'

'In which case, I must get a move on and make sure everything is spotless here in the house.'

Just after 3 p.m., I join Imogen on the short ride to school. I sit in the car whilst she goes up to the school gate to fetch Ava. When they appear, Ava is skipping with delight, so excited to be going to the fair.

'Can I go on the bumper cars?' she asks.

'I think you might be a little young for them,' Imogen replies.

'I'll happily take her,' I say. 'I love the bumper cars. Have you been to a fun fair before?' I ask Ava.

She shakes her pretty little head. 'No, but Issy has been and lots of my friends are going.'

The fun fair has been set up in a field on the outskirts of the village. We park in a field where they cheekily charge £10 per car. As soon as Imogen releases the child looking system, Ava jumps out and runs off ahead of us. I can sense Imogen's unease.

'Stay with us, Ava!' she shouts. Imogen shouldn't be chasing her daughter in her condition, so I run ahead and grab Ava's hand.

'There are scary people here, so it's important you stay with Gangan or Mummy,' I say in a quiet voice. 'You promise?'

She looks at me with a serious expression and nods. The first thing we come across inside the gates is a traditional carousel merry-go-round with old-fashioned horses bobbing up and down. 'Can I go on that, Mummy?' she asks, the excitement in her high-pitched voice contagious. Imogen pays for a ticket and the ride operator helps lift Imogen onto the horse. We watch her as she goes around and around. The tinny music reminds me of childhood memories I'd prefer to forget.

When she gets down from the merry-go-round she bounces up and down in front of Imogen. 'Please, can I have some candy floss?' Ava asks. 'Please, please!'

By now the fun fair is thrumming with people, children who have been brought here straight after school, like Ava.

Imogen laughs. 'Alright,' she says. 'But I don't want you eating so much you get sick.'

'I won't!' Ava claps her hands. Her delight is so innocent and pure, it's a joy to experience. There's a long queue for the candy floss.

'Should Ava and I wait here whilst you stand in the queue?' I ask Imogen.

'Thanks, that would be great.'

I hold onto Ava's hand and we move to one side, next to a stand where people are shooting with plastic guns, trying – and generally failing – to hit any of the toys. It's then that I look to my left and I see her.

Clare.

What the hell is she doing here?

I try to move Ava to my right, out of the sight line, but it's too late. Clare has seen us and she's striding in our direction.

She waves a hand. 'I've been trying to reach you. Did you get my messages?'

'It's not a good time,' I say.

She raises her eyebrows. 'How are you?'

'Fine.' I keep on glancing towards Imogen, who is now edging to the front of the queue.

'Ow!' Ava says, wriggling her hand in mine. 'You're hurting me, Gangan.'

I release my tight grip on her little hand, which I must have involuntarily squeezed too hard. 'Sorry, sweetie,' I say.

Clare bends her knees and leans towards Ava. 'And who do we have here?'

I don't answer. I can sense Ava looking up at me but my eyes are on Imogen.

'I'm Clare,' she says to Ava. 'What's your name?'

I'm about to pull Ava away, tell her not to talk to strangers, but it's too late. Her little voice rings out loud and clear. 'Ava Annabel Letwin.'

'That's a pretty name,' Clare says.

'We need to go,' I say. 'Come on, Ava. Mummy's nearly at the front of the queue and she'll need help carrying all of that candy floss.' I tug Ava and she comes with me willingly, dancing as we stride forwards. We reach Imogen's side just as she's finishes paying for the candy floss, which she hands to Ava. I glance back the way we came and Clare is still standing there, her arms crossed, her eyes narrowed.

'I saw some ponies on the other side of the fun fair,' I say. 'Shall we head over that way?' I start walking and fortunately Imogen and Ava follow. As we weave in and out of stalls and hordes of people, I glance back again. To my relief, the crowd has swallowed up Clare. I'm uneasy for the rest of our time at the fun fair, constantly looking out for her, terrified she'll just appear and introduce herself to Imogen. Although the next hour goes painfully slowly for me, I don't have to worry. I don't spot Clare again and when Imogen suggests it's time to go home, I've never been more relieved.

Ava is over-tired by the time we get to Fairview House, and I'm happy to leave them to it and disappear up to my room. I wish Ava hadn't told Clare her full name, because I know that Clare is resourceful. But the damage has been done. I'll just need to be on my guard.

The next day, Imogen has a report she needs to get out so she asks me to collect Ava from school, once again driving her car. I'm very careful; perhaps too careful, because a white van hoots me from behind and then overtakes, the driver sticking his finger up in the air as he does so. I can't help myself. I put my foot on the accelerator and I'm just centimetres from the rear of the van. But then I catch myself. What the hell am I doing letting my temper get the better of me? I'm in Imogen's car, I'm banned from driving; I mustn't draw attention to myself. I pull back and the idiot driver disappears into the distance. It leaves me a little shaky though, so by the time I've parked the car several streets over, I'm late to collect Ava. All the other parents are getting into their cars as I hurry up the school path.

'I was going to bring Ava home,' Tom says. He startles me. He gives me a look, as if I'm scum on his shoe, and I feel like slapping him.

'I'm here now. Say goodbye to Issy,' I tell Ava, who does as she's told. I don't understand what Imogen sees in Tom. He's a self-righteous idiot who has nothing better to do than be a stay-at-home dad.

I drive home a little faster but still well below the speed limit, so aware that I have the most precious cargo in the car. Ava is relaxed with me now and she witters about her day at school. She really is the sweetest little creature.

As we walk into the kitchen, Imogen says, 'Can I have a word with you, Maria? I've just had a phone call.'

My heart plummets.

'Run upstairs, Ava, and get out of your school uniform, please,' Imogen says.

I'm holding my breath when Imogen motions for me to take a seat at the table.

'I had a phone call from someone called Clare. She said that she's trying to get hold of you but you're not returning her calls and that it's urgent.'

Bloody Clare. She's found Imogen already. It's my fault for not stopping Ava from blurting out her name. I'm an idiot.

'She sounded really worried about you.'

'She's my daughter.' I sigh. 'I had two daughters. Clare is the first one and I'm sad to say that she has severe mental health issues. She's a great disappointment. Unfortunately I've had to distance myself from her for both of our sakes.'

Imogen looks shocked. 'I'm sorry,' she says, although I'm not sure what she has to be sorry about.

'Clare has a massive problem with prescription drugs. I did everything I could to help her, paid for therapy, even had her sectioned at one point, but despite all the interventions, she rejected me. She's the reason I've been living so frugally, why I was so thrilled to get work with you. I spent every last penny on trying to get Clare the help she so desperately needs. But she just spent the money on more drugs.' I stare off into the distance, thinking how Clare takes after me: damaged goods but impressively resourceful.

'And your other daughter?' Imogen asks.

Here it is. The massive moment I've been waiting for. My heart is galloping in my chest, blood rises to my cheeks and I take a deep inhale. 'My other daughter was adopted. My other daughter was wonderful and–'

There's the sound of tyres on the gravel outside. The slamming of a car door. The opening of the front door followed by the slamming of that, so strongly it reverberates through the house. Both Imogen and I sit there with bated breath, waiting for the storm to arrive.

Josh strides into the kitchen. I have never seen a man look so angry. His eyes are narrowed, his forehead furrowed and his lips pulled back over his teeth. It's terrifying and I fear not only for myself but most of all for Imogen.

'We need to talk.' He spits out the words as he glares at Imogen. 'Could you leave us, please,' he says to me.

I jump up from the table. The bastard has ruined my special moment. 'I'll go and check on Ava,' I say, feeling a surge of resentment.

When I'm in the downstairs corridor, I lean with my back against the wall, listening to their conversation.

'What's going on?' Imogen asks.

'This is what's going on. Would you like to explain this photograph?'

There's a long moment and I hear Imogen's gasp. 'It's not what it seems,' she says.

'Oh really?' Josh's voice is laden with sarcasm. 'A photograph of my wife hugging another man, and quite probably kissing him, is not what it seems? Couldn't you try to be a bit more original, Imogen?'

A smile flickers across my face.

'Who sent this?'

'I've no idea and I don't care. That's not really the point, is it? Someone has sent me a message telling me that my wife is having an affair with Tom Box and attaching this photograph. And all you're saying is, it isn't what it seems. It's bloody obvious to me that my wife is embracing a man who isn't me.'

'I was upset and he hugged me. There's nothing happening between us, I promise.'

'How long has this been going on for?' Josh asks.

'There's nothing going on!' Imogen cries.

'Is he the father of the child you're carrying? When were you going to tell me, Imogen?' Josh is shouting now. On the one hand I'm delighted how quick Josh is to anger; on the other I'm extremely worried for Imogen and Ava's safety.

'Of course he isn't! This is your child. Tom and I are just friends; there's nothing going on between us.' There's desperation in Imogen's voice now and she sounds like she's close to tears.

'So why would someone send me this?' Josh is yelling, his voice carrying throughout the sturdily built house. I hear running footsteps upstairs. I race along the corridor just as Ava appears at the top of the stairs.

'Why's Daddy shouting?' she asks. I run up the stairs and grab her hand, pulling her back towards her bedroom.

'Daddy had a bad day at work. You know what it's like. When you turned up at school and Mummy had forgotten that you needed to wear fancy dress, well, it's a bit like that. He's annoyed and upset.' I shut Ava's bedroom door behind us. I need to protect my little granddaughter, shield her from the disintegration of her parents' relationship. Josh is a bad father to Ava and she deserves so much more.

'Shall we play with your dolls?' I ask.

She looks at me with trusting eyes and nods her head. I smile. I will do anything to protect my granddaughter. Absolutely anything.

15

IMOGEN

I suppose I've been naive. I've been spending a lot of time with Tom and yes, he did hug me that day when I was feeling so low. But nothing inappropriate has happened between us. I don't even fancy Tom; he's just like a brother to me. So who is it that has been spying on me, who is spreading vicious rumours, who got hold of Josh's phone number? I think of the mums who sat next to us at the farm shop café. Was it one of those women? But why would they even care? And I can't help thinking of the time I really did do something bad and how I promised myself I would never, ever do that again.

It takes a huge amount of persuading but I swear to Josh that I would never cheat on him with Tom; that we're just good friends; that someone has sent a malicious message with no real evidence.

'Talk to Tom if you like,' I suggest. 'Or even Julia, his wife. I love you, Josh, and I would never do anything to hurt you, or anything that might ruin our marriage. You're all the family I've got.' It strikes me then that of course he isn't my only family – I have a father out there somewhere – and that I *have* been doing something that might ruin our marriage, just not the thing that Josh thinks. 'Have you tried calling the number the message came from?' I ask.

'The phone is switched off.'

'So it's some coward who is trying to upset us. Or maybe trying to upset Tom and Julia. Perhaps she received the same message,' I suggest. I try to put my arms around Josh but he pushes me away.

'I'm going for a run,' he announces. Josh uses running as a stress reliever so I don't dissuade him.

I have spent the last five years being scared that Josh might tire of me, that he might have an affair. Yet, in reality, it's been me who has come the closest to destroying our relationship. As much as I'd prefer to deny it, it was the affair I had with Josh that was the final nail in the coffin for his first marriage. Josh told me on numerous occasions that their marriage was already broken, that he and Guila had fallen out of love as quickly as they fell in it and they had been living apart under the same roof for years. To be fair, Guila later told me something similar, so I've never felt that weight of responsibility for destroying their marriage. But our relationship moved so quickly. We had only been together for four months when I discovered I was pregnant with Ava. I remember being terrified about telling Josh, but I didn't need to be. He was over the moon, utterly thrilled to be having another child. For us to spend the rest of our lives together. We got married in a registry office five months to the day of our first kiss. I've always been fearful that our marriage might not have the strongest of foundations, and now, for the second time in our six years together, Josh and I are being tested. And how ironic it is that both times it's me who has caused the rifts. I always assumed it would be Josh who would meet a younger, prettier version of Guila and me, and that he would disappear off into the sunset with my smashed heart.

I wish I could have a glass of wine but instead I pour myself a fizzy water. I carry it upstairs where I hear sweet chatter coming from Ava's room. She's sitting on the floor with Maria playing with her dolls. They seem fully engrossed, so I leave them to it and walk to our bedroom. The guests have left but I still haven't moved everything back into place. I'm carrying a pile of my sweaters when there are more footsteps and hushed voices.

'Hello,' I say, smiling at Kyle and the girl that is standing next to him. I'd forgotten that he was coming over tonight, or perhaps I never actually knew. I'm losing track with everything.

The girl looks very young, dressed in school uniform, her skirt extremely short and most probably rolled up at the waist.

'Hi.' She looks bashful.

'Who are you?' I ask.

'Carly,' she says. 'I'm a friend of Kyle's from school. We're working on a geography project together.'

'Does your mum know you're here?'

'Of course she does,' Kyle says, ushering her into his room.

I'm out of my comfort zone here. Is it acceptable for a fifteen-year-old boy to take a similarly aged girl into his bedroom? It makes me think of my birth parents. My mother was just fifteen when she was raped, when she fell pregnant with me. What if Kyle and Carly get up to things they shouldn't? Under normal circumstances I'd call Josh, but after our argument I don't want to disturb his run. I debate calling Guila, but decide not to. Instead I finish tidying up and then drag my weary body downstairs and start making tea for Ava. It's much later than normal, so I grill some fish fingers and boil up some vegetables. I haven't made anything for our supper and decide a takeaway will be the easiest, especially as Kyle is here and I don't know what his dietary requirements will be this week. In addition, I'm still hoping to go to my painting class this evening. I need to get out of the house.

Josh returns from his run.

'Kyle is here with a girl,' I say. 'They're in his bedroom. Are you okay with that?'

'Why shouldn't I be?' He frowns.

'It's just they're quite young to be alone in his room.'

'You always assume the worst, don't you?'

I let the irony of that statement pass; after all, it was Josh who was thinking the worst of me.

'Shall we order a Chinese takeaway?' I suggest. 'I'm sorry, I haven't had time to make supper and I'd still like to make my painting class.'

'Whatever. I'm going to have a shower. I'll have Peking duck and spring rolls.'

I follow Josh upstairs but turn the opposite way to walk to Kyle's room. I knock on the door and immediately open it. My assumptions were correct. Carly and Kyle spring apart. Her lips are raw and red and her blouse unbuttoned.

'You're too young for this!' I exclaim. 'You should leave now.' I point at Carly.

'Who the hell are you to tell us what we should or shouldn't do?' Kyle snaps. 'You're not my mother. You're nobody to me!' He jabs his finger at me. Carly looks mortified and quickly pulls on her sweater and grabs her coat.

'You don't talk to me like that, Kyle. You're living in my home with my young daughter and I expect certain standards of behaviour.'

'What, like you shagging my dad when he was still married to my mum? Talk about hypocrisy.'

'Please, Kyle. Don't talk like that. Carly, I think you should leave. Do you need a lift home?'

'No, thanks. I'll call my mum and wait outside.'

'Kyle, I'm ordering in Chinese takeaway. What do you want to eat?'

'Nothing. I'm going back to Mum's. Carly, wait for me. Can I hitch a lift with your mum too?'

The youngsters grab their bags and run down the stairs.

'At least tell your dad you're leaving,' I shout after Kyle, feeling totally undermined and ineffectual.

'You tell him.'

The front door slams once again.

Josh and I barely talk during our takeaway. He says that he accepts I'm not having an affair with Tom but he's also annoyed with me for 'pushing Kyle away', as he sees it. If I get into another argument with him, I'll break down in tears so I just accept it. For now, anyway. The bad blood between Kyle and me cannot go on.

It's such a relief to be driving away from home, knowing I can dump all my worries on Danielle. She's deep in conversation when I arrive at the village hall but when she sees me, she beckons me over.

'I was wondering whether the four of us could meet up for supper sometime,' she suggests.

'Okay,' I say. I'm not sure that Josh will want to spend the evening with the adulterous French painting teacher so I'm non-committal.

When we're settled down at our tables I tell her about my dreadful week.

'I'm totally losing it,' I say.

'It'll be the pregnancy hormones. You were all over the place when you were pregnant with Ava.'

'I wasn't!' I retort indignantly. Or is she right? Have I conveniently forgotten? I was infused in a bubble of love during that period.

'Alain has left his wife,' she whispers. 'We're moving in together.'

'Oh,' I say, because although I want Danielle to be happy, I can't stop thinking about Alain's wife.

'Josh thinks I'm having an affair with Tom. He got an anonymous text message.'

'Wow! But I'm not that surprised.'

'What do you mean? Tom's just a good friend.'

'You need to be careful. This is a small town and folk talk. I've already had to tell a few people that you and Tom are just friends and there's nothing untoward going on.'

'But you believe me, don't you?'

'Well, you are very friendly with him and he's fit with all the cycling he does.'

'I'm not having an affair.' I grip my paint brush too tightly and make harsh marks on the page. I never told Danielle what I did eleven months after Ava was born. In fact, I didn't tell anyone; the risks and the shame and the guilt were too monumental. Instead I pushed it into the recess of my brain. But I'm sufficiently self-aware to realise that Danielle's behaviour is a trigger for me. A trigger for waves of guilt. Danielle has well and truly destroyed a marriage. Josh and Guila's marriage was already broken when we met, so in that instance I wasn't to blame.

The irony of a malicious text message being sent to Josh when I'm truly innocent doesn't pass me by. Who has done that and why? Is Danielle jealous of my friendship with Tom because these days I spend more time with him than I do with her? Could it have been Danielle who sent the message – but if so, why? The turmoil in my head just doesn't let go. Or was it Tom himself because he wants more from me? No. I discount that. Tom has never made any romantic overtures towards me. It must be someone else, someone who is jealous of my life, or someone I've snubbed inadvertently. I think of the people I've fired in my work but as far as I'm aware, none of them live near me. No, it's got to be someone closer to home, another mother from school. Or Louise, perhaps. If anyone should have a grudge against me it would be Louise. But why take her revenge now, four years later?

16

MARIA

Tom is a very bad influence on Imogen. It's not natural for a married woman to have a close friendship with another man, and whatever anyone thinks, such relationships always slip into something more. If not a physical relationship, then an emotional co-dependency that is deeply unhealthy for a marriage. The text message to Josh doesn't seem to have changed things so I'm going to have to take another tack. All I want to do is save Imogen's perfect family; I'm looking out for her. With every-thing going on in her life she needs a guardian angel like me, someone to help focus her mind on her family.

Today, Imogen has her ultrasound. I wish I could go with her, hold her hand as a mother should do, but Josh is going instead.

'I'm not sure I'll be back in time to collect Ava from school,' she says. 'I've asked Tom to bring Ava back here.'

'Forgive me for saying this, but is that a good idea?' I ask.

A flicker of unease crosses Imogen's face. 'It's just that Tom's so often distracted on his phone and I've noticed that he's barely able to pay his own daughter proper attention, let alone accompanying two little girls. He's different when you're around.'

'But Tom dotes on Ava. She's Issy's best friend.'

'I'm just saying he's not that attentive when you're not around and I couldn't rest easy knowing that. I could get a taxi to bring Ava home or she could come on the back of my bicycle. I'm sorry my car is still off the road. The repairs are taking forever.'

Imogen scrunches up her face but eventually says, 'If I'm running late at the clinic, I'll call you and you can order a taxi.'

'Excellent,' I say. 'Good luck for the scan.'

I'm vacuuming one of the guest bedrooms when my phone rings. My stomach clenches when I see Clare's name show up. I'm tempted to ignore her like before but she's crossed the line contacting Imogen behind my back. She's going to get a piece of my mind.

'Yes,' I say. 'What do you want?'

'To check you're okay.'

'And you think it's alright to track me down via an innocent little girl? Well, it's not. You're not wanted, Clare.'

'Who is Imogen Letwin?'

'She's my other daughter and she's way nicer and more successful than you. She has a beautiful family and she's welcomed me in.'

'Oh, come on. Don't be like that. This Imogen needs to know the truth.'

'You just butt out of my life, do you hear me? I don't want to hear or see from you ever again and don't you dare go near the Letwins. All you ever want to do is ruin things for me. Well, you're not going to. Not this time.'

'Are you still driving despite your licence ban?'

'What I do or don't do is none of your business. I know where you live, Clare. Stay out of my life.' I end the call. But I'm shaking with fury. How dare she interfere! I clean the room with more vigour than normal, so much so that I scratch the top of the enamel bath. I position the freebie shampoo and conditioner bottles on top of the mark and hope that Imogen doesn't notice.

The unease continues though, and I'm worried that Clare will say something to Imogen. I'm going to have to tell Imogen the truth, sooner rather than later. As I pour the toilet cleaner into the bowl of one of the guest bathrooms, I realise we've run out of bleach – totally my fault as I'm meant to keep track of the cleaning materials Imogen needs to buy and leave her a list. I let out a screech in anger and thump the palm of my hand on the basin. I need to get out of here, get some fresh air and calm down. I decide to cycle to the village shop. Pedalling furiously does the trick, and by the time I arrive, I'm feeling a little calmer.

As luck would have it, I'm pulling up in front of the shop just as the black Porsche Cayenne with the personalised numberplate pulls away.

I saunter inside, and wave at Hazel. 'Who's the lady in the big black car?' I ask nonchalantly as I hand over a bottle of bleach. I tilt my head to one side and scrunch up my forehead. 'She looks familiar but I can't place her.'

'Oh, you mean Louise Devi?'

'Yes, and I know I've met her before, but I can't think– ' I let my voice fade away.

'She's married to Arun Devi. Your dentist Josh Letwin is a looker, but Arun Devi, now he's in a different league altogether.' Hazel winks at me.

I recall the personalised numberplate that looked like TEETH. 'Is he a dentist too?'

'Yes. Arun Devi and Josh Letwin used to run a dental practice together. Even the folk who were terrified of going to the dentist didn't mind visiting that handsome duo, but then something happened... I'm thinking four or five years ago. Arun Devi upped and left, set up his own practice over Crawley way. Local gossip said that the two of them had a serious bust-up but no one really knows what's gone on. I doubt you'd get your Imogen Letwin in the same room as Louise Devi. There's no love lost there.'

'Right, well, you take care,' I say to Hazel, before hurrying out of the shop. That's a very interesting nugget of information, something that needs further investigation.

Back at Fairview House, I take out my phone and do a search for *Arun Devi dentist*. Hazel is right. He's got a practice over in Crawley. I reckon I need to pay him a little visit. I haven't got enough money to afford a dentist appointment, especially as there's nothing wrong with my teeth, other than the yellowing from smoking and the missing molar thanks to crunching on a particularly hard piece of toffee a few years back, but I'm confident I can get to see him nevertheless.

I'm musing on the best way to play this when Imogen calls. She sounds chirpy.

'Everything was fine with the scan and I'll be on time to collect Ava from school.'

'That's fabulous news,' I say. 'Hope you don't mind but I've got a doctor's appointment at 5 p.m. with my old doctor in Crawley.'

'Oh goodness, I hope you're alright,' Imogen gushes. She's such a kind young woman.

'Nothing to worry about,' I reassure her. 'Just ladies' issues. I'll be back for supper.'

'No need to hurry. Josh is away tonight and I can manage alone.'

I smile. It's as if all the stars are lined up just for me. This afternoon I'll find out why there's animosity between the Letwins and the Devis and tonight I will tell my beautiful Imogen the truth.

I TAKE a bus to Crawley and walk to Arun Devi's dental practice. It's in a low-slung brick building in a residential area with a large sign at the front saying, *Devi's Dentistry for a Perfect Smile.* There are two black Porsches Cayenne out front. One has the numberplate T33TH LD and the other T33TH AD. How very cute to have matching cars and numberplates. I bet that cost them a fair bit. I wonder what Mrs Devi is doing here. Does she work in the practice too? I open the door and walk into an open plan area with a reception desk and a waiting room filled with brightly coloured armchairs. The place is empty other than Louise Devi, who is sitting behind the reception desk. She looks up as I enter, her smile dazzling, her teeth almost a fluorescent white.

'Good afternoon. How can I help you?'

'I need to see a dentist and I've been recommended your practice.'

'We're only taking on private patients at the moment. Is that okay?'

'Sure,' I say. *Not a hope in hell I can afford that.*

'In which case, please can you fill in one of our new patient forms?' She hands me a clipboard with a form attached to it, along with a blue biro.

'I was with Josh Letwin before,' I say, trying hard not to smile. 'I'm sorry about what happened.' I glance at Louise Devi and her face clouds over. 'Were you good friends with Imogen Letwin?'

It seems that my hunch is right. Louise Devi's eyes narrow and her plump lips tighten.

'No,' she spits.

'It's such a shame what happened,' I repeat.

'What do you know about it?' she asks with a hiss. Her cheeks redden and I realise I've touched a nerve.

'Imogen feels really sad about it,' I say.

'Sad!' Louise exclaims. 'She might have thought about our friendship before screwing...' Her hand springs up to cover her mouth.

I scribble down a fake address in Horsham and a false mobile phone number then hand over my completed form. I whisper conspiratorially, 'I'm sorry for how the Letwins treated you.'

'Not Josh, just Imogen. She's a bitch,' Louise Devi says. 'How well do you know her?'

'Well enough to agree with your description. I think she's up to it again.' I'm not positive what I'm suggesting here but I have a suspicion and I'm shocked. This isn't the Imogen I know.

'Poor Josh. He deserves better. Arun was a bloody idiot. He swore to me that it was a one-off, and I chose to believe him. He said that if I told Josh the truth, both our marriages would have been over and the dental practice destroyed, so I bit my tongue but I insisted we had nothing to do with the Letwins again. She got away lightly, did Imogen. If it had been up to me, I'd have told the world that she's a cheating bitch. We would have moved away; it's just the kids are so well settled in their school and it didn't seem right to move them.'

The door chimes as another patient walks in.

'I'll call you,' I say as I edge towards the door. 'Sorry about what Imogen did but it takes two to tango, doesn't it?'

Louise glowers at me, but I'm not hanging around to find out more. I dart out of the door and hurry back towards the bus stop.

Oh, Imogen, I think as I sit on the bus, my head leaning against the glass of the window. *What did you do? Is there a side of you that isn't quite so pure?* I can't decide if that makes her more interesting or whether I'm a little bit disappointed. Did she have an affair with Arun Devi, as his wife suggested, and if so, what can I do with that knowledge?

BACK AT FAIRVIEW House the hours pass slowly and I'm willing Imogen to hurry up and put Ava to bed and come downstairs. I make a jug of lemon water with a few mint leaves in it and put out a bowl of crisps. I'm debating whether to light a candle to create a calmer atmosphere, but suddenly Imogen is in the kitchen, opening the fridge door.

'There's something I need to tell you,' I say. 'Have a seat and we'll sort out supper afterwards.'

She frowns at me but does as I suggest. 'You're not leaving, are you?'

I laugh. 'The opposite, actually.' I put my photo album on the table. It's not a big, clothbound book like Imogen's, but a small plastic album with each photo slid into a plastic sleeve. 'Have a glass of infused water.' I pour her a glass from the jug. 'You know how you're adopted.'

Her knuckles are white as she clenches the glass.

'Hey, there's nothing to worry about,' I say, touching her arm. 'This is going to come as quite the surprise, but I may as well just say it.' I pause. 'I'm your mother, Imogen. I am your birth mother.'

'You're what?'

'I am your birth mother. The woman who gave you up for adoption.'

The glass of water slips from Imogen's hand and shatters onto the stone floor. 'No, you can't be,' she says, shaking her head and staring at the broken glass and puddle of water.

'I know it's a shock but a happy shock, I hope.'

She continues staring at the floor. I jump up from the table. 'I'll clear this mess up and then I'll show you my photos, the ones I kept of you before I had to give you away.' I hurry to the cupboard under the sink, grab a roll of paper towel and the dustpan and brush. I pick up the shards of glass and put them in the dustpan and soak up the water with the paper towel. I wrap most of the glass in old newspaper but I keep a couple of shards back. You never know when something like that might come in useful. I leave them in the dustpan and will collect them later.

'Now, where were we?' I sit back down and open up the photo album. Such sadness wells up inside of me when I see that very first baby photo. Guilt too. I contort my face, remembering how Seema in the video looked when she recalled her guilt for giving away baby Leo.

'This was you, straight after you were born,' I say, pointing at the tiny baby wrapped up tightly in a white woven blanket. I flip through the photos and I see flickers of recognition on Imogen's face. She recognises her younger self in photo after photo.

'I don't understand,' she says.

'Of course not, love. It's a lot to take in. I was too young. Much too young to have a baby, let alone keep you. I wanted to. Believe me, I desperately wanted to keep you. You know what that bond is like between mother and baby. It was overwhelming. But I was underage, and I had no control over what was happening. They whisked you away from me and it was the most painful, most horrific thing that has ever happened to me. I could hear your cries all the way down the corridor. I still hear them sometimes. I grieved for years. I don't think you ever get over being forced to give up your child. I looked for you everywhere. For over thirty years I looked, staring into the eyes of every little blonde, blue-eyed child I saw, knowing that the recognition would be there as soon as I saw you. And it was. The moment we met, it felt like my heart was going to explode with love for you and my perfect little granddaughter. I think you felt it too, that flicker of deep recognition, but unlike me, you didn't understand what you were feeling.'

Imogen stares at me, her jaw slack. I wish she'd say something.

'The only good news is that you were placed in such a loving home. Your adoptive parents gave you a life of privilege that I could never have offered you. Money, education, stability. Unfortunately I didn't realise what a fabulous childhood you had until I met you, and by then it was too late for me to say thank you to your adoptive parents for giving you such a perfect life. I worried for all those years, Imogen, but now I know that worry was for nothing. And I take great comfort in that.' She still says nothing but she's picking the sides of her nails and staring at the floor. 'I'm sure you have lots of questions to ask me.'

This is not going the way I anticipated. I'd hoped that

Imogen would throw her arms around me, tell me that she's so happy she has a mother, that I'm the missing part in her perfect life.

But all she says is, 'How did you find me?'

Clearly I can't tell her the truth about that, so I lean forwards across the table. 'I used an agency. I saved up every last penny and used an agency that specialises in tracking down adopted children. They found you for me and here we are.'

'But why didn't you tell me straight away and why did you accept this job?'

'The timing has to be right when sharing momentous news such as this. And I wanted to be sure that you were who I thought you were. Imagine if I'd disliked you but I'd already told you that you were my daughter? There would be no going back from that, just disappointment for both of us. No, I needed to get to know you first and make sure that you were strong enough to be told this happy news.'

And still Imogen doesn't say anything. The churning in my stomach is increasing. We should be hugging by now, shedding happy tears, running upstairs to awaken Ava to tell her that Gangan is her real granny. But Imogen seems shell-shocked, and this isn't at all the reaction I was expecting.

17

IMOGEN

I feel like I've been hit with a sledgehammer. My mind is all over the place. Maria, my birth mother? How can she be? Mum said my birth mother had taken her own life, so how does that add up? But why would she be pretending? And the baby in the photographs she showed me look just like me. I know Maria was expecting some reaction from me, but really I feel like I've been cast in concrete. No words came to me, it was such a shock. And now I'm in bed, missing Josh, who is away for two nights. It's the middle of the night but I've been tossing and turning for hours thinking about the woman down the hallway who may be my flesh and blood. Although I didn't say much, I do feel a bond with Maria but I don't trust myself. Maybe she's lying? But why would someone do something like that? It would be so cruel.

I think back to Mum lying in that nursing home room. She was moved to a palliative care centre the week before and we knew her time was nearly up. It broke my heart seeing her lying in that bed, hooked up to a machine, so thin, the bones jutting out at strange angles. Mum was on the highest doses of morphine and goodness knows what other drugs. They could have played with her brain; probably did. Maybe she got confused when she said my birth mother was dead. Perhaps that was easier for her to deal with rather than the thought that my birth mother might swoop in and relegate her to second best. But that would never happen. Whatever the circumstances of my birth, Mum was the person I loved.

Is Maria the nameless person referred to in the articles about rapist Anthony Stanbridge? It's all too much of a coincidence, isn't it? After all, Maria discovered I was adopted and only told me she was my mother afterwards. But maybe she didn't see my adoption certificate after all, because I was sure I hid it well. Maybe she already knew its contents and she just engineered the conversation for me to talk about it. I wish I could recall her exact words. My conflicting thoughts go around and around. Of course, it would be lovely if she was my mother. I'd have a proper family and Ava seems to adore Maria. But at the same time it feels like a betrayal of Mum. It's as if she died and another mother swooped straight in to take her place.

By the time Ava comes into my bedroom in the morning, it feels like I've only slept for five minutes. My eyes are gritty and my shoulders ache. Why didn't Maria tell me straight up when we first met? That's the thing I don't understand.

Maria is making breakfast for our guests when Ava and I go downstairs. She turns to us with a big grin.

'Good morning! How are we this morning? I've made you both a full English as a special treat. Do you like eggs and bacon, sweetie?' she asks Ava.

As my daughter is settling on her chair, I pull Maria to

one side and whisper, 'Please don't say anything yet to Ava. We'll talk to her tonight or over the weekend.'

Maria looks disappointed but nods in agreement.

It isn't until later, after I've dropped Ava at school and returned home, that I realise what has been bothering me. Mum said I was the product of rape, yet Maria hasn't mentioned it. In fact she hasn't said a word about my conception other than she was too young. Is that because she wants to spare me the horror of what happened? I need to find out.

'Maria,' I say, accosting her as she's cleaning a guest bedroom. 'Can you tell me about the rape?'

'Um...' She frowns.

'The rape. The trial. When you found out you were pregnant, what happened?'

'No. That's not... that's not something I like to dwell on.'

'I don't know if I believe you. I don't know if you're really my birth mother.'

Something happens to Maria now. It's like she's going to combust. Her breathing is short and irregular and big red blotches appear on her cheeks. 'Are you ashamed of me, Imogen? Is that what this is all about? Is it because I'm just a cleaning lady, a homemaker, someone who does menial work? Are you ashamed of your heritage?' She prods her finger towards me and I take a step backwards. 'Because I couldn't help what happened to me.'

I try to keep my composure but her behaviour has rattled me. 'What year were you born?'

'Why does that matter?'

'It does.'

'1973. I was born in 1973. I was 15 when I had you. Too young.'

'Okay,' I say, because that tallies with what Mum says and it tallies with the article about Anthony Stanbridge, but her intensity is making me uncomfortable. Perhaps it's because she wants to be my mother, that she's been looking for me for so many years, there's a sense of desperation and clinginess.

'Please, Imogen. Let's not argue. I realise this is a shock for you whilst I've had plenty of time to get used to our relationship. It's a strange situation for us all.'

I have another busy day but also I get the impression that Maria is staying out of my way. It suits me and gives me some breathing space. For a few hours I feel unusually calm, as if the conundrum around my birth has been solved. In many ways it would be wonderful if Maria is my birth mother. Ava adores her and I respect the woman. She's a hard worker with a positive attitude and we get on well. Perhaps I could even come to love her one day. I sleep surprisingly well and dream of Maria tucking us all up in bed.

THE NEXT MORNING, after I've taken Ava to school, the doubts set in. I go into the study and fire up my laptop. I need to find out facts. Online, I pay for a subscription on Ancestry. I wonder if Maria has given me her real name, so when I type in Maria Hinks and select her birth year from 1960 to 1980, I don't know what I'll find. There are several people with her name of that age but there is no Maria Hinks born in 1973. I feel a surge of fury. Maria has lied to me. She's taken advantage of the fact I shared my secrets with her and she's feeding off me. Why, I don't know, but I'm sure going to find out.

I storm through the house looking for Maria but she's

nowhere to be found. I hurry upstairs and see that the light is on in her bedroom, the door just a little ajar. I feel like pulling it open but I restrain myself and knock first.

'Come in,' she says. She's standing up next to the bed folding a hideous pink nylon nightdress. 'Sorry I'm running a bit late today, Imogen. I slept badly but don't worry, I'll make up the hours.'

'You've lied to me. There's no Maria Hinks born in 1973.'

'I don't know what you're talking about.' She crosses her arms across her chest.

'Why are you pretending to be my birth mother? Whatever you're doing is cruel.'

'I'm not lying, Imogen. You've got it all wrong.'

'Show me some paperwork then. Your birth certificate, my birth certificate, some proof that you are who you say you are.'

'You know I don't have anything like that, Imogen.' I don't know that, and why wouldn't she have the correct paperwork?

'But I'll get hold of a copy of my birth certificate and whatever else you need. It's just so disappointing that you don't believe me. What else can I do?'

'A DNA test. We can both do a DNA test,' I suggest.

'Oh no.' She sits down heavily on the end of her bed. 'I'm not doing one of those. That's just a far-right ruse to hold personal information about us that will be passed on to the government. I've heard that personal data is shared with insurance companies and doctors. It's highly dangerous to do a DNA test.'

'That's ridiculous,' I mutter. I wonder whether Maria really believes that or it's just an excuse not to take the test.

'I don't understand why you're rejecting me, Imogen. Am

I a disappointment? I suppose I'm not as attractive or intelligent or wealthy as your adoptive mother but I can't help any of that.'

'You haven't given me any proof to back up what you're saying.' My intuition is screaming that she's lying, but somehow she's been backed into a corner. 'I'm sorry, but this isn't working. I don't know what your game is but I'd like you to leave our house and get out of our lives.'

She stands up, narrows her eyes and fixes her gaze on me. A cold shiver passes through my body and for the first time I feel fearful in my own home. Her voice becomes a monotone. 'If you try to get rid of me, Imogen, I will tell Josh all about your heritage. About how you've lied to him regarding your birth parents and your adoption. About how you're having an affair with Tom, about how you had an affair with Arun Devi. Do you want to ruin your perfect life? Do you really?'

What the hell? How does Maria know about Arun Devi? I feel a surge of anger. How dare she threaten me! Then it all happens in a split second. She moves towards me, her arms outstretched as if she's going to grab me, but I don't want this woman touching me, so I push her backwards, fury giving me a strength I didn't know I had. But the room is too small and she stumbles, catching her leg on the side of the bed frame, and she tumbles to the floor. For a moment I'm stunned. She's sitting there moaning, rubbing her leg.

What have I done? As I look, I can see the swelling grow on her shin. I did that. I pushed her and now she's hurt. I've shocked myself. Is this proof that there really is badness inside me or were my actions commensurate with Maria's threats? Eventually I pull myself together.

'Are you alright?'

'Not really.' She's rocking backwards and forwards, rubbing her leg.

'It's not broken, is it?' I ask, frantic with horror at the thought of seriously injuring her.

She grabs the side of the bed and pulls herself up to standing, gently putting her weight through her leg.

'No. I'm going to have a humdinger of a bruise, though.'

'I'm sorry,' I say. 'I didn't mean for you to get hurt. I'll go and find you some arnica cream. Do you need a painkiller?'

'I don't need anything. Look, I realise it's the pregnancy hormones playing with your reasoning, making you violent. I won't press charges this time because I know how stressed you are. I won't say a word to Josh about Arun or Tom. I'll stay out of your way today to give you space to come to terms with everything.'

I leave her room because what else can I do? I feel like throwing things against the wall, screaming and shouting, because now Maria has me exactly where she wants me and I've no idea what game she's playing. I go into the bathroom and lock the door. How the hell does Maria know about Arun?

I think back to that time, a time I've tried to forget. In the weeks and months after Ava's birth, Josh began spending more and more time at Guila's. Kyle was behaving badly and was on the edge of expulsion from his school. He was an angry young boy, ready to throw a punch at any kid who was brave enough to stand up to him, swearing at his teachers and refusing to do his homework. It was obvious to us all that he wasn't coping well with his parents' divorce, that he resented me and Ava. Guila began calling Josh daily, at first to discuss Kyle, but then it seemed to me she'd call on Josh for anything in her life that wasn't going well. He would rush over to her house because the dishwasher wasn't working or she couldn't remember how to change the bags in the vacuum cleaner. Not an evening went by when he wasn't talking to her on the phone or disappearing to her house after work. I became increasingly insecure. Did Josh think he'd made a mistake divorcing her? Was he really helping her out or were they conducting a love affair?

One afternoon it got too much. Ava wouldn't stop crying. She was teething and in pain and I needed Josh's help. I rang the dental practice that he ran with Arun. The receptionist told me that Josh had left work early and then she put me through to Arun. He said he'd stop by on his way home and he'd bring some gel that would soothe Ava's gums. I rang Josh on his mobile and he apologised but said he wouldn't be home that night. He had to go to London to spend the evening with an American orthodontist who was unexpectedly in town, an orthodontist he'd met years ago when they were training. That little story didn't stack up for me. Josh had never spent a night away, and why didn't he know of this sooner? As far as I knew, he didn't even have any overnight things with him. I reckoned he'd created a little cover story so he could spend the night with Guila.

I stared at myself in the mirror and realised how frightful I looked. Frumpy, messy hair, as if I no longer cared about my appearance. Leaving Ava in her cot, I had a long shower, washed and blow-dried my hair, swiped on some make-up and put on a loose, flowing dress. For the first time since my little girl was born, I felt more like my old self.

I knew I looked good from Arun's expression when I opened the door to him. He kissed me on the cheek.

'Lovely perfume,' he muttered.

I welcomed him in and before long we'd opened a bottle

of white wine and we talked. He told me that he was going through a rough patch with Louise, but I wouldn't understand because I was newly married. But I did understand. And then we were kissing and soon our clothes were cast aside and we made love on the living room sofa. For a few minutes, it was magical, but we quickly realised what we'd done. As I watched him get dressed, I was horrified. And deeply ashamed. How could I have jeopardised my marriage like that? I'd never had a one-night stand before; it was inconceivable I could cheat on Josh.

'This was a mistake,' Arun said, barely able to meet my eyes.

'Yes, a terrible mistake,' I agreed, wrapping a throw tightly around my body.

'We'll never talk about it. Tonight never happened,' he said, before hurrying out of the house.

It was only later when Ava awoke crying, her cheeks red and her gums sore, that I realised Arun had forgotten to give me the gum-soothing paste.

I tried to forget about what happened but I was eaten up with guilt. I loved Josh. How could I have cheated on him? And worse still, with his dear friend and business partner. I knew that Arun had as much to lose as me and that the chances of him telling Josh the truth were slim, but what I hadn't counted on was Louise.

Somehow, she found out. I don't know how but I'll never forget the day she turned up on my doorstep.

'We need to talk,' she said, pushing past me and striding into our hall. She'd been inside on several occasions before, but this time she paced straight into our living room and stood in front of the sofa.

'Is this where you did it?' she asked, her teeth bared. She jabbed towards the sofa.

'I don't know what you're talking about,' I said, but my voice quivered, because I knew that she was about to rip my world apart.

'I know you had sex with Arun right here. He says just the once but as I don't believe a word he utters, perhaps he's lying about that too.'

I opened and closed my mouth unable to formulate a sentence.

'You're in luck, you cheating whore.'

I gasped.

'Arun has persuaded me not to tell Josh because he doesn't want to destroy the dental practice and he doesn't want to decimate our families. There are too many children involved: our three, Kyle and your baby. I don't suppose you thought of them when you opened your legs.'

I trembled.

'Arun loves me and promises that this was the first time he's ever cheated on me. We're in therapy to save our marriage. So this is what is going to happen. If I ever see you again, I'm going to pretend you don't exist. Arun is going to set up his own dental practice and our families will never see each other again. We are no longer friends.'

I wondered how that would work considering we lived in the same town. 'What are you and Arun going to tell Josh?' My voice sounded so distant.

'Nothing. But if this ever happens again, the whole world will know what a cheating bitch you are.' She then turned on her heel and strode out of the house leaving me gasping for air.

To be fair to Louise, she kept her word. The days spun into weeks and into months as I held my breath wondering whether she might still tell Josh the truth. But she never did. When Arun walked away from their joint dental practice, Josh was deeply hurt. He didn't understand it. They had a massive argument, according to Josh overheard by all their staff, when Arun announced he'd be taking their client list and the most expensive equipment. Josh couldn't understand why Arun had turned on him. He came home that evening, fury making his eyes flash and spittle collecting at the edge of his lips.

'Arun has screwed me over,' he said. 'He told me to talk to you. What the hell do you know about it?'

I froze, fear gripping my throat. 'Nothing,' I whispered. But my answer wasn't good enough.

'Why would he say that, Imogen?' he asks, his fists clenched.

And so I lied. 'I had a massive argument with Louise. I'm sorry.'

'An argument about what?'

I said the first thing that came into my head. 'About how you work so much harder than him, that you have more clients and are a better dentist, but you split the profits equally and it's not fair.' My voice petered out.

'What the hell! That's nothing to do with you! How dare you comment on my business. You've ruined everything, Imogen!'

Josh punched the wall then. He actually rammed his fist into the plaster of our living room wall and gouged out a chunk. I'd never seen him lose his temper like that.

I'm particularly ashamed of what I said next. 'Louise said you are still seeing Guila, that you confided in Arun that you made a mistake marrying me.'

'But that's not true!' Josh exclaimed as he examined his bleeding knuckles.

'I know, and that's why the argument spiralled out of control.'

Josh groaned, but he accepted my lies while I spent the next few minutes patching up his hand, and it was Josh who repeatedly told me that he was sorry.

And now, four years later, we never talk about the Devis, yet the guilt of what I did is a burden I'll carry until my dying day.

I think of Maria's threats. How did she find out about Arun? Is she a friend or confidante of Louise's? She knows too much about me. Much too much. She might be wrong about me having an affair with Tom but she's absolutely right about Arun. And I bet Louise would be only too happy to corroborate the facts.

There's only one solution. To tell Josh everything and then I'll be able to get rid of Maria. Yet the thought of it fills me with horror. I know for sure that if Josh finds out that I slept with Arun, that the reason their partnership collapsed was due to my disloyalty, our marriage will be over in an instant.

18

MARIA

I thought it best to avoid Imogen this morning, to give her some time and space to settle her emotions, so I stayed in my room until I heard her car leave. According to her diary, she has a client meeting this morning so I'm not expecting her back for a few hours. I meander downstairs and see that her guests are still eating breakfast in the small room at the back of the house.

'Is everything alright?' I ask them, injecting a cheery note to my voice.

The woman jumps. 'Oh,' she exclaims. 'We thought we were alone in the house. Mrs Letwin said to leave the keys in the box by the door.'

'I'm Imogen's mother. I live in the main house with them.'

'Oh, lovely,' the woman says. 'Was this your family home?'

'Yes. We are very lucky. Is there anything else you need?' I ask.

'No, thank you. We're just on our way out.'

'You will leave Imogen a lovely review, won't you? My daughter works so hard on this business.'

'If I can work out how to leave a review, I certainly will,' she promises.

That's a pathetic answer and for a moment I debate slashing their tyres or creating some other problem for them, but after taking a couple of deep breaths, I realise I'd rather they were just out of the house and gone for good.

After they leave, I strip their bedroom and throw everything into the washing machine but I'm not in the mood for cleaning and my leg is sore where I bashed it yesterday, so instead I make myself a coffee, select a book from Imogen's bookcase and sit down in the living room, my legs up on the sofa. This is such a lovely room with its south-facing patio doors and the grand piano in the corner. My eyelids feel heavy and I'm just dozing off when the front doorbell chimes. It makes me jump. Perhaps I'll ignore it. It chimes again and I wonder if Imogen is expecting a parcel or something. Or maybe it's a friend and I can invite them in and explain that I'm Imogen's mother and that they're welcome to wait in my house. After the third chime I hobble to the door and swing it open.

I wish I hadn't.

It's Clare. She's dressed smartly in a beige trench coat and brown knee-high leather boots, a matching handbag worn crossbody.

'What do you want?' I ask. 'I told you to leave us alone.'

'I'm worried about you. I'm worried that you're doing it all over again. It's not only you who'll get hurt. Imogen needs to know the truth.'

'This is none of your business, Clare. Just butt out of my life. I've got a wonderful daughter who actually cares about me and just when my life is perfect, what do you do? Come in and destroy it, all over again.'

She sighs. 'You need to see a doctor.'

'There is nothing wrong with me.' I speak through gritted teeth. 'It's all your fault anyway. As you won't give me grandchildren, I need to find my own.'

'But Imogen isn't your daughter. You're making all of this up! I don't know how but you've inveigled your way into their lives, into their house, and it's not right.'

'Imogen is my daughter. And she's a much nicer, more successful, prettier daughter than you are. Just piss off out of my life and out of Imogen's life too.' I make to close the door but Clare is quicker than me and she sticks her boot between the door and the frame.

'You need to be sectioned,' Clare stays.

That infuriates me. I feel a surge of anger course through my veins. I grab a long umbrella from the stand next to the door and tug the door open. Then I rush at Clare, trying to hit her over the head with the umbrella. But she's quicker and nimbler than me, running down the steps to her car.

'You're crazy!' she yells.

I try to chase her but my leg hurts and within seconds, she's inside her car, starting the engine. She actually looks scared as she throws me a last glance and puts her foot on the accelerator.

How dare she come here and threaten me! Clare has backed me into a corner and given me no choice. I am trembling with rage but I know exactly what I need to do. Two daughters will have to become one.

Having not wanted to clean earlier, now there is so much energy soaring through my body I can't possibly stay still. I scrub and clean and dust so that by the time Imogen and

Ava come home, the house is sparkling. The living room smells of furniture polish, the bathrooms of bleach and I even have time to spray the inside of the oven with that toxic cleaning stuff. I'm not in the mood to pick up the conversation Imogen and I had yesterday. My focus is all on Clare, so I excuse myself and say that I have a headache and need to lie down. To my annoyance, Imogen looks positively relieved. That deserves a little payback. I walk towards Ava and bend down.

'Hey, sweetie. How was your day at school?'

'Fine, thank you.' She's such a polite little thing.

'If you come to my room, I might have something special for you.' I'll have to tip my bag out because I've probably only got a packet of Tic Tacs or a piece of gum. But that'll do.

As I leave the room, I hear Ava say, 'Can I go now?'

'No. Maria isn't feeling well so it's best you just leave her alone until she's better.'

Oh, Imogen. It's not good to tell little white lies to your daughter. I'm going to have to change that.

But tonight my focus needs to be elsewhere.

I lie on my single bed planning the evening. When I hear Imogen put Ava to bed, and then the pinging of the microwave, I change into black clothes – a pair of black trousers and an old hoodie that's seen better days. I take a single shard of glass from the back of my wardrobe, still wrapped in newspaper to protect my hands. I place it carefully into my backpack. I don't want it to dig into me so I leave it wrapped in the paper and shove a sweater in there too for additional protection. I wonder if it might be easier to take a knife from Imogen's knife block, but decide against it. I don't want her to be linked in any way to what is going to happen. I tiptoe out into Imogen and Josh's bedroom and take a pair of Josh's trainers from his dressing room, shoving them into my bag. Standing in the hallway, I can hear the television on in the kitchen. I walk silently downstairs and slip out of Fairview House unnoticed. It takes a little over twenty minutes to cycle to my dreadful bedsit and it's not pleasant either, cycling on these narrow country roads in the cold dark, drizzle dampening my face. I tie my bike to a lamp post and then, making sure no one is watching, I unlock the driver's door to my beloved old banger. Despite its age and mileage, it starts up first time, so I carefully reverse out of the space and head towards Clare's house.

She lives alone in a little country cottage, all twee beams and low ceilings. I used to be worried about her, living in the middle of nowhere, without a partner to check she was safely home. I wondered what was wrong with Clare, divorced and childless by the time she was thirty, then admitting that she didn't want to have children and that was the reason her marriage broke down. She was young and attractive, able to have choices, but she ruined them by taking drugs, losing control. Clare's house is on the outskirts of Loxwood and as I approach it, driving at a snail's pace, I see the lights are on downstairs. I park the car a couple of hundred metres away, partially hidden by the overhanging branches of an oak tree, not that I really need to worry out here. There aren't going to be any surveillance cameras. Removing my shoes, I slip on Josh's trainers, which are much too big for me, but they'll have to do. I carefully unwrap the shard of glass and leave the scrunched-up newspaper in the car, putting the shard in the outer pocket of my backpack, perfectly placed for me to grab it. I pull on some gardening gloves that I took from Imogen's house. I'll need them to protect my hands and stop me from leaving fingerprints.

Now I'm ready. I lock the car and stroll down the lane, trying not to stumble over my unnaturally large feet, walking with conviction up the little path to Clare's front door. She has a bell that you're meant to jangle. I hit it hard.

The front door opens and there she is.

'What are you doing here?' Clare asks, fear contorting her features.

'I wanted to tell you that you're right and I was wrong. I've decided to go to the doctor, but in return I want you to leave me alone – and in particular, leave Imogen alone.'

She narrows her eyes. 'I don't believe you.'

'I was worried you might say that.' I try to look contrite. 'Can I come in? I thought you could ring the doctor for me and then perhaps you'll leave me alone?'

I don't give her the chance to say no and quickly barge past her into the hallway, kicking the door shut behind me. The damn bruise on my leg courtesy of Imogen throbs painfully.

'Are you home alone?'

'What do you want?' Clare asks. She shrinks backwards against the wall, her head knocking a painting of mountains in muted colours – a painting I never much liked.

I grab the shard of glass and plunge it into her sternum. The shock is immediate. Her eyes widen, her mouth falls open and she tries to defend herself, but I'm too quick. I stab her again and again in a frenzied attack and she drops down onto the wooden floor in the hall, blood pouring from her wounds. She's still gasping, trying to get up, so I kick her. I hurry into the kitchen where there's a pan of water boiling over. I switch it off and grab the biggest knife I can find from her utensils drawer and then I walk calmly back to the hall where she's lying on the floor, bubbles of blood coming from her mouth. I stab the knife into her heart with all the strength I can muster and I stand over her, watching life ebb away from her body.

No mother should be forced to kill her child, and I feel a momentary wave of sadness, but then I remember I'm sacrificing her to save Imogen and Ava. I don't hang around. I rush upstairs and into Clare's bedroom, pulling out the drawers in her bedside tables, chucking everything onto the floor, then I do the same with the chest of drawers. I find her jewellery box in the bottom of the wardrobe and I grab a handful of items, chucking them into my rucksack. Downstairs I ransack the living room, taking her laptop but crushing her mobile phone with the heel of my boot. The place looks like a bomb has hit it. I'm still wearing gloves, but all the same, I can't take any risks, so I wipe down the banister and the door handle from in and outside. I wonder how long it'll take for Clare's body to be found. Will her work send someone around to check on her when she doesn't turn up to the office? Or perhaps a friend will become worried that she's not answering her messages. I'm hopeful that she won't be found for a while and by then, any traces of this burglar will be long gone.

I take one look at her and then I leave the house, gently shutting the door behind me, wiping down the doorknob with a wet wipe. I walk back along the garden path and when I'm on the road, I tug off Josh's trainers and put on my own shoes.

A sense of relief settles on me as I drive back towards Horsham and I start singing "Happy" by Pharell Williams, because that's what I'm feeling. Now I can focus on my family. It's a new start for me; just what I need. I stop off in the centre of town and dispose of the newspaper I used to wrap the shard of glass. I'm happy for the police to find the glass wedged into Clare's body. They'll never work out what it's come from, although undoubtedly they'll work out that the knife sticking out of her heart comes from her own knife block. Poor Clare, to be subjected to such a violent burglary.

I park my car back in the space it was in earlier and hop back on my bike. By the time I get back to Fairview House, all the lights are off. I'm worried for a moment that Imogen might have bolted the door, thinking I was sleeping off my headache, but no. It's just locked. As quietly as possible, I creep back into the house, using my phone as a torch. Upstairs, in the bathroom I share with Ava, I peel off my clothes and run Josh's trainers under the cold tap, washing away any traces of mud or dirt or splatters of blood invisible to the naked eye, anything that might link the shoes to Clare's house. After a quick shower, I head for bed.

When I wake up in the morning I reckon I've never slept so well.

19

IMOGEN

I'm glad that Josh is home but how I wish I could confide in him about Maria. My confusion hasn't abated. Maria is still acting as if everything is normal, that we are some long-lost happy family, while all I want is for her to leave our home. But the woman is clever; certainly more conniving than me, because she doesn't hesitate in reminding me how kind she's being by not reporting her 'accident' to the authorities. She murmurs Arun's name under her breath and tuts about how sad it would be for my marriage to Josh to be over, and how she really doesn't want to tell Josh about my adoption but sadly she might be forced to... The threats are hanging there right over my head and frankly, it terrifies me. At best she'll tell Josh about my adoption and he'll be hurt and angry. At worst she'll tell him about Arun and I could lose everything: my marriage, the security it provides for Ava and our future baby, even my business. Maria knows too much, and she knows how to push my buttons. The woman is clever but I am too. Somehow I'm

going to have to get her out without her exposing my
secrets.

JOSH and I are in bed. He's relaxed and in a good mood after
a successful dentistry conference in Birmingham. He's
telling me about his couple of days away but I'm not really
listening. I snuggle up to him and although he hasn't
brought up Tom again, I feel the need to reiterate my
innocence.

'I promise nothing has happened between me and Tom,'
I repeat, relieved that that is indeed the truth. 'I love you,
Josh, and I never want to hurt you or our family.'

'The text message threw me.' He pulls me closer to him.
'But I can't imagine you with Tom. Deep down, I know you'd
never do anything to hurt us,' he murmurs.

I try not to think of Arun and as I'm lying in bed, clinging
to Josh, so glad to have his protective limbs around me, I
wonder, should I tell him now? Perhaps I can mention my
adoption but leave out the bit about Arun, come up with a
good reason why we need to let Maria go. But just as I try to
formulate the words, his breathing deepens and I realise he's
fast asleep. Another potential moment slips by.

The next morning I'm no clearer as to how best to deal
with Maria. One moment I decide to fire her, to hell with the
consequences. The next moment I realise I can't take the
risk. The woman knows too much. I spend the day in
Brighton at my client's and I'm glad for the excuse not to be
at home. After school I take Ava to the village shop to settle
my account and buy her a kiddies' magazine. She's been
such a good girl recently and with my mind elsewhere, I
wonder if I've been neglecting her. Generally, I prefer shop-

ping in the farm shop, not only because of the wider selection but also because I prefer to avoid Hazel. She's very much the village gossip and I don't have the energy to engage with her.

'Good afternoon, Mrs Letwin!' Hazel says cheerily.

'I'd like to settle my account,' I say.

'Ah yes, Maria was in here buying some bits and pieces for you, wasn't she?' Hazel delves into a drawer behind the till and takes out a cash book. 'Now, let's see.' She flicks through the pages. 'It's so lovely that Maria has made up with her daughter. She's even living with her now. You know, I told her that family is everything and one needs to stick together.' She takes out a calculator and does some calculations. 'Now, that'll be fifty-five pounds and thirty-two pence altogether.'

I don't hear what Hazel says. All I can think about is what Maria has told her. At least she hasn't said that I'm her daughter. Or has she?

'Mrs Letwin?' Hazel prompts me.

'Sorry,' I say, taking my bank card out of my purse. 'I'm miles away.'

Half an hour later, back at home, Maria accosts me in the kitchen. 'Would you like me to cook supper?' Maria asks. 'I thought we could have a relaxed meal, just the three of us.' She's acting as if nothing whatsoever is wrong and I've no idea how to respond.

'No, thank you.' I can feel myself bristling. 'If you wouldn't mind making your own supper, I'll do mine and Josh's. We need some time alone.'

'Of course, dear. A marriage is like a fire. It needs stoking from time to time and with all your secrets, I'm sure your marriage needs some serious attention. I'll just make myself an omelette whilst you're putting Ava to bed.'

That comment elicits a searing anger inside me. How dare Maria comment on my marriage! I could so easily lift up one of those frying pans and bring it down... The thought shocks me so I dart out of the kitchen and race upstairs to run Ava's bath. Half an hour later, I'm still stewing over Maria's words but I'm also scared by my reaction. Her threats are propelling me towards violence. Has that anger always been in my genes or has it just lain dormant until someone pushed all the right buttons?

It's a relief to hear Josh downstairs. 'Up here!' I shout from the top landing. He bounds up the stairs and into the bathroom where Ava is pulling on her pyjamas.

'How are my favourite people?' he asks, tickling Ava under the arms so she squeals with giggles.

'Is Maria still in the kitchen?' I ask.

'She was carrying a plate of food to her room.'

'Good,' I say.

Josh frowns at me. 'All okay?'

'Not really, but I'll tell you later.' I wonder what I can tell him without letting on the real reasons for my dislike and distrust of our live-in housekeeper. 'Can you put Ava to bed and I'll make a start on supper?'

'Of course,' he says, kissing me gently on the lips. 'Oh, I told Kyle to come over for supper. His mum is out tonight.'

'Alright,' I say, although I could do without surly Kyle joining us. It means I won't have the opportunity to talk to Josh about Maria over supper and I'll have to come up with a vegan meal, which is outside of my cooking comfort zone. As it turns out, Kyle and his dad spend the evening chatting about football and I zone out. I consider telling Josh the truth when we're in bed, but once again I go to bed long before him and I don't have the energy to start a conversation that will probably take hours when it's so close to midnight.

'Mummy, my school jumper has got a hole in it,' Ava says as she wanders into the kitchen the next morning. She points to a rip near the cuff edge of her right arm.

'Oh dear. Let's take the jumper off and see if I can sew up the hole so it doesn't rip anymore.' I can do without having to darn before getting Ava to school. She lifts her arms up in the air and I pull the jumper over her head.

'What's that on your arm?' I ask, dropping the jumper onto a chair and clasping her forearm. I push the sleeve of her blouse right as far up as it will go. My little girl has bruise marks on her upper arm, but they don't look like the typical bruises that she gets from tumbling from her climbing frame. These look like finger marks, strong finger marks.

'How long have you had these?' I ask, trying to quell any panic in my voice.

'Don't know,' Ava says.

'Do they hurt?' I stroke her arm.

'No.'

I think back to bath time yesterday evening. Surely I would have noticed them if they'd been there then. I remember lifting her out of the bath, wrapping a pale yellow fluffy towel around her, and then Josh arrived and he tickled her. It was all our normal, gentle fun. I'm almost positive that Ava didn't have any marks on her.

After supper, Josh went upstairs to check on Ava. He collected his car keys from the bedroom and drove Kyle home, and then this morning, he got her dressed. He's already left for work.

'Good morning!' Maria says cheerfully as she strolls into the kitchen. 'Oh goodness! What's happened to your arm, darling?' Maria says as she walks over to Ava. 'Those look like nasty bruises.' I quickly pull Ava's sleeve down. 'They look like the bruises I got on my leg when your mummy pushed me.'

I stare open-mouthed at Maria. How could she say something like that in front of my daughter? I pull myself together. 'Run upstairs and get your bag, Ava, otherwise we'll be late for school. And get your other school jumper. I'll fix this one later.'

I turn to Maria. 'Can you not talk like that in front of Ava?'

'I'm sorry, but it is the truth. Don't worry, Imogen, I'll stay out of your way.' She hurries out of the room, leaving me feeling totally confused.

When we're in the car on the way to school, I question Ava again about the bruises.

'Did you have the bruises yesterday?' I ask.

'I don't think so.'

'And last night?'

'I think a man came into my bedroom in the night. It was a bit scary but I was too sleepy and I'm not sure. It might have been a bad dream.'

I almost drive straight into the back of a car waiting at a set of traffic lights.

'A man? Was it Daddy or Kyle?'

'No, I don't think so.' Could she have got it wrong and it wasn't a man at all?

'Did Maria hurt you?'

'No! I love Gangan.'

My stomach clenches. 'Who's Gangan?'

'Maria. She's my other granny. She told me not to tell you but she gives me sweeties when you're not looking. It might have been Daddy who came into my room last night.'

'Daddy?'

'Maybe. We've got gym today and I'm going to do cart-wheels.' Ava might have changed the subject but it feels like there's a lead weight sitting at the bottom of my stomach. Surely Josh couldn't have hurt our daughter? I remember when he punched the wall four years ago, but that was a one-off and the only person he hurt was himself. Or could it have been Kyle? He nipped upstairs to get something from his room. Could he have crept into Ava's bedroom and hurt her whilst she was sleeping? I circle back to Maria, but just because I don't trust her, doesn't mean she would hurt a child, especially one that she considers to be her grandchild. Besides, Ava was adamant. She likes Maria, but then what child wouldn't if they were being bribed with sweets? And how dare Maria tell Ava to call her Gangan. It's totally inappropriate.

I spend the morning stewing over Ava's bruises, terrified that someone has been knowingly hurting her, and by late afternoon, I decide I have to talk to Josh, a conversation that needs to be had face to face. Of course, it would be better to talk tonight at home, but I need answers now. Questions around my daughter's wellbeing can't wait until later. I call Josh's clinic and ask the receptionist what time he's breaking for lunch. One p.m.

I drive quickly, my mind in too much of a turmoil to plan the conversation. Josh's new clinic is smaller than the one he shared with Arun, but he decided partnerships were no longer for him, so he employs two hygienists, a couple of dental nurses and two part-time dentists, both women. I park up next to Josh's Range Rover and walk into the glass and steel modern building. I don't know the woman on reception so I have to introduce myself. She telephones through to Josh.

'There's a woman here who says she's your wife.'

I feel like retorting, 'But I am his wife.'

A couple of minutes later, I'm pacing up and down the empty waiting room and Josh appears, wearing his white short-sleeved tunic and black trousers.

'This is a surprise,' he says, planting a kiss on my cheek.

'Have you got time for a quick chat?'

'Is everything alright?' He frowns.

'Not really.'

I follow him into his room. A dental nurse is in there busying herself with some equipment.

'Cath, would you mind stepping out for a moment. This is my wife.'

'Oh, hello, Mrs Letwin.' She turns to smile at me and I can't help but notice that she's stunning, with bright blue eyes and high cheekbones. She walks through a door to the side of the treatment room and I wonder what the sound-proofing is like. I perch on the end of the dental bed while Josh sits on his stool.

'What's up?'

I speak quietly. 'Ava has bruises on her arm that look like finger marks.'

His brows knot together. 'Have you spoken to the school?'

'No, because I don't think it happened at school. She

didn't have the marks when I bathed her last night, but they're there this morning.'

He tilts his head to one side. 'What are you saying?'

'Did you notice them?'

'Of course not. I would have said something.'

'You tickled her yesterday evening and then checked on her last night. Do you think you might have held her too tightly by mistake?'

'You've got to be joking!' Josh stands up and the stool rolls across the room. 'You're accusing me of hurting our daughter?'

'Shush! No, of course not. Keep your voice down.'

'I can't believe this, Imogen. You've driven all the way here, interrupting my day to accuse me of the most horrific thing possible. I love Ava. I would never do anything to hurt her. You're the one who has been behaving strangely these past weeks. Perhaps it was you? You're trying to deflect on to me because it's always the father, isn't it?' He's really angry now, a vein throbbing in his forehead. I need to backtrack.

'I'm not accusing you, it's just it happened last night. Maybe it was Kyle when he went in to say goodnight to Ava.'

'Don't blame my son for something like that!' He points his index finger at me. 'What about Maria? She's the stranger in our house.'

He's right. It could be Maria, and if it is, I will force that woman out of our home come hell or high water, marching her straight to the police station if I have to, but I can't let Josh start accusing her, as Maria will undoubtedly make good on her threats. It's up to me to find out the truth.

'I'm so sorry, Josh,' I say, because now I'm in the same room as my husband, I am positive that he would never knowingly hurt our little girl. 'I shouldn't have accused you or Kyle but we need to work out how she got the bruises.'

'It's best if you go home and we'll discuss this later,' Josh says, running his fingers through his hair.

'You're right,' I say. 'I'm really sorry.'

As I leave, I know the damage has already been done.

20

MARIA

Imogen is crumbling. It makes me sad to see my daughter like that, but I have to break her in order to get her exactly where I want her. It's what parents do, isn't it? Being cruel to be kind. That's what Dad said to me when he chucked me out of the house. It seems unreal, but I actually had quite a cushy childhood. We lived in a compact but detached house in a newish estate on the edge of Horsham. Mum stayed at home and I've no idea what she did all day, except being a hypocrite. How Dad didn't realise that she was drinking from the crack of dawn is beyond me. Or perhaps he did know but just turned a blind eye. He was the manager of a garden centre and most nights he'd return home with a boot full of plants or garden sundries which he sold on to his mates down the pub, or other dodgy people that used to come to the house. He told me it was excess stock, so it wasn't until many years later, when he lost his job, that I realised he'd been on the fiddle. When they chucked me out of the house, I was just a teenager. Terrible, really. But Dad told me it was for my own good. I needed to stand on my own two feet and not bring our family into disrespect. The sheer hypocrisy of it. Mum sobbed her eyes out but she didn't try to change Dad's mind. She was such a weak woman.

I have a look through the photos I took of Tom and Imogen on my phone. There's no doubt in my mind; they're having an affair. They must go back to his place when Imogen says she's at a meeting, or perhaps they're in some seedy hotel. But I've got the photographic evidence; the two of them hugging, their bodies pressed up against each other (particularly gross considering Tom's favoured clothing of Lycra); the way they gaze into each other's eyes; I even got a picture of them when they were at the farm shop having a coffee, where Tom removes a hair from Imogen's shoulder. Such an intimate moment caught on film. But it turns my stomach. Tom is leading Imogen astray at a time when she's so vulnerable. I despise Josh, but Tom is even worse. So now it's down to me to manage this household, to put them back together again.

I reckon that if Imogen didn't work so hard her whole life would be in better balance. I've looked at their bank statements and the Letwins are seriously wealthy. We're talking seven-figure wealth, so why on earth is Imogen pushing herself? She seems to be forgetting that she's incubating a child, and not any child, but my grandchild. If that foetus is damaged in any way, I'll never forgive her. Never. So it's up to me to come up with a strategy of care. Frankly, it's really Josh's job to look after his wife, but he's much too self-absorbed. Sadly, other than his looks and his bank balance, Josh hasn't got much going for him and he has a worrying short temper. I heard him yell at Imogen the other night and it took all of my restraint to stop myself from charging into their room and stabbing him with the left-over shard of glass. Josh's demise needs to come at a time when Imogen has lost all trust and respect for her husband, and that's not quite yet.

The easiest thing for me to control is the bed and breakfast business. It's demeaning to think of my daughter pandering to the needs of strangers in her own home. I simply don't understand why she's doing it. Once that little sideline business closes, then I'll suggest that I turn those two rooms into a suite for myself; quite literally a granny flat. Ava can sleep with me from time to time, especially after the new baby comes, so she's not wakened by the infant's cries.

This morning there is a hoity-toity couple eating their breakfast in the guests' dining room called Mr and Mrs Hetherington. They've been here for one night already and are booked in for another two. When I went to tidy their room, she looked down her nose at me as if I was a piece of insignificant dirt. I spat in her fried egg and I hope she enjoyed it. The man has a shock of white hair and tortoise-shell spectacles, which gives him the air of a professor. His wife has a long, sharp nose and a chin to match. Goodness knows what he sees in her.

'Excuse me,' I say as I interrupt their breakfast. 'I'm afraid you're going to need to leave.'

'We haven't quite finished our food,' Mr Hetherington says.

'I mean you need to pack up your bags and go. You can't stay here any longer.'

Mrs Hetherington drops her piece of toast. 'Excuse me, what are you saying?'

'It's pretty simple. You need to put your bags in your car and leave this house.' I stand with my hands on my hips and have to bite my lip to stop myself from laughing. The look on the woman's face! It's as if no one has ever told her what to do.

'Our relationship is with Mrs Letwin. Where is she?'

'Imogen is out this morning and I'm in charge. I've just been up to your room and found an ashtray with cigarette ends in it. As you are aware, this property is strictly no-smoking.'

'That's not possible,' Mr Hetherington says. 'We are non-smokers. Always have been. It's a filthy habit. Are you sure you've found the ashtray in our room?'

'Absolutely sure, because you're the only guests staying here at the moment. Imogen is pregnant and she has a young child. Surely I don't need to tell you, such upper-class educated people, that smoking is a great danger to the young.'

Mrs Hetherington stands up suddenly, her chair only staying upright because her husband grabs it. 'Woman, we do not smoke! How dare you talk to us like that! I will report all of this back to Mrs Letwin.'

'Feel free. Imogen's my daughter and we always talk off the same hymn sheet.'

The couple look shocked.

'Come on, Janet,' Mr Hetherington says. 'We will not be spoken to like this.'

'Let me know if you need a hand with your suitcase,' I say, as they storm out of the dining room. I chuckle. Five minutes later the door slams and I hear their car start up.

I decide to clean out their room later because first I need to nip to the village shop. Fortunately for me, Hazel isn't at the till and the shop assistant is a surly teenager who has no interest in the contents of my shopping basket. I buy a bottle of Calpol because I need to replenish the bottle stashed high up and out of reach of little people, in Ava and my bathroom. I gave her quite a lot an hour before I squeezed her arm. I wanted my little darling to be very sleepy and not cry out. I would never hurt an innocent child and particularly my own granddaughter. I'm also in desperate need of a pack of Benson & Hedges. I had to smoke quite a few cigarettes to get an ashtray-full to plant in the Hetheringtons' room. I hurry back to Fairview House and straight up to the bathroom. I fill up the existing Calpol bottle so it's at the same level as before, not that I think Imogen is likely to notice, but I do need to tie up all the ends, so to speak.

Imogen returns home looking out of sorts. Pale, with big rings under her eyes, she pours herself a glass of water and pops a couple of paracetamol.

'Should you be taking those when you're pregnant?' I ask. She throws me a strange look.

'Your guests, the Hetheringtons – they've had to leave early. Honestly, Imogen, it's just as well you don't have any guests now as you really look like you need to rest. Why don't you go and lie down and I'll bring you a nice cup of tea and a biscuit?'

'I'd rather–'

I cut her off. 'You're my daughter and I care about you. I'm sure you would have let your adoptive mother fuss over you when you were feeling ill. It's what mothers do.'

She turns to me and asks, with a hint of sarcasm to her voice which I don't like. 'How is Clare, your other daughter?'

I dig my nails into the palm of my hands and smile. 'It's kind of you to ask. Sadly, she's disappeared again and isn't answering my calls. It's always the same with Clare, this pattern of destruction. The reality is I lost her many years ago to drugs and mental illness.'

'She seemed fine when I spoke to her.'

'That's the thing with people like her. They're clever and conniving. When you meet them you have no idea anything is wrong. That's what makes it even harder.' I sniff loudly and take a piece of paper towel to dab at my eyes and blow my nose. 'What's up, dear?' I ask, stroking her arm. She pulls away from me.

'Have you got the paperwork yet to prove that you're my mother?'

'Of course not,' I say. I'm disappointed. 'It'll take weeks to get hold of everything; surely you know that?'

Imogen ignores my advice to lie down and instead she retreats to her little study, no doubt pushing herself to work when she should be relaxing. Despite offering to do the school run for her, the afternoon pans out like most afternoons. Imogen collects Ava from school, I do the ironing of the bed sheets in the utility room, and Josh comes home, a little earlier than normal. I sense an atmosphere between them. Normally he kisses Imogen and twirls Ava around, but today he mutters, 'I'm going for a run,' and disappears straight upstairs. Little red splodges appear on the apples of Imogen's cheeks and she opens her mouth as if to say something, but then thinks the better of it.

'Everything alright?' I ask.

She pretends she doesn't hear me and chatters away to Ava.

Ten minutes later, Josh comes hobbling into the kitchen. He has a trainer on his left foot but is holding the right one in the air.

'I've cut myself. There's bloody glass in my trainer, inside it! Did you put it there, Imogen?'

'What are you talking about?' She looks genuinely shocked. 'Oh my God! Let me look at your foot.' He sits down, crossing his right leg over his left. Imogen kneels down in front of him. 'That looks nasty. I'll grab the first aid box.'

'Do you need any help?' I ask, a concerned look on my face.

Ignoring me, which is extremely rude and out of character for Imogen, she fills up a bowl with water. 'I'm going to need some tweezers. Maria, I've got some on the bottom shelf in my bathroom cupboard. Please can you get them.'

'Of course,' I say, hurrying out of the room, happy to be useful.

I'm back downstairs in a flash, not wanting to miss any of the conversation. 'Here you go,' I say, handing them to Josh. He winces as Imogen tries to clean up his foot.

'I think I've got most of the pieces out. You'll be hobbling for a bit but I don't think there's any lasting damage and you won't need stitches.'

'What I want to know is how the hell glass got into my trainers?' He is still clearly livid and hasn't even thanked Imogen for her valiant attempt at first aid.

'Remember how you dropped that glass the other day?' I say to Imogen. 'Maybe some got into Josh's shoe. You do have them lying around from time to time.' Actually, that's not true – Josh is somewhat of a neat freak.

'That was in the kitchen,' Imogen says, defensiveness in her voice. 'And Josh keeps his shoes either upstairs or in the utility room in the cupboard.'

'Mmm, most of the time, but I seem to recall they were lying around. Or perhaps it was your trainers?'

Imogen throws me a filthy look, which is very disappointing. I would have thought she'd be pleased that Josh was hurting, especially after he caused pain to their little girl. He stands up and gently puts his weight through both his feet.

'Are you alright?' Imogen asks.

'Yes, it's not too bad. But for heaven's sake, both of you, keep this house tidy. What if the glass had got in Ava's shoes?'

Of course, I would never let that happen. Ava is the innocent around here and she needs to be protected. Her father though, well, that's another matter altogether. Think of this as a little initial warning.

'As I can't go for a run, I'm going to the pub for a drink,' Josh announces.

'Would you like me to drive you?' Imogen asks.

'No.'

Goodness, he can't even say thank you to his wife. Things really are a little broken in paradise. But I don't mind. It means that I'll be home alone again with my girls, and that's all I really want.

21

IMOGEN

I was asleep by the time Josh came to bed last night. In fact I didn't even hear him get back but I assume it must have been sometime around 11 p.m. He didn't return for supper, which I left on a plate in the fridge, just in case, but presumably he ate at the pub. He was still in a foul mood this morning.

'I still can't believe you came to my work and accused me of hurting my own child. Did you put the glass in my shoe as some sort of sick revenge?'

'Of course I didn't. Look, I wonder if Maria is behind all of this. What do you think?'

He throws me a pitying look. 'So you're blaming your behaviour on her now? That's cheap, Imogen. If you want to get rid of her, then do. But don't come running to me that you're exhausted and can't cope.'

And yes, I do want to get rid of her. I don't trust Maria one iota but she has the potential to destroy my marriage and we're on such unstable ground at the moment, it's not a risk I can take. What if she goes to the police and tells them I hit her? Or if she shows more photos of me and Tom to Josh? Or worse still, if she persuades Louise to tell Josh that Arun and I slept together? But if I find out that Maria has laid a finger on my daughter, I'll be reporting her to the police in a nanosecond. The trouble is, Ava clearly adores her and I haven't got any proof whatsoever that Maria has done a single thing wrong.

When Josh left this morning, he pointedly gave Ava lots of hugs and kisses but completely ignored me. I can't decide whether that was just childish or no more than I deserved for questioning my husband.

'Maria, we need to talk,' I say, as she's clearing away our breakfast things.

'Would you like me to take Ava to school?'

'No, Tom is stopping by to collect her so I can get to my meeting on time.' I have a meeting at 9.30 a.m. in Brighton, so yesterday I asked Tom if he could take Ava to school. I know I'm meant to be keeping my distance from him, but it's not fair to keep Issy and Ava apart, and it's not like anything is actually happening between us. I'm damned if I'm going to give in to malicious gossip.

She scowls as I mention Tom's name. 'Did you squeeze Ava's arm and leave those bruises?' I ask.

'So now you're accusing me!' Her eyes flash with anger. 'You're the only one in this household who has violent tendencies. I think it's best not to try to deflect the blame onto others. The consequences could be horrendous.' She lets that thought hang and walks out of the room.

8.30 am comes and goes. It's not like Tom to be late, especially as he said he'd be coming by in his car. I try calling him but there's no answer on his mobile. That is really strange. Realising that I'm going to have to take Ava myself, I bundle her in the car and drive full-pelt towards school. We hurry up the path. Ava's teacher, Miss Smith, is standing by the gate welcoming the children.

'Have you heard anything from Issy's parents this morning?' I ask, wondering if perhaps Issy is sick.

'No, not that I'm aware of. Is everything alright?'

'I'm not sure,' I say. 'Hopefully.' I give Ava a kiss goodbye, and she disappears into the throng of kids with a happy skip.

Back in the car I try calling Tom again, but it goes straight to voicemail as if his phone is switched off. I don't really have time to be taking a detour but something feels off. What if some malicious person has told his wife that we've having an affair? Could she have been sent a message like Josh has? If so, this needs nipping in the bud immediately. As it's only five minutes out of my way, I decide to swing by their house just to be sure everything is all right. Tom and Julia live on a new estate of big five-bedroom houses, each with their own unique design, quite suitable for an architect even though Tom didn't design the house. Although it's newly built, their home looks like a converted barn from the outside. Inside there is a vast wooden frame, with a fabulous open-plan kitchen living area that looks like it's been taken straight from the pages of a homes and gardens magazine. As I pull into the close, my heart starts pounding. There's a police car parked in front of their home.

I dump my car and run up to the front door, pressing the electronic doorbell. A woman I don't recognise answers the door.

'Is everything alright?' I garble, hopping from foot to foot.

'And you are?'

'Imogen Letwin. A friend of Tom and Julia's. Well, Tom

mainly, and I'm Ava's mum. Ava and Issy are best friends. Tom was meant to have picked Ava up and take her to school this morning but he didn't turn up. Is everything alright?' Obviously it's not, because there wouldn't be a police car in front of the house or a stranger answering the door.

The woman steps forwards, forcing me back slightly. She pulls the door closed behind her.

'My name is Olivia Jones and I'm a police officer. I'm afraid that there has been an accident.' My hands jumps up to cover my mouth. 'Tom was involved in an accident whilst riding his bike last night.'

'Is he alright?'

'He's in hospital.'

'But is he going to be okay?' My heart is hammering.

'He is currently in a coma.'

'In a coma! Oh my God! Can I see him?'

'Family only, I'm afraid.'

'And Julia? Is she alright?'

'She's been at the hospital all night.'

'What happened? Tom is such an experienced cyclist. He goes everywhere on his bike. He's fanatical about it.'

'So we've been led to believe. But from his injuries, we think that he might have been the victim of a hit and run. Information will be given to the media shortly as we begin our investigation.'

'No!' I mutter. 'How could anyone do that?' I feel dizzy and I gulp in the fresh, damp air.

'Could you give me your address and contact details, Mrs Letwin?'

'Um, yes, of course.' I reel off our address and my phone number, which the police woman writes down in a little lined notebook.

'And where were you yesterday evening between 7 and 10 p.m.?'

'At home with my daughter, husband and housekeeper.' Why on earth is she asking me that? 'Which hospital is Josh in?'

'He was taken to Worthing Hospital via air ambulance.'

'Air ambulance,' I repeat, shock reverberating through me. Poor Tom. This is so terrible. 'Who is looking after Issy? Do you need any help?'

'Her grandparents are here; Julia's parents.'

'Can I be kept in the loop? Tom is a very close friend. We see each other almost every day.'

'I'm afraid it's family only that are notified of changes to his condition. But I will let Julia know of your concern.'

'Thank you,' I murmur. I watch as Olivia Jones produces a key from her pocket, unlocks Tom and Julia's front door and walks back inside. She throws me a sympathetic look before shutting it behind her. My legs are so shaky I struggle to walk straight back to the car.

I sit in my driver's seat for a couple of long minutes trying to get my head together. I'm meant to be at my client's in half an hour but I know I won't be able to concentrate. I telephone them and explain that there's been an accident and I won't make it in today. I imply that it's a member of our family because I don't suppose they will understand if I say it's just a friend. Tom and I may not have been having an affair but he really is like a brother to me and I'm shocked to the core. I start the car and head for home.

I'm still trembling when I walk into the kitchen. I pour myself a glass of water and my hand is shaking, droplets falling onto the floor.

'Goodness, you look like you've seen a ghost,' Maria says as she bustles in.

'Tom was severely injured in a hit and run accident last night. He's in a coma in hospital.'

'Oh my, that's terrible,' she says, slapping a hand over her mouth. 'I hope he pulls through.'

She walks to the dishwasher and starts unpacking it. Maria doesn't look at me when she talks. 'Where and when did Tom's accident happen?'

'Between 7 and 10 p.m. Knowing Tom, he might have been on his way home, probably after going to the gym.'

'Near the Hanging Gate pub, then?' Maria suggests.

I nod.

'I expect they'll be interviewing everyone who went there yesterday evening.' She throws me a strange look and then I realise what she's suggesting. Josh went out to the pub last night.

I take my glass of water and walk through to the study, shutting the door behind me. Josh was out last night. He was so angry when he received that text message, when he thought Tom and I might be having an affair. And he was angry again yesterday when I accused him of hurting Ava, and then he hurt his foot, and I suppose he might have blamed me for that too. He went to the pub last night and it's undeniable that my husband was out driving when Tom was hit. But Josh would never do something like that. He's a good man. I remember when we were driving back from the theatre in Chichester years ago and a deer ran out onto the road in front of us. Josh slammed on the brakes but it felt like we might have hit the animal. He stopped the car, raced outside and spent over ten minutes looking for the deer. He didn't find it. Josh is not a man to knock someone off his bike and then flee the scene. I wonder if it was a deliberate hit and run, whether Tom was actually targeted. But if that was the case, then it's attempted murder, isn't it? I can't help but think of the bruises on Ava's arm, my husband's fury at the text message. 'No,' I say out aloud to myself. No. It wasn't Josh and it would be easy enough to check. After all, he would have been at the pub amongst other people, and if he'd hit someone, his car would have a dent in it, wouldn't it? But he left for work early this morning and he could have gone to a garage today to get it fixed.

I groan as I run my fingers through my hair. What has our marriage come to that I'm even considering my husband might do something so terrible?

I find it impossible to concentrate, to get anything done, and I know that I need to go to the hospital, if for no other reason but to support Julia. I don't know her that well, but they're family friends and if the shoe was on the other foot I think I'd want support.

I say silent prayers the whole way down the A24, hoping that Tom will pull through this. I turn on the radio and then switch it off again. I try calling Danielle, but unsurprisingly for a teacher, her phone is turned off. I leave a message and ask her to call me urgently. I'm tempted to call Josh, but I don't think he'll appreciate being disturbed during his clinic. At the hospital, I can't find a parking space, so I have to park across the road. I walk quickly, my head down, towards the main reception.

'I'm here for Tom Box. He's in the ICU.' If he's in a coma, I assume he must be in ICU.

'I'm afraid no visitors are allowed in ICU.'

'I want to support his wife. Where might I find her?'

'ICU is over in the West Wing on the second floor. You might find her in a waiting room.'

'Thank you,' I say. I walk hurriedly, following the signs, but my insides are jittery with fear of what I might see and the worry that Julia might not want me there, especially if she's been sent a text message similar to Josh's. What I'm not prepared for is to find Julia crouched on the floor in the lobby to the lifts. She's being comforted by a nurse as she rocks back and forwards, letting out horrible moans.

'Julia?' I say, crouching down opposite her. She ignores me.

'What's happened?' I ask the nurse.

'Are you here for Julia?'

'Yes.' Not that I am, really.

'I'm afraid that Tom passed away from his injuries. We did our best but it was just too much. I'm trying to encourage Julia to go to the bereavement suite but she's not hearing a word I'm saying.'

Tears spring to my eyes. Tom can't be gone. He's so full of vitality, such a wonderful father to Issy. Much too young to die. But I know I need to be the strong one. It's not me who has lost their husband. I stroke Julia's back. 'I'm so sorry,' I murmur.

'Why are you here?' she asks in a hiccupy voice. I feel a bit embarrassed, as if I'm pretending to be family when I'm not.

I don't answer. 'Can I do anything for you?'

'Call home. Get Dad to come and pick me up.' She then collapses into tears again, her grief all-consuming. I feel sick at the thought of having to give Julia's parents the terrible news but then I wonder whether perhaps the police officer at their house already knows. Julia stands up and the nurse puts her arm around her shoulders.

'I want to be with Tom,' Julia hiccups.

The nurse leads her away through the locked doors and I just stand there, trying desperately hard not to burst into tears.

The rest of the day passes in a haze, my heart bleeding for Issy, who will be growing up without a father. I wonder what I should tell Ava, how being touched by death at such a young age will affect her. But all the time my mind circles back to Josh. He was out last night. He was angry. I didn't see him until this morning, when he was still angry. Could he have been driving too fast last night? And how much did he drink at the pub?

Josh returns home at his normal time and he seems to have calmed down because he does his normal trick of throwing Ava up into the air.

'I just need to take the bins out,' I say, which is an odd thing for me to do at this time of day, but Josh doesn't seem to notice. I slip out of the back door and run across to the garages. I use the torch on my phone rather than switching the light on in the garage and study the front bumper of Josh's Range Rover. I can't see anything untoward, although it does strike me that the car is very clean. There aren't even any specks of mud or dead insects. Could he have had the car washed today? I creep back to the house. Josh is sitting next to Ava at the kitchen table, their heads close together.

'We need to talk,' I say quietly.

'Really?' he asks sarcastically. 'Again?'

'Something terrible has happened,' I whisper into his ear.

We leave Ava to her colouring and Josh follows me into the living room. I shut the door behind us.

'Tom died,' I blurt out.

'What?' Josh pales. I'm scrutinising his every reaction.

'He was the victim of a hit and run whilst on his bike last night and he died today in hospital. I went to Worthing to see how he was and–'

'What? You went to the hospital? Why? You're not family.'

'No, but he's a good friend.'

'That's awful,' Josh says. 'Poor Julia and poor Issy.'

'Did you see anything on your way to or from the pub last night?'

'No. What do you mean?'

'It's just that you might have passed Tom.'

There's a long pause. 'What are you suggesting?'

'Nothing. It's just you were very angry last night, you still are, and you might have hit a bike, perhaps without even realising it. The Range Rover is such a big car.'

A vein in Josh's forehead is pulsating, his upper lip slightly snarled, and his eyes are flashing.

'What the hell are you suggesting?' Josh asks.

I take a step away from him because I'm scared of the reaction I've triggered. I've never seen Josh look so furious, as if he's going to explode, and I realise I've gone too far.

'I'm sorry,' I say, but it's too late.

'How dare you accuse me of something like that! Firstly you accuse me of hurting our daughter and now this!' His hands are balled into fists at his sides. He throws me a look of such disdain before striding to the door and pulling it open. I hear his footsteps on the flagstone floor and the front door opens and closes with a slam that reverberates through the house. I follow him into the hallway and watch as the rear lights come on in his car. He reverses out of the garage and then puts his foot on the accelerator, his tyres spinning a little as he speeds away.

He's not the only one to feel anger. It surges through me, boiling and boiling. My dear friend has died. And Josh has driven away without us resolving our argument. I'm not sure who I'm more angry with: him or myself. Without thinking, I pick up a glass paperweight that someone gave us for our wedding and hurl it across the hall. It slams into the white wall, gouging away a bit of plaster. I collapse into tears, crouched on the ground, feeling a mixture of grief, sorrow for myself and sorrow for our tattered marriage, edged with a little remorse because I did just accuse my husband of murder.

'Mummy?'

I jump up. I'd forgotten all about Ava. What sort of a mother forgets about her own daughter? Did she hear our argument or see me throw the paperweight?

'What's the matter, Mummy?'

'Oh darling,' I say, reaching out my arms, but she hesitates to come to me and that shatters my heart. What have I done?

22

IMOGEN

Somehow I manage to pacify Ava, although I'm conscious I'm telling her a pack of lies. I say that Daddy had to go and fix someone's teeth. That Mummy is sad because someone she knows has gone to heaven. That Mummy and Daddy weren't really shouting at each other. Oh, the fibs we tell our children to try to protect them, but is that what we're really doing? Perhaps we're simply trying to protect ourselves from having to deal with the painful reality that is the truth.

To ease my guilt I've let Ava have a bubble bath and I'm sitting on the stool in her bathroom wondering whether I've pushed Josh over the delicate edge of our marriage. My mobile phone pings with an incoming email that lands in my bed and breakfast account. It's from the Hetheringtons who left early.

Dear Mrs Letwin,

We are writing to express our dismay in the way that

your mother spoke to us and demanded that we leave your property. She accused us of smoking cigarettes in the bedroom, which we most certainly did not do, as neither my husband nor myself smoke. She was extremely belligerent and she totally ruined our mini break. Rather than hunting for somewhere else to stay, we decided to return home. We trust that you will refund us in full and we expect some further compensation to make up for a ruined holiday.

Yours sincerely,

Janet and Wilfred Hetherington

'What the hell!' I exclaim out aloud. Maria falsely accused my guests, lied to me, and it looks distinctly like she's trying to destroy my business.

'What's the matter, Mummy?' Ava asks, splashing some bubbles onto the floor.

'Just some annoying work stuff,' I fib again. 'Are you ready to hop out of the bath?'

'No. Please, a bit longer.'

I force myself to smile and remember how something as simple as a bubble bath can bring such pleasure. It's Saturday tomorrow, and I know I'm going to have to break the terrible news of Tom's death to Ava over the weekend.

'What shall we do tomorrow?' I ask.

'Can I go to Fencer's Farm with Gangan?'

'She's called Maria, not Gangan,' I say a little too harshly. 'And it's the weekend so you'll spend it with us.'

Ava puts on a whiny voice. 'Please. She said she'd take me and Issy and we can ride on the ponies.'

'No, it's not appropriate. Why was she even suggesting that?' I realise I said that last bit out loud when really it was a question for me.

'But Gangan is my other granny. She said I can stay with her at her house during the school holidays. Gangan said that she's got two children but one of her daughters is sick and she's disappeared. She said it's a shame I can't get to meet my Aunty Clare.'

'Do not call Maria Gangan,' I say too harshly. 'And Clare is not your aunt!'

Ava stares at me and her bottom lip starts to tremble.

'I'm sorry, darling, I didn't mean to shout at you. I've got a lot going on at the moment. Come on, let's get you out of the bath before your skin turns all wrinkly like a walnut.' That elicits a little smile from Ava.

As I'm rubbing my little girl dry, I think about Clare. I wish I'd spoken to her and found out more about Maria. I'm livid with Maria. Not only has she treated my guests terribly but she insists on telling Ava that she is her granny. I can't have the woman in my house any longer. Whatever the consequences might be, she's going to have to go.

'How are you, dear?' Maria eyes me with a look of concern. She's stirring something on the Aga and it fires up annoyance in me. Who is she to be using my kitchen, inveigling her way into our family?

'We need to talk,' I say, crossing my arms and trying to bolster myself. I've fired people hundreds of times before but this is personal and dangerous, as if I'm about to light a terrifying fuse. 'I'm very sorry but it's not working out, you being here. I'll pay you a month in lieu of notice but I need you to leave.'

She drops the wooden spoon into the pan and lifts it off

the Aga, placing it on the countertop. I want to tell her that the hot pan might leave a mark but Maria's lips tighten into a thin line, her eyes narrow and redness crawls up her neck.

'Are you sure about that, Imogen? Throwing out your own mother? After everything I have done for you, you're just going to discard me on a whim?'

'It's not like that,' I say, shifting from one foot to the other. 'I received an angry email from the Hetheringtons and you haven't given me any proof that you're really my birth mother. I appreciate the cleaning you've done but I don't think I want a housekeeper.'

'You don't want a housekeeper or you don't want a mother?'

'She might be dead but I already have a mother.'

Maria nods slowly and speaks in a sarcastic voice. 'So this is how it's going to go, Imogen. If you turf me out, I'm going to tell Josh that you lied to him, that you had an affair with Arun and Tom, that your father was a rapist and that evil blood flows through your veins. I'm going to tell him that you hit me, and rest assured he'll be interested in the photographs of my bruised leg.'

'I don't care what you say. I'm going to tell Josh the truth myself.'

'And what about poor deceased Tom? This photograph doesn't look too innocent, does it?' She takes her mobile phone out of her pocket, fiddles with some buttons and turns the phone to face me. It's another photograph of me and Tom hugging.

'It was you!' I exclaim. I'm shocked but perhaps I shouldn't be. 'It was you who sent the anonymous message to Josh! Why are you doing this, Maria?'

Nothing is making sense. Why does Maria want to undermine my marriage?

'You know, I'm so disappointed in you,' Maria says, shaking her head. 'You're as bad as my other daughter, but at least she wasn't the child of a rapist. Look at how you lose your temper, how easily you've ignored your wedding vows. It's obvious that you take after your evil father and I wonder how your bad genes will show up in your children. I've been watching Ava, you know, and she's a mean child. She pushes Issy down the slide when Issy doesn't want to go. She steals and hides other children's toys. There's evil there whether you see it or not.'

I lose it. I completely lose it. It's one thing saying bad things about me but to talk like that about Ava is unforgivable.

'Get out!' I scream. She just smiles at me, which angers me more. I have to clench my hands together to stop me from grabbing the pan and chucking the burning contents in Maria's face.

'You do realise that you can't force me to go, don't you?' Maria says. It's as if she's enjoying this exchange.

'Oh yes, I can force you,' I speak through clenched teeth. I grab a couple of bin liners from the cupboard under the sink then stride out of the room and storm upstairs, flinging open the door to Maria's small bedroom. I start grabbing Maria's belongings, her clothes that are hanging up, her shoes neatly lined up at the base of the wardrobe, and chuck everything into the bin liners. I glance up and she's standing in the doorway, leaning against the door frame, a grin on her face. I've never felt such rage, felt so close to physically hurting someone. It scares me and I know I need to get a grip. I try to ignore her and carry on chucking her belongings into the bin liners. When they're full I bend down and tug a suitcase out from under her bed.

'Have you finished yet, Imogen?' she taunts me. 'Do you really want your marriage to be over? Because I can make that happen. And do you want me to take down your business? It's so easy to write fake reviews. You remember that glowing review you had? Well, I can as easily write terrible ones. It takes years to build up a business, doesn't it? Yet it can be destroyed overnight.'

'Get the hell out of my house!' I yell.

'I look forward to seeing you in court, where I'll be suing you for unfair dismissal. I'll also report your attack on me to the police. My leg is still bruised, you know. But it's Ava I feel most sorry for. What terrible luck, to have two violent parents.'

'Shut up!' My breathing is rapid and it feels as if my heart will explode out of my chest.

'I'll ask Louise Devi to tell Josh the truth about your affair. And then, when the police discover how you attacked me and how Josh purposefully hurt Ava, you'll lose custody of your daughter. I mean, those bruise marks on her arm, they were just horrible.'

'Please get out!' I throw one of the bin liners towards her but she just steps backwards. I am trembling all over now.

'But don't worry. As Ava's grandmother, I'll intervene and take care of your little girl. The courts always favour family, don't they?'

What is she talking about? Could she really convince the authorities that we have hurt Ava? I freeze. It's as if my logical brain has disintegrated and I can't think properly. All I know is that I have to protect Ava from this mad woman and she has to get out of our house. I decide to change tack.

I take a deep breath and try to control my quivering voice. 'I would really appreciate if you would leave our house. I'll pay you anything you want and put everything in writing.'

'Now that's more like it. No need to get all worked up and angry. That doesn't help anyone. I won't be going anywhere tonight and it would be unreasonable of you to throw me out. It's not like I've done anything that can be construed as gross misconduct. Why don't we all calm down and sleep on it. If you decide you really want me to leave, then I will go tomorrow, but you need to think about the consequences rationally, because you have a great deal to lose, my dear Imogen.'

She steps into the room and I hop over the bin bag, needing to get away from her.

'Don't worry, I'll stay in my room this evening and give you and Josh plenty of time and space to have those difficult discussions. We'll talk again in the morning.' She stands back with her right arm outstretched, indicating for me to leave the room. And I do. As soon as I'm in the corridor, she closes the door and I realise that once again, Maria has got the upper hand.

I feel nauseous and take myself into our ensuite bathroom, where I sink onto the tiled floor and learn my head against the cool enamel stand of the sink. I'm terrified about how much Maria knows. Would the police really believe her if she told them her lies? What makes her so clever is that everything is rooted just a little bit in the truth. Yes, I did cause those bruises to her leg. Ava does have bruises on her arm. Yes, I did sleep with Arun and I've lied about it ever since. And she's still spinning the yarn that she's my birth mother but has given me absolutely no proof to back up her claim. All I know for sure is that she's deluded and quite possibly dangerous. At the thought, I lever myself up, splash some cold water onto my face and tiptoe down the corridor. To my relief her door is still closed. Gently, I open Ava's bedroom door and pad over to her bed. She's fast asleep, clutching her little rabbit toy. Would Maria do anything to harm Ava? I simply can't risk that. I pull back Ava's duvet and as carefully as I can I lift her out of her bed. She whimpers slightly and puts her arms around my neck. She's getting big and as the new baby grows, I don't suppose I'll be strong enough to carry her much longer. I walk back along the corridor to our bedroom and place her in the centre of our bed, tucking the duvet in around her. I'm going to keep my little girl by my side all night. I climb onto the bed next to her where exhaustion settles on me, and before I know it, I'm fast asleep.

'Imogen,' Josh is whispering. I open my eyes and blink hard. I'm fully dressed and the lights are on.

'Is Ava sick?' he asks.

'No.' I sit up in bed and glance at the clock. It's 10.32 p.m. 'I'm sorry about earlier. I should have never accused you like that.'

'No, you shouldn't.' He sits on his side of the bed.

'I've fired Maria. She's totally unstable and she's freaking me out.'

'What do you mean?'

'She's doing her best to undermine my business. She accused my guests of smoking in their bedroom and told them to leave, yet they're non-smokers. And she's been leaving false reviews.'

'Why would she do that?' He frowns. 'And what about

you? The whole reason for employing her was to ease your workload. I thought she was doing a good job.'

'Good enough but I can't have her around anymore. She's making all these wild claims, pretending she's a member of our family.'

And so the moment presents itself. Both Josh and I are talking calmly, Ava is fast asleep, and we have our privacy. I need to apologise for keeping my secret to myself for so many weeks. I need to eat humble pie and just pray that Josh will be understanding.

'There's something I need to–'

The front doorbell chimes.

'Who's here at this time of night?' Josh frowns and stands up. Our bedroom looks onto the garden at the back of the house so we can't see the driveway. The doorbell rings again.

'I'll go downstairs,' he says. I listen to his footsteps bound down the stairs and then I heave myself up from the bed.

I hear a woman's voice ask, 'Can we come in?'

I switch off the light and shut our bedroom door and follow Josh downstairs. I come to a halt two thirds of the way down, gripping the handrail so tightly my knuckles are white. It's two police officers dressed in uniform.

Oh my God. Was I right? Did Josh really hit Tom?

'Mr Letwin, could we have a word, please.' The police officer looks up and sees me. 'Mrs Letwin?'

'Yes,' I reply, hurrying to the bottom of the stairs. 'What's happened?'

'Would you like a cup of tea, some water perhaps?' Josh asks. How can he think about being polite at times like this?

'No, we're fine, thank you.'

'Right. Well, come through to the kitchen,' he says. I glance back upstairs and just pray that Maria doesn't appear.

My legs are shaking as I follow them through. Josh indicates for them to sit at the table and I follow suit.

The male officer introduces himself as Sergeant Thomas and his colleague as Police Constable Alice Simons. 'We've received an anonymous tipoff that you, Mr Letwin, were seen hurting your daughter, Ava.'

I lean back against my chair. I'm so relieved that they're not here to accuse Josh of hitting Tom it takes me a moment to absorb what they're really saying.

'That's nonsense!' Josh says. 'Malicious nonsense, and I've no idea who would say such a thing.' My husband glances at me for a nanosecond. *Please don't let Josh think this was my doing!* 'I adore our daughter and I'm in the medical profession. My work is all about making people better.' I'm not sure that being a dentist will sway the police in any way. 'What am I meant to have done?'

'We understand that there are bruises on your daughter's arm. Finger-mark bruises.'

Josh glances at me again. 'Yes, that's correct. My wife noticed them yesterday morning. We assumed they were the result of boisterous play at school. They didn't seem to bother Ava.'

'She's a tomboy,' I explain. 'Forever climbing up play equipment and bashing herself.'

'Right.' The police officer glances at his colleague, his face impassive.

'Where is Ava now?' Constable Simons asks.

'Asleep in our bed.'

'Your bed?' Simons questions. 'You've got a big house. Doesn't she sleep in her own room? She's five years old, isn't she?'

'That's correct,' Josh replies. 'She had a bad dream earlier so my wife brought her into our bed. She's normally in her own room.'

'I'm afraid that we'd like to see Ava. I realise it's not ideal to wake her, but please, can you bring her downstairs.'

Josh opens his mouth as if he's going to object but I get in there first. 'Of course. I'll go and get her.'

I walk out of the kitchen, my back ramrod straight, but when I'm in the hall I collapse against the wall. I know I accused Josh of hurting Ava but I did so in the heat of the moment. I don't really believe that he would do such a thing. Or do I?

I manage to awaken Ava surprisingly easily. The harder thing is deciding what to tell her. I carry her down the stairs.

'Darling, there are two police officers in our kitchen and they want to talk to you.'

'Have I been naughty?' she asks, her eyes big saucers.

'Absolutely not. They're worried about the bruises on your arm.'

'But they don't hurt,' Ava says, her little forehead in a frown.

When we get into the kitchen she clings to my neck and doesn't want to look at the police officers. I don't blame her.

'Ava munchkin, these police officers want to ask you a couple of questions.'

I sit Ava on my knee but she keeps her back to the officers. She reaches towards Josh, who holds her hand.

'We're sorry to wake you, Ava, but could you show us the bruise marks on your arm?' Constable Alice Simons asks.

Ava looks at Josh, who says, 'It's fine, sweetheart. Do as they say.' Ava wriggles around and I help her pull up her sleeve. The marks are already fading.

'How did you get those bruises, Ava?' Constable Simons asks.

'Dunno,' she whispers.

'Has anyone hurt you, because if they have we need to know.'

She shakes her head vigorously.

'Mr Letwin, would you mind leaving the room for a moment, please,' Sergeant Thomas asks. Josh opens and closes his mouth but he does as they ask. I feel so vulnerable and alone.

'Ava, has your daddy ever hurt you?'

'You're putting words into her mouth!' I exclaim.

'Mrs Letwin, please.'

'I love my Daddy,' Ava says. 'Daddy never hurts me. Never.' Her little voice is high and emphatic and in that moment I'm so proud of her. She wriggles off my lap and runs to the door.

'Ava!' I say, but she ignores me.

I stand up. 'Sorry.'

Ava's voice carries. 'Daddy. Daddy, where are you?'

'Do you have any idea how she might have come to get those bruises?' Constable Simons asks. I pause for a moment. Maria claims to love Ava and Ava seemingly adores her too, but could Maria be behind all of this? Should I mention Maria or rather discuss it with Josh first? I shake my head.

'I really think she got those marks at school. I'll discuss it with her teachers.'

Sergeant Thomas stands up. 'I'm not of the opinion that your daughter is in any imminent danger but I'm afraid we will need to refer this matter.'

'Refer? What do you mean?'

'Any report of injury to a child gets investigated by the police and social services.'

'You mean social services are going to get involved? Come here and talk to us? Are you saying that despite you thinking this is a fuss about nothing my husband is still under suspicion?'

He nods at me. 'We have procedures that we need to follow, Mrs Letwin. We'll see ourselves out, shall we?'

I'm too numb to respond.

23

MARIA

What a night! I had first row seats to the hilarity of the visit by the police. Imogen and Josh clearly forgot that my small room is directly above the kitchen and if I lie on the floor and put a glass to my ear I can just about hear every word that is being said. I got lucky, because if they had taken the police officers into the living room, I wouldn't have heard a thing.

I'm up at the crack of dawn and in the kitchen, preparing a veritable feast for breakfast. I want the Letwins to feel as if they're staying in a fancy hotel, with a fabulous choice of foods from a full English to pancakes, fresh fruit salad to cereals. I lay the table using their best china and cutlery and keep the food warm in the special warming oven in the Aga. I'm getting used to cooking on it and I'll miss it if I have to leave. I shake my head. No negative thoughts. I'm a member of this family and I intend to stay.

Unusually, Josh and Imogen come down to breakfast together.

'Good morning!' I say cheerily. 'As you had a tough night, I thought I'd prepare a treat. What can I offer you, Josh? Fruit salad or yoghurt to begin with? I've got a full English and pancakes ready in the warming oven.'

Josh stares at me as if I'm crazy but then snaps out of his rudeness and says, 'This is unexpected.'

'That's the plan, sir,' I say. I catch Imogen's scowl out of the corner of my eye. He sits down and unfolds the white linen napkin I put on top of his plate. 'Where's Ava this morning? Still asleep?'

'What's going on, Maria?' Imogen asks. Interesting that she's finally found her voice.

'It's clear we needed a chat so I thought I'd make it more pleasant and do it over a delicious breakfast. After the horrors of the past twenty-four hours, I thought you deserved it.'

Imogen plonks herself down. She's not happy and makes no effort to conceal her emotions. 'What can I get you, Imogen?'

'A black coffee,' she says without adding her normal please.

I hand Josh his regular freshly squeezed orange juice and then pour myself a milky tea and sit down at the table, next to Josh, who sits at the head of the table (so horribly patriarchal) and opposite Imogen.

'I've been thinking.' I glance at Imogen, who has paled. 'I'd like to go to the police and vouch for you, Josh. I can tell them that you're a wonderful father and in my opinion, having lived in your house, you wouldn't lay a finger on your daughter. I can tell them that Ava got those bruises whilst playing with her friend Issy.'

'But–' Imogen interrupts me.

'May I finish?' I ask politely.

'Go ahead,' Josh says. I can sense Imogen bristling.

'In return I want to keep my job.'

'No!' Imogen exclaims, spilling her coffee as she pushes it away from herself.

'Hold fire,' Josh says. 'Let's talk this through at least.'

'But it's a lie,' Imogen exclaims. 'Issy has just lost her father and you're going to blame her for hurting Ava. I know categorically that those bruises appeared overnight. Did you hurt Ava?'

'I am deeply offended you could even suggest such a thing! All I've been trying to do is help you and it's pretty obvious that Ava adores me. She's even been calling me Gangan, Josh! Did you know that? It's because she views me as her substitute grandmother. You can ask her yourself.'

The tension oozing out of Imogen is so tangible it feels as if I could slice it into pieces.

'If it wasn't me, it wasn't Josh and it wasn't Kyle – because he was barely here that night – then that leaves you, Imogen. Did you hurt your own daughter and have you tried to deflect your guilt onto Josh and now onto me? After all, you do have a violent temper and it wouldn't be much of a stretch to think you grabbed Ava a little too hard.'

Imogen's face is scarlet and she's trembling. Her hands are tight fists and her left foot is bouncing up and down. She opens her mouth but shuts it again as if she doesn't trust herself to speak.

'What do you mean, describing Imogen as having a temper?' Josh asks.

'Just leave it, Maria,' Imogen says through clenched teeth.

'Unfortunately you don't seem to know your wife very well, Josh. She's obviously hidden her temper from you but sadly I've seen it, haven't I, Imogen?'

'Ignore her, Josh,' Imogen says.

'So what exactly do you intend to say to the police in my defence?' Josh asks. Imogen looks startled and so she should.

Oh, Josh. What a self-centred man you are. I've fed you information on Imogen but you're only interested in saving your own skin, aren't you? Can't you see that your wife is about to explode, that she needs your support and understanding? Josh is not good enough for Imogen. He should be coming to her defence yet it's all about him. I thought the glass in his trainer would be a good warning for him but it clearly wasn't enough. The only way Imogen is going to be completely safe is if Josh is out of her life altogether.

'I suggest I speak to the police officers who visited last night and explain that there was no way that you could have hurt Ava. What else would you like me to say?' I smile at Josh.

'I'd appreciate that,' he says. 'They've told us that social services will get involved so you might need to speak to them too.'

'Of course. I'll do anything for this family.'

Imogen literally can't sit still. She's a ball of nervous energy. Poor darling, she obviously thinks I'm about to spill her secrets to Josh. But actually I'm not. That would be cruel and I'm here to protect my daughter, guide her onto a path of happiness.

'Are you ready for your full English?' I ask. 'I've made the bacon super crispy and eggs well done, just as you like them, Josh.'

'Thanks. That's very thoughtful of you.'

I place piled-up plates in front of Josh and Imogen, although Imogen just plays with her food. I'm worried that she's not eating properly at a time when it's so vital to her baby's growth. Perhaps I'll have a little word with Josh when she's out of earshot, make sure he knows how much I care for her.

They both eat in silence, which I suppose is understandable with so much on their minds, but any awkwardness is broken when Ava pads into the kitchen, her hair standing up on end, still wearing her pyjamas and clutching a soft toy.

'Good morning, sweetie,' I say before her parents can speak. 'Did you sleep well?'

'Why was I in your bed?' she asks Imogen before clambering onto a chair.

'Mummy and Daddy wanted some snuggle time with you last night,' Imogen says. 'Do you remember what happened?' I suspect they were rattled by the arrival of the police.

'Yes, the police people wanted to look at my arm.' She pushes up her pyjama top and the bruises have practically disappeared.

'Would you like a pancake?' I ask Ava.

'Yes please!' She jumps off her chair and flings are arms around me. What a sweetheart.

When Josh has finished his food, he stands up. 'I'm going to the garden centre to pick up some plants.

'Good idea,' Imogen says. Josh and Imogen have a little debate over Ava's head as to what they need.

'Can I come too?' Ava asks. Surely Imogen isn't going to allow that when there's a question mark whether Josh hurt their daughter?

'Sure,' she says. *Oh Imogen, you've disappointed me.*

Josh disappears upstairs with Ava to help her get ready, so I sit down on the chair Josh has vacated and bring it closer to Imogen.

'This is what I suggest,' I say. 'I'll take a couple of days off work, which will give you the chance to tell Josh the truth about everything. Your adoption, the bastard that raped me, that I'm your birth mother, your affairs with Arun and Tom–'

'But it's nonsense!' Imogen interrupts me. 'You're just pretending to be my mother and I don't understand why.'

I'm not going to dignify that statement with a response, so I carry on. 'Tell Josh about how you hit me and that you were in an inappropriate relationship with Tom, but you regret it.'

'But I wasn't!'

'Calm down, Imogen. Either you want my help or you don't. I can make the police and social services go away or I can make things so much worse for you. That's the last thing I want, as I love you and want to protect you, but we need some honesty around here.'

She stares at me, her mouth agog. 'I think it's a good idea that you leave. How soon can you go?'

'Well, that's not very kind, is it?' I chuckle. 'I'll wash up here and then I'll be on my way.'

'I can wash up. I'd rather you leave now.'

'As you wish,' I say, throwing her a wink. 'When would you like me to speak to the police? I could go over to the station later.'

'We'll give your phone number to them and they can contact you.'

'If that's what you really want. Good luck with the tricky conversations.' I laugh.

As I cycle away from Fairview House, I can't wipe the

smile off my face. I've got the Letwins exactly where I want them, right under my thumb. It's annoying that I've got to stay away for a couple of days, because I'd hoped I never need return to my bedsit, but so be it.

The single room feels cold and damp so I crank up the night storage heater and keep my coat on inside. I take the laptop out of my rucksack and fire it up. If Imogen and Josh think I'm out of their lives, they're totally wrong. I've installed a couple of hidden cameras, one in the kitchen behind a shelf of cookery books that Imogen never seems to look at and another in their bedroom. I know that's a bit creepy and it's not like I want to be a voyeur or anything, it's just that I expect the two of them to have their most intimate conversations in the bedroom and I want to be privy to those. I'm hoping that I'll be able to listen in when Imogen tells Josh the truth about me. Of course, I've still got my key to their house, although as a precaution, I got it copied. Better to be safe than sorry.

Even if Imogen rejects me, which I'm hoping she won't, I've still got Ava and Kyle. They, along with the new baby, are my only hope of grandchildren and I'm not going to give them up easily. I know that Kyle will stay in touch because I'm his source of free booze and cigarettes, and darling Ava, well, she just loves her Gangan.

I'm settled down in front of my laptop and switching between the cameras at Fairview House – which so far haven't yielded any conversations because I assume Josh and Ava are still out – and catching up on *Love Island*. I know I'm a bit old for it, but the programme is my guilty secret.

But then the doorbell rings.

I ignore the first ring but when it rings again and

someone knocks on the door, I haul myself up and go to the door. The landlord was too much of a cheapskate to put a peep hole in the door, so I speak through it.

'Who's there?'

'It's the police. We need a word with you so please can you open up.'

I'm not stupid enough just to swing the door open, because it could be anyone pretending to be the police. I keep the chain attached and open the door a fraction.

Surprisingly – and not in a good way – it is the police, a couple of whippersnappers barely out of nappies dressed in uniform standing in front of me.

'Maria Hinks?'

'Yes.'

'Please can we come in.'

I undo the chain and hold the door back. Well, that was quick. Josh must have rung them the second he got in the car. I suppose that's what desperation does to you.

The young woman's nose wrinkles up ever so slightly and that irks me. I know this place is horrible but it's not my fault. Besides, I've got a proper home now.

'I'm more than happy to confirm that Josh Letwin is a model father.'

'Excuse me?' the older of the two women says. 'I think we're talking at cross purposes.'

I freeze. Surely not.

'We're here to ask whether you've used your car recently.'

'My car?' All of a sudden my insides feel icy.

'Yes.' She glances at her notebook. 'You are the registered owner of a silver Ford Ka, registration number DG57 XUE?'

'Yes. But it's off the road at the moment.'

'We've received a tipoff that you've been driving your car even though you have lost your licence and are banned from driving for one year. You were convicted for being in charge of a vehicle while being unfit through drink and received a three-months prison sentence, a fine of £2500 and a year's ban. Have you driven a car since receiving that sentence?'

'Of course I haven't!' I say, doing my best to sound indignant. 'What proof do you have, or is this just tittle-tattle?'

'We can't give you any further information at this stage but we do want you to understand that if you have driven your car whilst being banned, this could result in you being readmitted to prison.'

'I let my daughter drive my car but I haven't driven it. That's why I've got a bike. The knackered blue bike locked up in the hall that you passed on your way in belongs to me.'

'Very well, but please understand that if any CCTV or automatic numberplate recognition system throws up your registration plate, then we will be bringing you into the police station for questioning.'

'I get it and rest assured, the last place I want to end up is back in jail.'

I wonder whether I should tell them about Josh but I decide that these two officers are too junior and it's better not to bring any further attention to myself. When they've gone, I lean back against the door and let out a long breath. That was a very close shave. Too close. I've driven my car and Imogen's car, but worst of all, what if my car was spotted near the scene of Tom's hit and run or near Clare's house? I'm positive there's no public CCTV on those country roads but nosey neighbours have their own cameras, as do other car owners, so it's not impossible that someone has picked up my details. But I was so careful, knocking Tom off on a dark country road lined with hedges and overhanging trees, and when I visited Clare I didn't park outside her house. So who would have reported me? It can only have been Clare before she died. No one else knows where I live or that I've been banned from driving. What a betrayal. 'Oh, Clare,' I mutter. 'I'm glad you're dead.'

24

IMOGEN

When Maria cycled off down our drive, I felt the tension ease from my limbs and I sank down into a chair and sobbed, safe in the knowledge that I was alone in the house. I've let delusional Maria get to me, but in a weird kind of way, it's a relief that she's backed me into a corner, because now I have to tell Josh everything.

Josh and Ava are going to be out all morning, visiting the garden centre followed by a trip to Fencer's Farm. There was no way that I was going to let Maria take her there, so this is a good compromise. It means Josh can go with her to pet all the farm animals and take her on a pony ride, and hopefully the horrible accusations of last night can be forgotten for a while.

After feeling sorry for myself for a few long minutes I decide to take advantage of having the house to myself. I need to prove once and for all that Maria isn't my birth mother and then I can tell Josh everything, including how Maria is delusional and that she's been blackmailing me. If the woman thinks she's returning to our house, she's got another think coming. My number one priority is to protect Ava, and I don't want her anywhere near our daughter.

I stride to my study and pick up my laptop, taking it back into the kitchen. I've rather buried my head in the sand regarding Anthony Stanbridge but assuming he is my birth father, I need to find out more about him. I do a Google search using his name and the words *prison* and *jail,* and after scouring pages and pages, I find a one-sentence newspaper article. It simply says:

Convicted rapist Anthony Stanbridge, 22, has been released from jail after serving 4 years of an 8-year sentence.

How come he only served half his sentence? Does that mean anything? So he was released at the age of 22. I've been searching for him in the south of England because he originally came from Guildford in Surrey, but of course, he could be anywhere now; perhaps not even in the UK. And perhaps he changed his name to distance himself from the horrors of his crime.

I open up my subscription to Ancestry and type in his name and the year of his birth, looking through the Births, Deaths and Marriages register in England. And then I strike lucky. Anthony Ian Stanbridge married a Luda Kowalska fifteen years ago in the registry office at Lambeth Town Hall. Could that have been him? The dates fit. That means he would have been 38 when he got married. How helpful that he married a woman with an unusual name, Polish perhaps? I type in Luda's name and up pops lots of information. I click on LinkedIn first and see that Luda Kowalska works for an estate agency in central London. Looking back through her profile, I reckon she must be mid-forties right now, so she'd just turned thirty when she married Anthony. I go onto Facebook and although her settings are private, under her relationships it says she's divorced. I hope Anthony Stanbridge hasn't committed any further crimes. That would be too horrible.

With plenty of trepidation, I pick up the phone and dial the number for Red Rafters Estate Agency in Bloomsbury, London, hoping that they're open.

'Good morning.' I try to inject some cheeriness into my voice. 'Please, can I speak to Luda Kowalska?'

'Who should I say is calling?'

'My name is Imogen Letwin. She doesn't know me.'

'And what's in regard to, please?'

'A new listing,' I say, immediately feeling guilty for potentially getting Luda's hopes up.

'One moment, please.'

The phone rings three times and then it's answered. 'Luda Kowalska speaking.' Her voice is quite low and accentless.

And now I'm a bit tongue-tied because I haven't prepared what I want to say. 'Hello. This is a bit of a strange request but I'm trying to track down Anthony Stanbridge. I understand you were married to him and I was hoping you might be able to point me in the right direction.'

There's a pause and then she says, 'Why are you looking for him?'

'I believe he's a relation of mine. I know this is an odd request and I'm sorry, but it's really urgent that I find him.'

'We're divorced.'

'Yes, I gathered that. Do you mind me asking how long

you were married?' I wonder if they have any children together, whether I have any stepsiblings.

'Only eighteen months. I should never have married him.'

'Oh. Was that because of his conviction?' There's a long silence on the end of the phone. 'I know about his rape conviction when he was eighteen,' I say.

'In which case you know more than I did when I married him.' I want to punch the air because Luda has just admitted that I have the right man.

'What was he like?'

'Sorry, but why are you asking me all of these questions? I haven't seen Anthony in years.'

'I think he might have been my father.'

There's another long silence before Luda says, 'Oh.' I'm about to cut through the next silence when she says, 'He wasn't a bad man really. Just troubled.'

'Do you know how I might be able to find him?' I ask.

She sighs. 'You haven't heard it from me but he's a roofer and he lives in Brighton. At least he did the last time we spoke. He goes by the name of Tony now and he's got his own business so you should be able to track him down. TS Roofing, I think it's called.'

'Thank you so much,' I say. 'I'm really grateful.'

I lean back in my chair and take a few deep breaths. I might just have found my birth father and now I'm terrified. Steeling myself, I search for TS Roofing in Brighton and up comes an address and a mobile phone number. I hope he's not up a ladder when he answers my call. I dial the number and it rings about six times before going to voicemail, one of those prerecorded messages using a female voice. I don't leave a message.

I'm not sure if I'm disappointed or relieved. I get up to make myself a cup of tea but then my mobile rings.

'Hello,' I say.

'I just missed a call from this number. It's TS Roofing.'

My heart starts pumping and I lean against the counter-top. 'I'm looking for Tony Stanbridge. Is that you?'

'Yes. How can I help?'

'This will probably come as quite a shock but I think I'm your daughter.'

'You what?'

'I think I'm your daughter.'

'I don't have any kids, unfortunately for me.'

'Are you the Anthony Stanbridge who went to prison for four years when you were eighteen? Because I think I'm the child of that...' I can't bring myself to say the word rape. 'That... incident.'

There's silence on the other end of the phone and I wonder if he's hung up on me, but then there would be a beeping sound.

'Mr Stanbridge?' I say.

'Are you telling me that you're Amy's kid?'

'I don't know. In fact I only discovered I was adopted three months ago, but the dates fit and what my late mother told me – my adoptive mom, that is... I think I'm your daughter.'

'Well, blow me down,' he says.

'I was wondering if we might be able to meet. I live near Horsham so it's no distance.'

'Of course we need to meet. Tonight? Tomorrow? The next day? Just name a place and time and I'll be there.'

'Really?' This is going so much better than I expected.

'It's not every day that some lass calls you up and says you're her dad.'

'No, I suppose not.'

'And I don't want you to believe everything you read in the papers. You need to hear the truth from me.'

'Okay,' I say. 'How about tomorrow morning?'

'That's fine. You'll want to meet in a public place, won't you, so how about Downsview Park? If you walk in from Eastern Road, there's a bench just along the path there with trees behind and a nice view down to the sea. There are always lots of people walking their dogs, playing with their kids. I can meet you there at 11 a.m. if that's good for you?'

'Yes, that's perfect. Downsview Park at 11 a.m. Thank you.'

'You didn't tell me your name,' he says.

'It's Imogen. I'm married so I'm now Imogen Letwin.'

'Imogen,' he says. 'That's a nice name. I'll see you tomorrow then, Imogen.'

I can't believe it. I can't believe that he wants to see me, that he seemed to accept I was his daughter, that he wasn't even that surprised. Did he know that I existed, that I was adopted? And then I recall him saying her name. Amy. Why didn't I ask Tony for Amy's surname? I could ring back and ask but decide that's too desperate. I'll have to wait until tomorrow. And then it strikes me. He said Amy, not Maria. It was just as I assumed. Maria is nothing to do with me. She's just a desperate woman who for some reason has latched onto our family.

The landline rings. We don't often use it and I've debated giving it up altogether.

'Hello, Mrs Letwin. Just confirming your appointment at the optician's for your annual checkup on Monday.'

'Yes, fine,' I say, totally distracted. All I hear are Tony's words and the eagerness in his voice to meet me. I put the phone down and only then do I glance at my diary. No, I can't make my optician's appointment. I've got a Zoom call with a client then. I pick up the landline to call back and hear the *beep, beep* sound that indicates I have a message. I dial 1571.

'Hello. This is a message for Imogen. My name is Clare Hooper and I contacted you previously. I need to talk to you urgently about Maria Hinks. There are things you need to know about her. Please can you call me back as soon as possible.' She leaves me her mobile number and her landline number. I jot them both down on a piece of paper. I call the optician's first and rearrange my appointment, and then I think about Clare. Maria said her other daughter – Clare – was unstable and on drugs. Should I call her back? Or was Maria lying about that too? Clare sounded perfectly compos mentis in her message and this is the second time she's contacted me so there must be some urgency. I want to know the truth about Maria, so I dial both numbers. There's no answer on either phone and I don't leave a message.

With a couple of hours to spare until Josh and Ava come home, I decide to tackle the ironing. I carry the ironing board from the utility room to the kitchen and plug in the iron but I'm really not in the mood. Instead I call Josh and suggest we all meet up for lunch at the local pub. As I leave the house a strange and uncomfortable feeling settles over me. That sense of doom that I've had a few times recently, as if something truly terrible is about to happen.

25

MARIA

I created a photo montage wall in my bedsit. Before I moved to Fairview House there were just photos of Clare, but now I've got lots and lots of photos of the Letwins. That's why I was so scared when I realised the police weren't here to talk about Josh but about my driving. Because if they'd put two and two together and they'd known about Clare's death, well, I would have been a goner. As it was, Clare's death has only been announced today. It's rather sad, isn't it, that a thirty-year-old woman isn't missed for two whole days. What did her colleagues at work think? That she'd taken a sickie and not told them, or she'd upped and left? But now Clare's face is everywhere and she needs to be off my walls. I take each photo down and rip every one into as many pieces as I can manage. It's a relief not to see her face anymore. Then I put all the little pieces in a china bowl that I bought for £4.99 at Tesco; I open the window as wide as I can and I burn the photos. I hold the bowl carefully because I don't want any smoke alarm to go off, but this place is such a dump, I doubt the fire alarms even work.

When Clare is reduced to ashes, I tip them out of the window. It's a bit like a cremation, and for a moment I'm sad as the ash is lifted up by the wind and then scattered onto the parking lot below. But then I remember what she was really like and that she doesn't deserve my commiserations.

Now it's time to change up the wall. I take all the photos of the Letwins out of my rucksack. I've got dozens. I've got an ancient phone and it doesn't take great photos, but all the same I took my phone to Boots and printed off the best of my pics. I have some adorable pictures of Ava, some taken when she was fast asleep, her face angelic and her arms outstretched. Others from when she was colouring, her little tongue wedged into the side of her mouth, and then there are those of her in the park, hanging upside down on the climbing frame when she's acting as a daredevil. Kyle was harder to catch but I've got a fabulous photo of him with a cigarette between his fingers, the smoke billowing out of his mouth, and he looks quite the cool dude. I think he'd be pleased with that picture. Imogen, of course, takes pride of place. My clever, beautiful daughter. I have printed off the profile photos from her hotel consultancy website but I've also got plenty others. They range from her working, her forehead furrowed in concentration, her back rounded over her laptop. (She has to be careful about her posture.) There's a glorious shot of her, Josh and Ava playing in the garden. I've chopped Josh out of the picture and it captures the joy in both of my girls' faces. I've also taken a few photos from Imogen's family albums because I feel left out of the early years. I roll little globules of blueback and carefully arrange the photos on the wall. When I'm finished, I stand back and admire my work. My heart swells with love for my family. The pièce de résistance is a photo I took of me, Imogen and

Ava when we were at the fun fair, Ava's face sticky and pink with candy floss. You don't have to look hard to see the resemblance between the three of us.

When I'm finished, I lie on the bed. The wooden slats underneath the lumpy mattress feel as if they're poking into my back. Balancing my laptop on my knees, I log into the camera system I've set up at Imogen's. It's amazing what technology you can buy at low cost these days. I go into the history and see Imogen in the kitchen, again hunched over her laptop. I wonder what she's doing. I listen as she makes a call to someone called Luda. She seems tense and awkward, but when she asks, 'Were you married to Anthony Stanbridge?' my heart plummets. What is Imogen playing at? I sit up straighter on the bed. It's hard to follow the conversation as I'm only hearing what she's saying, but when she puts the phone down, she seems even more agitated. *Oh, Imogen, you don't know what you're doing, my love. You're playing with fire.*

And then to my dismay, she calls him. The rapist. Why the hell would she do that? And she's smiling and laughing, walking around the room as she talks to him, and agreeing to meet him at Downsview Park tomorrow at 11 a.m. Is she out of her mind? She's willingly going to meet someone who has committed the most terrible crime? Doesn't she realise how dangerous this is, that her life could be in jeopardy?

I'm feeling restless now. I need to help Imogen but it's impossible to do that from a distance. What if Anthony Stanbridge tracks her down first or even gets to Ava? Darling little Ava, the most precious child in the world. She's with Josh this morning – although I'm appalled that Imogen thought it was safe to send her daughter off with her husband considering the man has been questioned about hurting the child – but this afternoon, Josh will probably be off playing a game of golf or something equally self-indulgent, and then what? The more I think about the situation, the more I realise that Josh is a selfish man, bigoted too in light of Imogen not wanting to share her adoption story with him, and he's doing nothing to support Imogen. If he is out of the picture, then my girl will only have me for support. Josh is where I need to focus my attention.

I switch off the playback of the camera. I'm a ragged bundle of nerves now. Imogen needs me. I stare at the photos and lose myself for a while in happy memories and dreams of what will come. And then I glance at my watch, and this is what happens sometimes. Time just melts away. An hour or so has passed. I switch the link back on to the cameras at Fairview House, live this time.

Imogen is on the phone again. 'Sure. That's a good idea. I'll meet you at the Hanging Gate in twenty minutes. Alright. If I get there first I'll order the chicken nuggets for Ava. What would you like? See you soon.'

If I deduce that correctly, the Letwin family are going out for lunch. That's perfect. They'll be out for at least an hour, which gives me time to pop back home. Yes, it is my home too. I pull on my jacket, hurry out into the hall and unlock my bike. And then I'm pedalling as fast as I can along the now familiar route. I hide my bike under a tree and walk up the driveway, keeping in the shadows. I need to be sure that Imogen's Volvo has gone. As I approach the garages, I'm relieved to see they're both empty. I walk up to the front door, turn my key in and disable the alarm. It's a relief that they haven't changed the code. I walk into the kitchen and sigh. It's a mess. Imogen has made a start on the ironing but there's still a big pile. I run upstairs and see that the beds are unmade. I quickly smooth out the sheets on the master bed, stretch out the duvet and open the curtains properly. In the master en-suite, I run a cloth over the sink and base of the shower, pour some bleach down the toilet and fold the towels, neatly placing them back on the towel rail. I hurry into Ava's room and do a quick tidy-up. Then it's back downstairs.

I finish the ironing and leave Josh's ironed shirts and dentist uniform on hangers, attached to the ironing board. I chuckle. Imogen's going to think a fairy godmother has turned up whilst she's been out and finished all the household chores. I switch the dishwasher on and grab the vacuum, running it along the kitchen floor and out into the hallway. I'm putting the cleaning materials away in the utility room when I find a spare bottle of bleach. I take it out and sniff it. The smell is pungent. In my mind's eye, I see Josh, still a bit sleepy, strolling into the kitchen, grabbing the bottle of freshly squeezed orange juice from the fridge and pouring himself a glass. He'll tip it back in one and then return upstairs to have a shower and shave before changing into his work clothes.

I find it fascinating how humans are such creatures of habit. We think we're original, unpredictable, with brains so superior to other mammals, yet we're not. We crave the framework of the banal, the regularity, the ordinary. Most of us get up at the same time, eat the same breakfast every morning, and our days follow the same paths as yesterday and the day before that. Josh, who thinks he's so superior because he's a highly educated professional at the top of his tree, is the same as everybody. Every morning he has that glass of orange juice. No one else in the family touches it. What a boring man he is.

I carry the bottle of bleach into the kitchen and take the

top off the plastic bottle. Very carefully, I pour the bleach into the juice, adding perhaps another fifth to the liquid already in the bottle. I put the top back on and shake the bottle, hoping that the bleach will mix well. When I settle it back into the door of the fridge, I wait to see if the liquid separates, whether the colour of the orange juice has changed substantially. To my inexpert eyes, it looks exactly the same. But how much will Josh need to consume to finish him off? And will he be able to taste it? I hope not.

I glance at the time. I need to leave because the Letwins could be back at any time. I reset the alarm, lock the door behind me and hurry down the drive. As I climb onto my bike, I look back at my house. A warm buzz flows through me knowing that next time I'm here, I'll be staying for good.

26

IMOGEN

In the car, I switch on the radio, tuning it to a local Sussex radio station. I catch the end of a song I don't recognise and then the news comes on and the leading piece is about a woman's body found in her home near Loxwood. I'm concentrating on the road and an idiot in a black BMW overtakes me on a bend, so I'm not listening carefully, but then the presenter says the name, and I nearly drive into a hedge. Gripping the steering wheel so hard my fingers hurt, I turn the sound up.

'Police went to the house at about 9.30 p.m. last night in response to medical concerns for the deceased. Neighbours say that Clare Hooper was a much-liked member of the close-knit community and that they're in shock. Sussex police are treating her death as murder. The force is asking anyone with information to get in touch.'

Did I hear her name correctly? I swing the car into a lay-by, which is actually the entrance to a field, and turn off the engine. With trembling fingers I grab my phone and do a Google search for Clare Hooper, Loxwood and murder during the last twenty-four hours. To my utter dismay, I heard correctly. What are the chances of there being two Clare Hoopers within a short radius of Horsham? That means two people I know have been killed this week. Two premature deaths. And they're both connected to me.

And to Maria.

I stare out of the windscreen to the country road ahead of me. Tom and Clare. Both dead. Maria's daughter, dead. She told me that Clare was on drugs but the news report said the police are treating it as murder. If she'd died from taking an overdose, then that would be accidental death. And Maria didn't like Tom; she made that perfectly obvious. I send Josh a text message telling him I'm running late and then I dial 999.

'Hello. Emergency service operator. Which service do you require? Fire, police, or ambulance?'

'Police, please,' I say. My voice sounds unnaturally high.

'I'll just connect you now.'

There's a pause and then a male voice comes on the line.

'Hello. Where are you calling from?'

'Um, I'm on a back road near the Hanging Gate pub, but that's not why I'm calling. I need to speak to someone about the hit and run involving Tom Box and Clare Hooper's murder.'

There's a slight intake of breath.

'What is your name, address and your own phone number, please?

I reel out my details.

'Thank you, Ms Letwin. And what information do you have?'

'There's a woman called Maria Hinks who worked for us as a housekeeper for a short period, who we've now fallen out with, and I think that she's something to do with both of their deaths.'

'Why do you think that?'

'Clare Hooper is Maria's daughter. They didn't have a good relationship and Maria told me that Clare was on drugs and that they were estranged but I'm not sure if that's the case. The messages Clare left me were articulate, and on top of that, Maria didn't like Tom at all. She tried to make it look like Tom and I were having an affair but we weren't. We had the police around last night because someone has falsely accused my husband Josh of hurting our daughter, Ava, and I think it's Maria who was behind all of this because she's trying to blackmail me.' As the words tumble from my mouth and I struggle to take a breath, there's a long pause on the other end of the line.

'Right,' the police officer says eventually. My shoulders sink down because I realise everything I've just told him is muddled and sheer speculation. I've given him no evidence whatsoever.

'I'll pass this on to my colleagues on the investigations team and they'll get back to you if they require any further information.' I can hear the cynicism in his voice. Just another time waster trying to push the blame onto someone they don't like. I realise it might come across like that because I don't have any hard evidence and without evidence no one will be the slightest bit interested. But my intuition is screaming that I'm right. The problem is, how am I going to prove it?

By the time I arrive at the pub, I see Josh's car parked at the front, so I hurry inside. Josh and Ava are sitting at a table near a far window that looks out onto the garden with the

South Downs in the distance. Ava jumps up when she sees me.

'Mummy!' she exclaims. 'We've had such a fun morning and I rode a pony and Daddy let me go on the big girls' zipwire.'

'I'm glad you've had a lovely time.'

I feel a relief being here, safe in a public place, away from Maria, in the heart of my little family. Although I'm perfectly aware that with everything I'm going to be telling Josh this afternoon, I need to savour this lunch because it might be the last time we're sitting together in relative harmony.

'You look pale. Is everything alright?'

'Just had some bad news but I'll tell you later,' I say, speaking over Ava's head.

Josh frowns.

'Don't worry. No one you know.'

Our food comes quickly, largely because Josh has already ordered for me, choosing my favourite beer-battered fish and chips with mushy peas and the best tartare sauce in the south of England. Ava chatters away, which suits me because my brain is totally full with the implications of Clare Hoopers' death, Maria's behaviour, the fact that social services might be contacting us any moment and the magnitude of what I've got to tell Josh later. By the time we're driving home, separately in our cars, my heart is pounding. But it's now or never.

I walk into the kitchen and stand stock still. The ironing is all done, but I only managed a couple of shirts earlier. The dishwasher is running but I know I didn't switch it on. I run upstairs, into our bedroom, and see that our bed has been neatly made. The bathroom smells of pine disinfectant and there's loo cleaner in the bowl. I race along the corridor to Maria's room, swinging the door open, but she's not there.

'Maria!' I shout as I run back down the stairs and then I realise she can't be here because the alarm was on when I came home and I've just switched it off. Ava and Josh are in the kitchen now but I need to study the alarm panel. I go through the menu and find recent history. The alarm was switched off shortly after I left for the pub and switched back on again just ten minutes ago.

I stride into the kitchen. 'Maria's been here in our absence,' I tell Josh. I'm furious. 'She's finished off the ironing and cleaned the house.'

Josh throws me a strange look. 'Isn't that what she's employed to do?'

'Yes, but I told her to get out. I watched her leave on her bicycle earlier this morning and she said she'd be gone for a couple of days, but I can see from the alarm panel that she came back whilst we were out and now she's gone again. She's playing games with us.' I realise that Ava is listening in to this conversation and I don't want that. 'Sweetheart, why don't you go into the playroom and I'll put a film on for you. What would you like to watch?'

'Can I watch *Khumba*?'

It's Ava's favourite animation about a half-striped zebra who has to earn his stripes and save all the animals of the Great Karoo.

'Of course, darling.' I settle Ava in front of the television and return to the sound of our second television blaring out in the living room. Josh is sitting on the sofa, his feet up on the coffee table.

'Is this an important match?' I ask.

'No. I'm just scrolling through.'

'I've got something I need to tell you,' I say, sitting down on the sofa next to him.

'Alright,' he replies, wariness in his voice. He switches the television off.

'I haven't been honest with you.'

'So you did have an affair with Tom?' He looks crushed.

'No, nothing like that. And I absolutely didn't.'

'So what is it?'

'A day before Mum died, she told me that I was adopted, and that my birth father raped my birth mother and was subsequently sent to prison for four years. He was eighteen. My birth mother took her own life after I was born.'

'Raped? My God, Imogen. And you didn't know any of this?'

'No. I had no idea I was adopted, let alone what a terrible thing my birth father did.'

'But why didn't you tell me?'

I wring my hands and can't bring myself to look my husband in the eye. 'I thought you'd be disgusted, that you'd reject me.'

'What?' He looks totally astounded.

'You've always said that genes are so important and how Rhiannon and Dom shouldn't have had children because of the mental health issues in their family.'

'Yes, but I didn't really mean it.'

'I was so scared that you might reject our children, particularly if we have a boy. What if he takes after his grandfather?'

Josh shakes his head and rubs his eyes. I can tell he's finding it hard to take this in. 'So why are you telling me now?'

'Maria. She found out that I was adopted and she's been

trying to blackmail me. She's even tried to convince me that she's my birth mother. It's ridiculous, because Mum said my birth mother is dead. And then I heard on the radio this morning that Clare Hooper was found murdered. She's Maria's real daughter. And what with Tom dying too, there are two deaths related to Maria.'

'What's she got to do with Tom?'

'I'm not sure, but she didn't like him and she took some photos of me and Tom hugging, and I agree they do look a bit ambiguous but really, he was just like a brother to me. It was Maria who sent you the messages about me and Tom.'

Josh rubs his head. 'Maria? But why would she do that? I can't believe you've kept such a big secret from me. I'm your husband, Imogen; you should be able to tell me everything.'

'I'm sorry. I really am.'

'It doesn't matter who your parents were. I still love you.'

But Josh doesn't reach out to hold me or even take one of my hands. He just stares straight ahead and I get the sense that he's in shock and holding back from me. 'I don't understand why Maria sent those messages,' he mutters, shaking his head.

'I've made contact with my birth father,' I say. 'I spoke to him for the first time this morning. He's got a roofing company in Brighton and I'm going to meet him tomorrow.'

'I'll come with you.'

'That's kind of you but would you mind if I do that by myself?'

'But what if he's still dangerous?'

'He was let out of prison when he was twenty-two and that was thirty-one years ago. He only served half his sentence. I don't think he'd be running his own business, living in the community all these years if the police thought he was dangerous.'

'Still–'

'I'm meeting him in a public place. You don't need to worry. He sounded really excited to meet me on the phone.' I feel such a relief that Josh has reacted calmly to my revelations. I suppose I thought he'd be angry, that he might storm off, but he just seems reflective and unfazed. 'I rang the police and told them about Maria. I'm not sure they'll take my tipoff seriously though.'

'What did you tell them?'

I try to repeat my conversation. Josh frowns. 'It's pure speculation, Imogen. Honestly, I think it's best if we stay right out of it. You don't know anything about this Clare Hooper, and if Maria's her mother, then the police will have been in touch with her anyway. With regards to Tom, we just have to be there to support little Issy and that's it.'

'But I want the police to look into Maria.'

'With this false allegation against me, we need to keep our heads low.'

I'd forgotten all about that. 'But Maria has been behaving so weirdly,' I say.

'Look, if you insist, we can go to the police station tomorrow and have an informal chat with them,' he suggests.

'Okay,' I say. 'But I don't want Maria anywhere near us. I don't trust her when she says she'll speak to the police to vouch for you. I suspect she was the one who gave the tipoff in the first place. In fact I don't trust her at all; we don't know what she's capable of.'

'But why would she have done that? It doesn't make sense.'

I wonder if now is the time to admit to my one-night stand with Arun, but then I decide I've dropped enough bombshells for one afternoon. 'I know you probably think I'm over-reacting regarding Maria but I want her out of our house. Most of her belongings are packed up. Can you take them round to her place and we'll pay her off – a month's pay, three months, whatever we need to be shot of her.'

'I don't think we should do anything too hastily regarding Maria. Let's issue her with a formal letter saying we're terminating her employment and I can speak to a solicitor early next week. In the meantime, we can change Maria's alarm code. Agreed?'

I nod. Josh has been so reasonable, and for that I'm immensely grateful. Nevertheless, when nighttime falls I check that every door in the house is locked and bolted, that every window is closed. I remove Maria's code from the system, and for the first time I switch the house alarm on when we go to bed so that if anyone tries to break in, the alarm will go off.

27

IMOGEN

I barely sleep. I'm on edge, wondering if Maria will try to come back into the house, and I can't imagine how the conversation is going to go with Tony. Josh came to bed late and now he's still asleep when I get up. Once again, he's offered to look after Ava for the day. Later we're going to tell Ava that Issy won't be in school for a while and that Tom has very unexpectedly gone to heaven. I'm not sure that she'll fully grasp what that means. Josh has asked me to leave Find Friend on my phone and to message him when I arrive at the park and when I leave again. I know he only means well.

And yes, I'm nervous. Terrified even. I'm about to meet my father, a rapist. Will he try to usurp Dad's place in my life now both my parents are dead? Will we look alike or even like each other's company? There are so many unknowns and no guidebook on how to deal with such a bizarre situation. I park the car along the road that runs parallel to Downsview Park. I've checked on Google Maps several times which entrance I'm meant to take, and now it's ten minutes to eleven and I'm here. It's a blustery day, so I pull on a beanie and wrap a scarf around my neck, then I wonder whether that's a good idea. Could someone strangle me with the scarf? I tell myself not to be ridiculous. I'm going to meet my father, and just because he did something bad when he was young doesn't mean he's a violent person today.

I step out of the car, lock it and walk with my head bent down against the wind, striding quickly to the park entrance, my hands deep in my pockets. I only have to walk a few metres inside the park when I see the bench. I stop for a moment. There's a man sitting there. He's got balding hair and is wearing jeans and a navy-blue anorak, the collar pulled up high. My heart is hammering. Is that him? Just as I pluck up the courage to walk towards him, he turns around and sees me.

'Imogen?' he says, jumping up from the bench.

I nod and walk towards him. He holds his hand out and I shake it awkwardly. His palm is rough but his handshake firm.

'My God, you look just like her.' He stares at me and I feel uncomfortable. 'Sorry, love, it's just quite a shock. A happy shock. Come and sit down.' He pats the bench next to him. 'You mentioned you've only known you were adopted for three months. That must have come as quite the surprise.'

'Yes, it did. My mum – my adoptive mum – told me just before she died. And after she'd passed I found the adoption certificate.'

'And how did you find me?'

'Newspaper articles, dates that matched up, speaking to your ex-wife.'

'Ah, Luda.' He smiles wryly.

'Can you tell me what happened? Tell me more about my birth mother – Amy, you said her name was.'

'My Amy.' He looks wistfully out towards the sea. 'We were so young, me and Amy. I adored her. I mean, it was the real thing but no one else believes it when you're so young. I was eighteen, Amy only fifteen, although the naughty lass swore to me she was sixteen. She told me she loved me and I certainly loved her. We got up to the hanky-panky that the young get up to and yes, with hindsight – and believe me, I've had a lot of time to think about it – it was wrong of me. I've regretted it every day. Not you, obviously, but Amy was too young. As I said, we were in love. The day we slept together her mum found us and she went totally ballistic. The next thing I know I'm being accused of raping an underage girl. I was arrested. She never liked me, Amy's mum. Thought I wasn't good enough for her daughter, and perhaps I wasn't. My parents didn't have any money to buy the services of a good solicitor, so I got banged up. Amy continued writing to me for a while and I knew she was pregnant. She said she'd keep the baby and we'd all be together when I got out of jail, but when it came to the trial, her solicitor read out a statement from Amy. I knew she hadn't written it, that it was her parents' words, but it was horrible. It cut right through me. Said I was violent and controlling and made her have sex with me when it wasn't like that at all. Not at all.' Tony's voice cracks. 'That never happened,' he reiterates. 'Anyway, I got convicted and banged up. I carried on writing to Amy, begged her to tell me how the pregnancy was going, but I heard nothing. Not a word. My parents disowned me and there I was, surrounded by violent men and the loneliest I've ever been in the whole of my life. I didn't hear until much later. Got a letter from my solicitor to say that Amy had given birth to a baby girl who was adopted and that Amy took her own life three months later. I've had to live with that, knowing that my Amy died because of me.'

'That's so sad.'

'I liked to believe that Amy couldn't live without me and that she carried such a heavy burden of guilt. I know she was only a wee girl at the time, but if she'd stood up to her parents and said that it was consensual, then I'd never have been banged up.'

'Have you ever forgiven her?'

'Of course. I never held it against her. I was in the wrong for sleeping with an underage girl and Amy was totally controlled by her wealthy, domineering parents. It's just one of those things. The worst was that Amy died. Such a waste of a life.'

We sit in silence for a while. It's so much for me to absorb and all the time a little voice at the back of my head is asking, should you believe him? You've only got his word for what happened and he's had over thirty years to perfect a palatable theory. But as I sit next to this man who in some ways is a total stranger but in others seems so very familiar, my gut is telling me that he's telling the truth.

'What was Amy's surname?' I ask, wondering if I can trace relatives on my mother's side.

'Amy Swanborough. She would have kept the same initials when we married.'

'It's an unusual surname,' I say.

'Yes. The thing that I'm most sorry about is how all of this impacts on you,' Tony says. 'Have you had a good life, Imogen?'

'A wonderful life. A blessed life. My parents gave me a

fabulous childhood and they never stopped telling me that they loved me. I wanted for nothing.'

'That at least is a blessing. I know I shouldn't ask you for forgiveness, but I'm deeply sorry for any hurt I've caused you.'

I take Tony's rough hand and squeeze it. 'You haven't caused me any real hurt.'

'What the hell are you talking about? You're not really going to believe or forgive this man, are you?'

I jump to my feet.

Maria is standing right in front of us. She's wearing a black top with the hood over her head and black trousers. 'This man, he's evil, a rapist!' She jabs her index finger at Tony.

'What are you doing here, Maria?' I gasp.

'I'm here to protect you. That's all I want to do – to protect you, to be there for you, to be a true mother.'

'But you're not my mother! This woman isn't Amy, is she?' I turn to Tony.

'Never seen her in my life before.' Tony gets to his feet.

'You need to leave us alone, Maria. I don't know what you think you're doing but I don't want you here.'

'You need saving! Look at you, here alone with a rapist, vulnerable, pregnant. Are you even thinking about your unborn child? I've saved you from Tom; now I need to save you from him.'

'What!' I exclaim, interrupting her.

'I stole his bike helmet, rammed him off the road because you couldn't see what damage he was doing to you and your family. I even had to kill my own daughter to stop her from talking. And Josh – let's hope he's gone too by the time you get home. So you see, I have to save you from this violent, horrible man!'

'Who are you? What's going on?' Tony asks.

Suddenly there's a flash of metal. Tony grunts and bends forwards.

'No!' I scream. Maria has a huge knife and she's already jammed it into Tony once. 'Help!' I cry.

'Shut up, you stupid girl,' Maria yells. I kick out at her, my foot catching her shin, and she stumbles as she tries to push the knife into Tony once again. He staggers away and I put myself between Maria and Tony. Her eyes are flashing and there's froth at her mouth.

'Get out of my way!' she screams and holds the knife high up in the air, its blade dripping red, its serrated edge catching the low sunlight.

'Put it down, please!' I beg her. 'You don't have to do this, Maria.'

'But I do. You need me, and I need you, and this monster needs to die.' She lunges towards Tony once again and I know without a shadow of a doubt that she's going to kill my only living parent. I run towards her and punch her in the jaw with all my strength, her head snapping backwards like a doll's, but rather than crumpling down, Maria lets out a laugh much like a hyaena's cry and the blood freezes in my veins. I left this woman alone with Ava and she's evil through and through. How couldn't I have seen that? How will I ever be able to trust my own judgement again? Tony is crawling now, on his hands and knees, fingers grabbing at the meagre grass. Maria leaps towards him but this time I put out my foot and she falls over it, tumbling to the ground, the knife flying out of her right hand. I dive towards it, grabbing it before she has a chance to pull herself to standing. I stare at the blade with horror. What am I meant to do now?

Maria runs towards me, her head down, her arms outstretched. 'Give me the knife!' she screams. I hold the blade outwards, pointing towards her, and yet still she doesn't stop, and at the last moment everything pans out in slow motion. She trips over the leg of the bench and falls towards me, the angle of the blade perfectly poised to plunge straight into her heart. Her momentum provides little resistance to the blade, which goes into her with ease. She falls, her knees giving way, and I jump backwards, away from her, letting go of the knife. Her head crunches against the side of the bench.

There's silence.

How can there be silence when a scene of such horror has just unfolded in front of me? I can hear the birds singing, the sound of traffic from the nearby roads, the distant horn of a boat on the pale grey English Channel, the soft sound of the breeze swaying the branches behind us.

'Imo–' Tony is on the ground, looking back at me. I spring into action, running to his side, pulling off my coat whilst I look at his wound. He's been stabbed in his thigh and blood is pulsating from his leg.

'What the hell's going on here?' A man appears, his black Labrador pulling hard on the lead.

'Please call an ambulance and the police.' Why does my voice sound so calm when there is such chaos and horror around me?

'On it,' the stranger says. 'You need to put a tourniquet on that leg.'

I nod, tugging my belt from my waistband. 'Stay with me, Tony,' I say as I wrap the belt around his leg, pulling it as tightly as I can. He groans. 'You're going to be okay and I'm going to introduce you to Ava, my daughter, and as you might have gathered, I've got another baby on the way. A ready-made family for you.'

'I don't deserve you,' he murmurs.

'If what you've told me is true, then I think you do.'

'It's true,' he murmurs as his eyes flutter closed.

'Stay awake, Tony. The ambulance is on its way.' My voice quivers.

The stranger has tied his dog to a tree and is hurrying towards me. 'I did some first aid training for my job. Do you want some help?'

'Yes, please.'

'The woman over there?' he asks.

'Yes, you need to help her, but be careful; she's violent.' I realise that Maria is horribly disturbed, psychotic probably, but does she deserve to die?

'I don't think she's going to be doing any harm in the state she's in,' he says.

I leave the kind stranger to care for Maria and I turn my attention back to Tony, whose eyelids are closing, his breathing shallow. 'Stay with me, Tony,' I repeat, squeezing his hand.

It feels like hours until I hear sirens, but it's probably less than five minutes. The longest five minutes of my life. 'Please look after this man first,' I beg the paramedics. They bend down besides Tony and start working on him immediately.

'She's gone, anyway,' the stranger says, angling his head towards Maria. I can't bring myself to look at her.

'Are you sure?' I ask, because it would be just like Maria to arise again from the dead.

28

IMOGEN

A police officer is standing next to me as I watch Tony being stretchered onto an ambulance. The scene is chaotic, with uniformed officers securing blue and white tape around the bench and the area where Tony fell, his blood soaking the grass. Blue lights are flashing from the vehicles parked on the road just behind us, and now a second set of paramedics are carrying Maria. She's been zipped into a bag and both the paramedic and police officer have confirmed that she died at the scene. I had wanted to go to the hospital with Tony, but the police officers need me here for questioning, plus the paramedics have confirmed that Tony will be fine. I pray they're right.

'Shall we go and sit down over there?' The police officer has thick dark hair and gentle eyes. I follow him to another bench. I'm still trembling and wonder if I'll ever get warm.

And then suddenly, Maria's words come back to me. 'Josh! I need to call Josh!'

'Josh is?'

'My husband.' I tug my phone from my pocket and dial

his mobile. It goes to voicemail. I call the landline but only get the answer machine. 'No!' I jump up and pace backwards and forwards. 'Before she died, Maria said something about saving me from Josh. Something about him being gone before I get home.'

'That could mean anything,' the officer suggests.

'No, I think it's something bad. Really bad.'

I try calling both the phones again. What if Maria has done something to Josh or to Ava? I'd never be able to live with myself. If only I'd been honest about my parentage, none of this would have happened. Maria wouldn't have hooked into our lives as she did. 'Come on,' I mutter, willing Josh to answer the phone. This time, when the landline beeps for me to leave a message, I do so.

'Josh, please answer the phone. I'm really worried something has happened to you or Ava. Just pick up the phone or call me. Please Josh, just answer.'

'Mummy?'

'Ava!' I yelp. 'Are you alright?'

'Daddy's lying on the floor and I thought it was a game because we were going to play hide and seek but he's in the living room and he's not moving.'

'Oh my God! Darling, I need you to go into the kitchen and when the doorbell goes, have a look out of the window. If it's the police or an ambulance, you must let them in. I'll be home as quickly as I can.'

'I want you here. I'm scared.'

'I'll be there really quickly. I'll see if Danielle is around and if she can come over. She knows where we keep the spare key.'

'Okay, Mummy.' Ava's voice sounds very small.

'My husband is unconscious. We need to get paramedics

to our house, now!' My voice is edged with hysteria. 'And my five-year-old daughter is home alone.'

The police officer jumps up and starts talking into his two-way radio. He then turns back to me. 'What's your home address, Mrs Letwin?'

I reel it off. All I can think of is I need to be there with my family. Now.

'We've got paramedics on the way.'

'I need to go home. Immediately.'

'I'll take you there. We can use the blue light and get you there much faster than you driving yourself. I wouldn't want you driving in such a state anyway.'

I nod my acceptance because fear is choking my throat. I've never been in a police car before but I'm so relieved when he starts weaving in and out of traffic, putting his foot down so we're driving faster than I've ever been on English roads.

'Is it okay if I call my friend to get her to be with Ava?' I ask.

'Of course.'

I call Danielle.

'Where are you?' I ask.

'In Horsham shopping. Is everything okay?'

'No. Josh is unconscious and Ava is home alone with him. Paramedics are on their way and I'm going home with a police officer. It's a long story. Can you go to my house to be with Ava?'

'Of course. I can be there in ten minutes.'

I say prayers for Josh the whole way home. I barter with myself, promising that I'll be a better wife and mother if only Josh survives. I try to imagine what my life would be without my husband, how Ava and my unborn child would cope without a father. And then I think of Tom and feel an over-whelming pang of guilt. He died because of his friendship with me. My fingernails are torn and bleeding by the time we pull up in front of Fairview House. There's an ambulance by the front door, its rear doors open, and Danielle's car is parked haphazardly to the side. I pull open the police car's door and race into the house.

'Where are you?' I shout and then skid to a stop. Two paramedics are leaning over Josh, who has his eyes closed and an oxygen mask over his face.

'What's happened? Is he going to be alright?'

The police officer appears besides me. 'This is Mrs Letwin and your patient is her husband.'

One of the paramedics stands up, his face serious. 'We hope he'll pull through. We think that Mr Letwin might have ingested something poisonous but as soon as he's in the hospital we'll run tests. We'll be leaving now.'

Thank goodness for Danielle. She takes charge. She gets the police officer, who I now know is called Ric Martland, to drive me to the hospital. Ava is tearful when I leave but I promise her Daddy will be all right. Danielle will stay with her for as long as it takes, and with the promise of back-to-back films and ice-cream, she calms down. Danielle even organises for Alain to get a lift with a mate down to Brighton to collect my car.

'I think Maria poisoned Josh,' I say to Ric Martland as we head towards the hospital.

'We'll have to search your house. I'll organise for a team to get over there as soon as possible. Have you and Ava got somewhere you can stay?'

Danielle sorts everything out at our house, even packing overnight bags for Ava and me, and she whisks my little girl off to her place, promising we can stay as long as needed. It's horrible to think that the police are going through our house when we're not there, that Josh may never go home. I try to stay positive, I really do, but it's so hard.

The next forty-eight hours are a blur of hospital visits, police interviews and sheer terror. Josh arrived in hospital in a very poorly state but two days on and he's over the worst, and thank heavens, is expected to make a full recovery. Tony is being discharged from hospital today, and as soon as Josh is over the worst I'm hoping to have a family reunion. The police worked out that Josh drank his normal freshly squeezed orange juice for breakfast, and we're still waiting for the full toxicology report but it's thought it might have had anti-freeze or bleach added to it. Maria was clever in that respect. She knew that Josh was the only person who drank orange juice in our house.

Ava and I moved back home last night but somehow the place feels tainted. I hope that feeling will vanish in time. This morning she's gone back to school for the first time. I know it will be very difficult for all the children, but nothing compares to the grief Issy will experience. I'm restless, unable to focus on work, so I decide to search my birth mother's name. I start looking through the births, marriages and deaths, expecting to find her death in the year of my birth, or perhaps the year later. Weirdly, I find an Amy Swanborough whose age fits, but she's not dead. Instead she's been married for eighteen years to a man called Peter McCabe. I do a Google search for Amy Swanborough and, to my astonishment, she lives right here in Horsham. Her Facebook profile shows her face alongside her husband and two daughters, the girls probably in their mid-teens. I send Tony a message.

> Where did Amy's parents live?

He replies immediately.

> In Petworth. Probably still do, in a big house on the outskirts called Mayfield Manor. Went to see them when I got out of prison but they threatened to call the police on me if I didn't leave immediately. Haven't heard from them since.

I search that address along with the surname Swanborough, and Tony is right. Giles and Annika Swanborough are still there. They must be in their mid-seventies now. My grandparents. I go back onto Ancestry and it's correct, their daughter is the Amy Swanborough I found married to Peter McCabe. I'm stunned. So she didn't die, she didn't take her own life, she just gave me up for adoption. I feel so sorry for Tony, who has lived with her death on his conscience for the best part of his adult life. Yet she's been living all this time nearby and is now married, with a family of her own. I have a ready-made family that I didn't even know existed.

A warmth and excitement envelopes me. I could have passed my mother on numerous times, perhaps when I was queuing up at Tesco's or browsing in John Lewis. Maybe I've even spoken to her. I send her a message via Facebook.

Hello, Amy.

My name is Imogen Letwin and I've recently discovered that I was adopted and that you were my birth mother. I realise that contacting you out of the blue like this might come as a shock but it would be wonderful to talk to you or see you. Bizarrely, we both live near Horsham. I had a

very happy upbringing with loving parents and I only
found out I was adopted three months ago, when my
adoptive mother passed away. I can't wait to have the
opportunity to meet you.

Best wishes,

Imogen

I wish I could tell her that Tony has missed her every day of his life, but I know that wouldn't be fair to Amy. She's married, with a family. Tony can't just pick up where he left off over thirty years ago. I press send and keep my fingers crossed.

The next morning I still haven't heard back from Amy. I'm disappointed. Josh calls to say he's being let out of hospital, which is such an overwhelming relief. When I arrive, he's fully dressed and waiting for his discharge papers. My phone beeps with an incoming message. When I see it's from Amy, my fingers shake. I read it slowly.

Dear Imogen,

I'm happy you had a good childhood but I have a family
of my own and I don't need another daughter. I wish you
well but request that you stay out of my life.

Regards,

Amy McCabe

'Oh,' I say. Unexpectedly, tears spring to my eyes. How

naive I was not to prepare myself for rejection. It's under-standable that she doesn't want anything to do with me, but it stings, hard.

'What is it?' Josh asks, edging closer to me on the bed and putting his arm around mine. I show him the text message.

'I found my birth mother and she doesn't want to know me.'

'You don't need her, Imogen. You've got your own family and you had wonderful parents who loved you.'

'And I've now got a bonus dad,' I say through my tears.

'Exactly.'

It's now or never for me to tell the truth. I take a big gulp of air. 'I've got something to tell you. Something bad. I cheated on you, Josh. I had a one-night stand with Arun and I've regretted it every single day since.'

He stares at me uncomprehending. 'Arun?' he asks eventually.

'Ava was eleven months old. You were out of the house a lot, with Guila, and I was scared and lonely. It's no excuse, I know.'

I wait for my husband to explode, but it doesn't happen. His shoulders sag.

'Just the once?' he asks.

I nod. 'And Louise found out. She confronted me.'

'I was the only person not to know?'

'I'm so sorry,' I say.

'I wasn't looking after you at that time.'

'But you weren't meant to look after me.'

'What I mean is I was still under Guila's thumb. When she called, I went running because I was so scared she'd contest custody of Kyle. She was threatening me with that, you know.'

'You never told me.'

He shakes his head. 'You were struggling with a newborn; I was struggling with an angry son and didn't know which way to turn.'

'Aren't you furious with me?' I ask.

He sighs. 'I suppose Arun was his normal charming self.'

I nod. 'It should never have happened.'

'So that's why he stormed off with more than half the dentist's practice?'

'Yes. It's all my fault.'

'Honestly, Imogen, we were both to blame.'

'Are you going to forgive me that easily?' I ask.

He smiles grimly. 'I'll need some time to process it, but we were both at fault back then. Of course, you shouldn't have slept with Arun but you weren't his first conquest and you won't be his last.'

'Oh,' I say.

'And I wasn't a good husband then.' He pauses for a moment. 'But you didn't have an affair with Tom, did you? You haven't lied about that?'

'Absolutely not. It was the once with Arun four years ago, and I promise you, it will never happen again. It's eaten me up all of this time. I regret it every single day.'

Josh edges closer to me. 'Can we go home? I want to see Ava.'

'Of course.'

He doesn't say much during the car journey home. As I park the car outside our house, I murmur again, 'I'm so sorry, Josh.' He squeezes my hand.

'I know you are.'

There is surprisingly little media coverage about Maria Hinks but I do get regular updates on the police investigation from Detective Sergeant Ric Martland; we're on first-name terms these days. About three weeks after her death, Ric calls me with two updates.

'We've discovered that Maria had been anonymously reported for driving without a licence.'

'What? She didn't have a licence?' I feel sick. She drove Ava to school in my car on several occasions.

'She'd lost her licence a few months ago for drink-driving. Anyway, we've taken her car in for a forensic examination and the report confirms that there's a dent on the front bumper and splatters of blood that match Tom Box. Based on your evidence, it looks like she ran him down on purpose. We even found his bike helmet in her car, so she didn't try very hard to conceal his murder. She had the audacity to put it up for sale on Facebook Marketplace. In addition, Maria's DNA was found all over the crime scene at Clare Hooper's house and we're positive that she killed Clare. I know it's a lot to take in. And then of course, she tried to poison your husband.'

'I feel sick to my core that I had a murderer living in our house.'

'Any investigation into your husband hurting Ava is being dropped. We found CCTV footage of Maria buying a bottle of Calpol the morning after the bruises were found. We think she might have drugged Ava before bruising her.'

'It makes me feel like a terrible mother, having exposed my daughter to someone like Maria.'

'You mustn't blame yourself. She was a psychopath and an accomplished liar. You were far from the only person taken in by her. The other thing I wanted to tell you, although I don't suppose you really need to know, is that Maria's funeral will be held at Crawley Crematorium tomorrow at 10.30 a.m.'

'Is it weird for me to want to go?' I ask.

'Not at all. It could give you closure.'

That evening, I tell Josh I'm going to Maria's funeral and he offers to come with me, but there's no need for him to take even more time off work. I tell him I'm fine going alone. I don't wear black, just a pair of jeans and a thick sweater with a navy coat over the top. Maria doesn't deserve my respect. There is only one other person there; a woman at a guess in her late fifties, who bears a resemblance to Maria. She nods at me as I take my place on the other side of the aisle. The service is the shortest I have ever attended. Barely ten minutes, and then her simple coffin has gone. I walk out and the stranger touches me on the shoulder.

'Thanks for coming,' she says.

'I'm sorry, I don't know who you are.'

'Maria's sister, Pauline. You're Imogen Letwin, aren't you?' I nod.

'Maria was obsessed with you.'

'You knew?' I'm surprised.

'Have you got time for a quick drink? There's a pub over the road.'

I glance at my watch but I've got all the time in the world. We head over to the pub, which is dark and smells of beer. Pauline has a small glass of white wine and I have sparkling water. We sit at a small, sticky table in the corner of the quiet pub.

'I want to apologise for what Maria did to you. We were estranged but she was still my sister. She had a lot of mental health issues and was sectioned a couple of years ago.'

'I'm sorry that she killed your niece.'

'My niece?' Pauline frowns.

'Clare Hooper, Maria's daughter.'

Pauline shakes her head and sighs. 'Maria didn't have a daughter. She didn't have any children. A long time ago she got pregnant but the baby was stillborn and she never had any more. It was a girl who she called Joy. Ironic really, since that experience brought her anything but joy. She never got over it, and her whole life was spent trying to get a family. Clare Hooper was just another woman Maria hooked into, like she did to you.'

'Clare got in touch with me. She wanted to talk, but we never got the opportunity.'

'I think Clare was trying to warn you about Maria. Clare was a good woman. She tried really hard to help Maria but it was to no avail. I think she realised that Maria was grieving and desperate to belong, to be part of a family. Clare offered to pay for therapy, to get Maria the medical attention she needed. But Maria didn't think there was anything wrong with herself so Clare's attempts to help were in vain. Tragically, when Maria discovered that Clare had no intention of having children, she had no use for her anymore. Clare paid with her life for trying to help Maria. I knew my sister was troubled but I had no idea she was evil.'

I'm shocked. Maria was so convincing when she described Clare as her daughter.

'I'm so ashamed to admit it, but my sister was a pathological liar. She's always been that way, even when we were children.'

'Do you know why she was like that?'

'No. We had a happy childhood. Mum stayed at home, Dad worked in the post office, and although they didn't have

much money, Maria and I wanted for nothing. I tried so hard
to protect my little sister but it was useless. I think sometimes we like to believe mental illness runs in a family, a bit
like certain forms of cancer, but in our case it was indiscrimi-
nate. Sometimes these things just happen.'

We chat for a little longer but it's clear that we are both
deeply hurt by Maria's actions. When I get up to leave we
shake hands but we don't exchange numbers.

About a week or so later, I'm pottering around our
bedroom and my eyes settle on Mum's urn. 'It's time to let
you go, isn't it, Mum?' I murmur. Just the thought chokes me
up but I know it's something that has to be done.

Kyle is joining us for supper. With all the upheavals and
his dad being sick, he hasn't stayed here for well over three
weeks. Ava is excited. She's missed her older brother.

'Do you want me to lay the table?' Kyle asks as he saun-
ters into the kitchen. I glance up with surprise. It's the first
time he's ever offered to help with anything.

'Sure,' I say.

'You know I don't mind you having another child.'

'Oh.' I'm not sure where that thought has come from but
I wonder if he's holding out an olive branch. It must have
been scary for him to realise his dad could have died.

'It really doesn't make any difference to me,' he continues. 'If you and Dad are happy, I'm happy.'

'Thank you, Kyle. That's a really kind thing to say.'

'But I was right about Maria, wasn't I? She was totally
creepy.'

'Yup, you were right.'

'So you'll listen to me in future?' he asks, with a cheeky
grin on his face.

'I can't promise that, but we'll see.'

'Don't tell Dad, but she gave me cigarettes and booze. I mean, that's kind of weird for someone old enough to be my gran, to want to have a smoke with me behind the garage.'

'Yes, that is weird. I think she was trying to get you to like her. It seems that she was desperate to be liked.'

'She gave me a pack of Benson & Hedges and a bottle of vodka. I don't really like them. I could sell them to my mates but I thought maybe you'd buy them off me. What do you reckon? A tenner?'

I turn to look at Kyle, my mouth agog. I can't work out if I'm admiring him or I'm a bit shocked. But then his face crumples and he howls with laughter. 'Got you there!'

'God, Kyle! What are you like?'

Ava runs into the room. 'What are you two laughing at?'

'I'll tell you when you're all grown up,' Kyle says, reaching for Ava and tickling her sides.

When the four of us are seated around the table, I can't stop smiling. I don't think any of us have been this relaxed for months.

'I was thinking it was time to scatter Mum's ashes,' I say, hoping I'm not going to spoil the levity off the evening.

'Where do you want to do it?' Josh asks.

'Up on Cissbury Ring. She loved it up there and she'll be able to see for miles.'

'Can Grandma really see for miles?' Ava asks.

'Of course. She's in heaven,' I say. 'The forecast is good tomorrow, with no wind. I think I'll do it then.'

'You can't scatter her ashes alone,' Josh says. 'I want to come with you.'

'And me,' Ava says. I know she doesn't understand what we're going to do, so I'm reluctant.

'Mummy might be feeling very sad because she'll be saying goodbye to Grandma all over again,' I explain.

'I'll come with you,' Kyle says. 'I'll look after Ava.'

'Are you sure?' I ask.

'I liked your mum. She was kind to me. Yeah, I'll come too.'

IT'S a week since we scattered Mum's ashes and yes, it was a sad day but cathartic too. Today it's all about new life as we go for the first ultrasound scan where Josh and I will be able to find out the gender of our new baby. It's also the first day that Tony is spending alone with Ava. At first she was wary of her new grandfather but now the two of them have developed a deep bond, probably because Tony is happy to push Ava on the swings for hours, and despite his injury, he chases her around the playground until they both collapse with exhaustion.

When Tony arrived at our house this morning, he'd written down an extensive list of questions including what time Ava should eat, what treats he's allowed to give her, what are her favourite games, and much more. It was obvious that he was taking his grandfather role very seriously and he was nervous. For the first time, I felt a real connection, perhaps even a little love for this man. I gave him a hug before we left and told him not to worry. I pretended not to see, but he wiped a tear off his cheek.

'Do you want to know if we're having a girl or a boy?' I ask Josh as we drive towards the clinic in Hove.

'Yes, but ultimately it's your decision.'

I'm quiet for a while. I remember how just a few short weeks ago I was terrified that I might be carrying a boy. But then I think of Tony and the mistakes we all make when we are young and I know that I'll be happy and relaxed whether we have a girl or a boy.

'Let's find out,' I say.

'You know, I really don't care about our child's heritage. No one should have to be judged on the behaviour of their ancestors.' He pauses for a moment. 'But I've got one big request.'

'Okay,' I say, placing my palms over my stomach.

'That you never ever keep secrets like that from me again.' He glances at me before returning his eyes to the road.

'I promise,' I say.

'And I promise too. We need to accept each other warts and all.'

'Excuse me,' I joke, 'I don't have any warts.'

'I know you don't, darling, but we all have faults; we're only human, and we need to forgive each other. I hate what you did with Arun but I wasn't a good husband to you at that time. Perhaps nearly dying has made me soft.'

I laugh.

Josh continues. 'And although it's great for you to have Tony in your life, it's your mum and dad who really matter. They're the people who brought you up, who turned you into the beautiful, kind and intelligent person you are today. The woman I fell in love with and still love.'

'Thank you,' I murmur.

Of course Josh is right. I need to remember Mum as the loving woman she was and not think of her through the lens of her last days on earth. Mum would have thought she was doing the right thing by telling me about my adoption. The fact that she'd kept it secret for the whole of her life must have been eating her up. I'll never understand my parents' reasoning but I have to accept their decision. I think of Maria, and how Tom and Clare died so needlessly. I recall how desperate she was to create a family, to ensure that Ava and I were happy, and despite the evil and the delusions, Maria succeeded. Josh, Ava, Kyle and I are a tight unit now, secure in our love for each other and excited to welcome a new baby into our family. Yes, we can learn from the past, but it doesn't really matter. What counts is today, and today the sun is shining.

A LETTER FROM MIRANDA

Thank you very much for reading *The Homemaker*. If you've read any of my other books, you'll know that I like to use this letter not only to say thank you but also to explain why I wrote the book. Most of my novels are rooted in something that has happened to me personally or the storylines have been inspired by a place I know well. *The Homemaker* is a bit different. The idea for this psychological thriller came about when I heard how an adopted celebrity had a successful meeting with her birth mother. I wondered how it would feel to only discover you're adopted as an adult, and how difficult it would be to learn you were the child of rape. The debate on nature versus nurture has always fascinated me, and this book gave me the chance to explore that a little. I realise these issues can be difficult for people who have experienced them first hand, and I hope that I have dealt with them as sensitively as possible, which sometimes isn't achievable when writing a thriller.

It seems incredible, but *The Homemaker* is my twentieth psychological thriller. It's been quite the ride these past few years, especially as I never thought it would be possible to be a full-time author. And yet, that's exactly what I am. My heartfelt thanks to you for reading my books. You've made my dreams come true!

None of this would have been possible without the team at Inkubator Books. Thank you to Brian Lynch, Garret Ryan, Line Langebek, Stephen Ryan, Claire Milto, Alice Latchford, Elizabeth Bayliss, Ella Medler and the rest of the team. Thank you also to Lucy Macdermott for your help. All mistakes are very much my own.

I owe so much to the book blogging community who take the time to review my psychological thrillers, share my cover reveals and talk about my books on social media. I would like to name every single book blogger but I worry I might inadvertently leave someone out! You know who you are, and I thank you from the bottom of my heart for sharing your thoughts on my books.

Finally, and most importantly, thank *you*. If you have a moment to leave a review on Amazon and Goodreads, this helps other people discover my novels and of course I'd be massively grateful.

My warmest wishes,

Miranda

www.mirandarijks.com

Please do join me on my exclusive Facebook group!

I'll share the latest news on my books, offer fabulous giveaways, sign books and let you know what I'm reading. Join the fun here:

https://www.facebook.com/groups/mirandarijks

ALSO BY MIRANDA RIJKS

(Book 1)

FATAL FLOWERS

(Book 2)

FATAL FINALE

(Book 3)

Made in the USA
Columbia, SC
28 October 2023

25123232R00171